ENVY & ELEGANCE
LEIGHTONSHIRE LOVERS
BOOK TWO

JONI HARPER

Copyright © 2024 Joni Harper

The right of Joni Harper to be identified as the author of this work has been asserted in accordance with the Copyright, Designs and Patents Act 1988. All rights reserved.

No part of this publication may be reproduced, stored in or transmitted into any retrieval system, in any form, or by any means (electronic, mechanical, photocopying, recording or otherwise) without the prior written permission of the publisher. Any person who does any unauthorised act in relation to this publication may be liable to criminal prosecution and civil claims for damages.

This is a work of fiction. Names, characters, businesses, places, events and incidents are either the products of the author's imagination or used in a fictitious manner. Any resemblance to actual persons, living or dead, or actual events is purely coincidental.

Cover design by Louise Brown.

Cover images @[Anna Subbotina] via Canva.com @[Bombdesign] via Canva.com

Please note: cover images are models and are not related to any characters in the story.

ALSO BY JONI HARPER

Leightonshire Lovers

1. Grit & Glamour
2. Envy & Elegance
3. Tinsel & Temptation

Also available is The Chase, a short story set in the world of the Leightonshire Lovers, exclusive digitally to members of the Joni Harper Readers Club – sign up at joniharperwriter.com

CAST

The Humans
In alphabetical order by last name

Tony Alton
British husband of Willa. Mobile phone billionaire. Lover of golf and Hawaiian shirts. Lives at Palisade Heights.

Willa Alton
Aspiring American dressage rider. Loves gossip and #RoséAllDay.

Lady Patricia Babbington
Eccentric aunt of Robert. Recently widowed. Jolly good sort.

Sir Harold 'Harry' Babbington
Lady Patricia's late husband. Hattie's father.

Robert Babbington
Banker and polo-playing party-boy nephew of Lady Patricia Babbington.

Jem Baulman-Carter
Dressage diva. Instagram influencer. Grade A bitch.

Fergus Bingley
Show jumper turned event rider. Known for absolute precision.

Alexander Bovey
Local dressage star. Married to famous theatre actor Dillan Bovey.

Peter van de Burgh
Groom for Jem Baulman-Carter. Dressage hottie.

Steve Burrows
Farrier. Mate of Wayne Jefferies. Loves karaoke.

Susi Doppler-Mung
Model turned dressage rider. Married to Edward Mung, property tycoon.

Liberty Edwards
Runs a homemade luxury vegan candle company from the kitchen of her home, Badger's End. Neighbour of Hattie Kimble.

"Mucker" Elliot
Friend of Wayne Jefferies. Moderate pool-playing skills. Likes a beer.

Eddie Flint
Daniel Templeton-Smith's kind-hearted head groom.

Lucinda Gray
Up-and-coming dressage rider. Full-time criminal lawyer.

Jenny Jackson
Local vet and amateur eventer. Friend of Daniel Templeton-Smith.

Detective James
Firm, determined and known for his trademark flinty gaze.

JaXX
Reclusive singer-songwriter. Frontman of the Deciders. Lover of hats. Patron of My Last Wish charity. High Drayton Horse Trials takes place on his land. Liberty's boyfriend.

Wayne Jeffries
Local farrier. World-class fuck boy. Mr March in the 'Rural Pleasures' charity calendar.

Tyler Jordon
Wannabe rock star. Gamer. Boyfriend of Jem Baulman-Carter.

Harriet 'Hattie' Kimble
Horse whisperer. Event rider.

Detective Lanson
Efficient, kind and good at her job. Marathon runner.

John Mackie
Farrier. Mate of Wayne Jeffries.

Kevin McDonald
Friend of Wayne Jeffries. Keen but rubbish pool player.

Evelyn Millar
Megan's bitch boss and co-owner of Doxford Millar. Polished. Poised. Icy.

Nancy Neale
Amateur dressage rider. Married but keen on extracurricular activities.

Helga Neilson
Greta's blonde head groom.

Rosalie Porter
Groom for Jem Baulman-Carter. Highly competent and much put-upon.

Bunty Saunderton
Daniel Templeton-Smith's yard hand and working pupil.

Jonathan Scott
Medal-winning Australian rider. Known for vigorous pursuits.

Netta Sharpe
Mother of pony eventing superstar Tilly Sharpe.

Michelle Sawyer
Home help. Friendly, kind – a jolly good sort.

Gerald Talbot
Private secretary to Lady Patricia. Loyal in every way.

Megan Taylor
Big dressage dreams, small budget. Works at Doxford Millar.

Daniel Templeton-Smith
Gorgeous and talented event rider. Broke. Owns Templeton Manor.

Rachel Eydon

Jovial landlady of the Red Lion pub, Saundersford.

Greta Wolfe
Medal-winning German rider. Likes to be on top.

CAST
The Animals
In alphabetical order

Albert
Wayne Jeffries' Jack Russell terrier. Likes to chase balls.

Bugsy
Big chestnut warmblood gelding. Owned and ridden by Jem Baulman-Carter.

Bubbly
Leggy grey youngster. Owned by Netta Sharpe.

Dinky
Jenny Jackson's pint-sized event horse.

Dodger
Fergus Bingley's less-experienced Advanced horse.

Dora
Wayne Jefferies' small but opinionated tortoiseshell cat.

Downton X
Jem Baulman-Carter's top dressage horse. Impressive but repressed.

Gertrude

Daniel Templeton-Smith's small black cat – chief mouser of Templeton Manor.

McQueen
Eddie Flint's swift three-legged collie. Proud rescue. Partial to pork scratchings.

Mermaid's Gold
A gift horse. 100% firecracker. Owned and ridden by Hattie Kimble.

Pink Fizz
Roan gelding with talent and attitude. Owned and ridden by Daniel Templeton-Smith.

Poppet
Red male cocker spaniel puppy adopted by Hattie Kimble.

Popsy
Red female cocker spaniel puppy adopted by Jenny Jackson.

Rosalind
Fergus Bingley's championship-winning bay mare.

Slinky
Sensitive ex-racehorse mare turned eventer. Owned by Tyler Jacobs and ridden by Daniel Templeton-Smith.

Star Child
Jem Baulman-Carter's highly strung youngster. Chestnut gelding. Good at airs above the ground.

The Rogue

Daniel Templeton-Smith's top horse. Bold over fences. Fan of ginger biscuits.

Velvet Mimosa
Uber-talented young black gelding. Owned and ridden by Megan Taylor.

Washford Bay
Bright bay mare. Owned and ridden by Greta Wolfe.

Westworlder
Ridden by Greta Wolfe. Owned by Mrs Clifford.

Zayanne
Jem Baulman-Carter's second top dressage horse. As sensitive as she is talented.

CHAPTER ONE

HATTIE

*H*attie wakes with the dawn.

It's always in the early morning light that the bedroom looks its most romantic, glamorous even, with the ancient chandelier high above the four-poster bed, the huge sash windows with their flowing voile curtains, and the cast iron fireplace with original floral tiles. But the low light camouflages the problems: the cracked ceiling plaster, the draughty gaps between the windows and bricks. Combined with the draughts, the temperamental, clanking heating system and lack of insulation means the place never feels truly warm.

Shivering, Hattie can't face getting up and into the chilled February air just yet, and as the horses won't expect their breakfasts until it's fully light, she decides to have another ten minutes in bed. It makes things much easier that her diminutive event horse, Mermaid's Gold, now lives here at Daniel's yard. Hattie is renting a little cottage up the lane, so she's less than ten minutes away if she's at home, but when she stays overnight with Daniel her commute from bed to stable takes less than a minute.

Staying with Daniel overnight is something that's been

happening increasingly frequently in the past few weeks. Their relationship is still new – their first date was on Christmas Eve – but things are moving fast, far faster than previous relationships she's been in. She's happy, though, even if Templeton Manor is ridiculously cold.

Shivering again, she burrows down further under the duvet and rolls over, pressing herself against Daniel's back, trying to warm herself with his body heat. It's a losing battle, though, because the air in the bedroom is frost-tinged and frigid. She wraps her arms around his waist and pulls herself tighter to him. He's warm and she snuggles in closer, kissing the skin on the back of his neck just below his black hair. She doesn't know how he can stand to sleep bare-chested in just his boxers, but then he grew up here; he's never lived in a place with modern central heating and double glazing.

Really, the only room in the manor that feels cosy is the kitchen, because the Aga throws out heat all day and night, and the plentiful stacks of old *Horse & Hound* magazines provide the best insulation. Although, thinks Hattie, smiling to herself, there are other ways to create heat here in the bedroom.

She runs her hand down Daniel's stomach, over the downy hair from his navel, and under the waistband of his boxers. He groans in his sleep as she takes him in her hand. Slowly, she runs her hand up and down his length, feeling him harden beneath her fingers. As he turns onto his back, she pushes herself up and astride him.

Daniel's eyes are still closed as he murmurs her name. She guides him inside, and as the pale sunlight begins to stream in through the gaps between the curtains, she rides him. Steadily at first; a warm, fuzzy, comforting pleasure that flows and builds. Until she can't hold back any longer, her rhythm quickening, her breath coming faster. Fully awake now, he grasps hold of her waist and thrusts hard into her. She leans back, enhancing the angle, feeling all of him. Lost in the moment, the sensation. Then she cries out. Daniel bucks beneath her. And the pleasure ricochets through her as they climax together.

Collapsing forward onto Daniel's chest, Hattie smiles.

Now *that* is the best way to start the day.

CHAPTER TWO

JEM

*I*t's not even 8am, yet Jem doubts her day could get any more shit. All her careful timings for this morning have been blown out of the water, and now she's going to be battling the clock to get her two top dressage horses – Downton X and Zayanne – schooled, and herself showered, glammed and all set for brunch with Mummy by ten thirty.

Standing in the middle of the yard, she scowls as she watches her idiot groom, Rosalie, tap the security code into the keypad to unlock the tack room. The girl has no style. Frankly, with her mousey hair scragged back in a ponytail, and dressed as drab as ever in black jodhpurs, grey polo, a faded navy gilet and some cheap long boots, she looks more like a hobo than the groom to an important dressage rider.

Jem shakes her head, watching as Rosalie pulls the tack room door open far too sluggishly. Bloody staff. She wouldn't be feeling this stress if they'd just done their jobs as they were paid to do. But no, her other groom, Peter, who was rostered to feed this morning, apparently has some vomiting bug so he couldn't be bothered to get up. That has left feeding the twelve stabled horses to Rosalie and she didn't get started on the yard until seven thirty, meaning the breakfast feeds were given an hour too late. As horses need a minimum of an hour to digest, Jem won't be able to start schooling her first horse until after eight thirty now. It's beyond irritating.

Tutting, she checks her watch for what seems like the hundredth time already this morning. It's seven fifty-nine. She should have been on-board Downton by eight, but that's obviously not going to happen. Blasted Rosalie is only just entering the tack room now to collect Downton's equipment, and the horse needs a proper groom before getting tacked up. The girl is such a sloth, it'll take her an age to get the horse ready.

Jem taps her foot.

What the hell is Rosalie doing?

Every second the girl wastes is making Jem later, and that just isn't acceptable. She promised Mummy that she wouldn't be late to brunch at Villa Rouge. It's an important day. The new Gucci collection is landing and they both have bags reserved. They *have* to collect them today. It's *vital*, obviously. So it's infuriating that her grooms are so damn selfish that they've put her whole day in jeopardy. Jem can't possibly be seen using last season's bag after today, can she? That would be ridiculous.

Jem hears Rosalie gasp, followed by some incoherent mumbling. It's muffled because the damn girl is still inside the tack room. Sighing, Jem strides across and yanks the door open. It seems as if she has to do everything herself. 'I don't know why the hell you're being so slow to…'

It takes a moment for Jem to fully comprehend what she's seeing. On the other side of the tack room there's a human-sized hole in the wall where the bricks are missing. Through it, she can see the muddy bank that leads up to one of the footpaths in the woodland bordering her property; it's strewn with broken bricks. 'What… what the…?'

'It's gone,' stammers Rosalie. Her usually pale face is red and blotchy.

She's not wrong. The whole place has been cleaned out. Every bridle, saddle, pad and girth has been taken, leaving rows of empty bridle hooks and saddle brackets lining the walls. The bastards have even taken the fancy coffee maker that Jem had installed in the room for her personal use only, along with the kettle the grooms used to boil water for their rubbish instant coffee. 'How could they…?'

'It was locked,' says Rosalie, a hint of fear in her voice. 'I had to punch in the code to get in here, you saw me. It was locked.'

'You don't need the code when you make a great hole in the wall,' says Jem. Her voice has an unfamiliar quiver to it. She turns to Rosalie, fury mounting. 'How the hell didn't you hear this going on? They would have needed sledgehammers to take the bricks out, and it would've been loud.'

'I… I…' Rosalie's cheeks flush red. She doesn't meet Jem's gaze.

'How?' shouts Jem. 'Tell me, for God's sake.'

'We were at the pub last night,' says Rosalie. 'It was a friend's birthday. We had drinks and a pizza.'

'We?' says Jem.

'Me and Peter,' says Rosalie, eyes downcast.

'Jesus!' Jem can't believe this. What's the point in having staff if they aren't around to keep an eye on the place at all times? 'So the yard was unattended all evening and then you came back drunk?'

'We'd already finished the horses,' says Rosalie, looking tearful. 'And we came back in time for late-night stable checks at half eleven.'

'You didn't check the bloody tack room though, did you?' snaps Jem.

Rosalie's face turns redder. 'We didn't need to open the tack room when we—'

'Fine, fine,' says Jem, angrily, thrusting her palms towards Rosalie to get her to shut up with her whining and excuses. 'Well, your night out has just lost me all my tack and equipment, so I hope it was bloody worth it.'

'It's not unreasonable for us to go out sometimes,' says Rosalie softly. 'You go out all the time.'

Jem feels the anger bubbling inside her. Clenching her fists, she glares at Rosalie and yells, 'Competing at my level is very stressful. I deserve some me time away from here, but I pay *you* to look after the place. Something you are obviously incapable of doing.' Jem gestures towards the door. 'Get out. Just get the hell out of here. Now.'

Rosalie scuttles out of the room, leaving Jem alone. Standing in the devastation of her once-pristine tack room, Jem feels tears prick at her eyes. Taking her phone from the pocket in her breeches, she switches the camera view to selfie, and sets it onto video mode. Taking a couple of deep breaths, she smooths down her long, blonde-highlighted hair and presses record.

'I've been robbed. Everything's gone,' says Jem to the camera, her voice even more shaky than before. 'All my tack, equipment and even the kettle.' She pauses to shake her head, and takes a big, shuddering breath before continuing. 'I'm totally devastated.'

She switches to the front camera view and slowly pans around the room, lingering over the empty saddle brackets and bridle hooks, the empty equipment cupboard, and finishing with a long shot of the huge, brick-less hole in the back wall.

Jem flips the camera back to selfie mode and looks imploringly into the lens.

Her lower lip trembles.

'Whoever did this,' says Jem. Her words are stilted and laced with despair. Black mascara tears stream down her face. 'You've stolen my dreams.'

CHAPTER THREE

HATTIE

By the time she's coaxed a lukewarm trickle of water from the shower and got dressed into her warmest yard clothes, Hattie feels ready to face the frosty February morning. She follows the smell of coffee and bacon towards the kitchen and finds the rest of the Templeton Manor gang in there. At one end of the oak table, there's Eddie, Daniel's kind and supremely knowledgeable head groom, who's tucking into scrambled eggs with his girlfriend Jenny, the local horse vet, and their three-legged rescue collie, McQueen, who is sitting on his own chair beside Eddie. Next to Jenny is Bunty, the shy but dedicated working pupil, who is doing her best to stop Gertrude, Daniel's small black cat, taking a piece of sausage from her breakfast roll.

'Coffee?' asks Daniel, looking up from the Aga where he's frying some bacon. 'Bacon and sausage butties?'

'That sounds perfect,' says Hattie, suddenly feeling ravenous. She smiles at the sight of a small, ginger cocker spaniel puppy who is dancing around Daniel's feet in a state of perpetual excitement, driven to distraction by the smell of bacon and sausage. 'Poppet!'

On hearing his name, the puppy turns and races across to her, pressing his body against her legs, his little tail wagging at double speed and his tongue licking her hands.

'Good morning, baby-dog,' says Hattie, crouching down to stroke him.

Poppet is her newest friend. He's one of two spaniel puppies who were dumped outside Jenny's veterinary practice on Christmas morning. Jenny was on call that day, and decided to go into the practice to get some additional supplies after being called out to a particularly nasty colic in the early hours. It's lucky she did. It had snowed overnight and the two barely four-week-old puppies inside the damp cardboard box left on the steps outside the practice entrance wouldn't have survived for much longer.

Hattie hadn't intended to get a puppy, but having moved out of Robert Babbington's Clover Hill House – the place she'd been house sitting – and looking after Robert's two dogs and two goats, while he was in America for the best part of last year, she had found it awfully quiet and, to be honest, a bit lonely in her new cottage without any dogs for company.

When Daniel told her about the puppies, and how Jenny was keeping one but needed to find a home for the other, she said she'd like to adopt him. It's one of the best, if most chaos-inducing, decisions she's ever made.

'Sorry, I let him out of his crate because as soon as we came downstairs he started bouncing about and squeaking,' says Jenny. As she speaks, something on her lap, hidden beneath her zip-up fleece, moves. Moments later, Popsy, the other small red spaniel, pokes her face out over the top of the zip, blinking.

'How is Popsy so calm when Poppet's so energetic?' says Hattie, smiling as the cute pup gives a huge yawn. Poppet, suddenly spotting her, rushes over to see his sister, jumping up and trying to get her to play with him. 'It makes no sense.'

'He really wanted to join you guys in bed this morning,' says

Eddie, mischief in his tone. 'But we figured you might like your privacy for a bit longer.'

Hattie feels her cheeks flush. Surely the benefit of Templeton Manor being an old building is that it has thick, if not well insulated, walls? But it seems, from the smirks on Jenny and Eddie's faces, that they're not as soundproof as she hoped. She pulls an apologetic face. 'Sorry about that.'

'No worries,' says Jenny. 'We're all adults here.'

'Yeah, I got earplugs when these two started their sleepovers,' says Bunty, gesturing at Eddie and Jenny. 'A bomb could go off and I wouldn't notice.'

'Here you go,' says Daniel, handing Hattie a mug of coffee and a plate with two sausage and bacon rolls. 'I've put equal parts ketchup and brown sauce, just as you like it.'

'Thanks,' says Hattie, taking them from him and sitting down beside Bunty. 'You're a lifesaver.'

Daniel smiles and feeds a tiny piece of sausage to each of the puppies, then goes back to the Aga to fetch his own coffee and breakfast. As he does, Jenny pushes her chair back and stands up. She gives Eddie a kiss and ruffles the hair on McQueen's black-and-white head, then heads over to put her dirty plate and mug in the sink.

'I'll sort that out,' says Eddie.

'Thanks,' says Jenny. She looks at the rest of them. 'Duty calls. I'm on the long shift today, so I'll see you all for supper.'

'Have a good one,' says Daniel, carrying his breakfast across to the table and sitting down opposite Hattie. As Jenny, still with Popsy in her fleece, opens the door and heads outside, Daniel looks at Hattie and says, 'So what's your plan for today?'

'It's a hacking day for Mermaid's Gold so I was going to head off on her after mucking out.'

'Good idea,' says Daniel. 'I can bring The Rogue if you fancy some company?'

'Sounds good.' Hattie takes a bite of her roll.

She's thankful that Daniel hasn't asked why it is that she's able to hack out on a Tuesday morning rather than rushing off to a job like Jenny. It's been over two months since Robert Babbington returned from the States and her house and animal sitting job with him ended. She's looked after the animals a couple of times since then when he's been up in London for various glitzy events, but that's been as a favour rather than paid.

The simple truth is that she hasn't thought about getting another job yet, but as the months are rolling on, she supposes she should; for show at least, if nothing else. Because she doesn't want to tell Daniel why it is that she doesn't especially need to earn money, not yet anyway. Not until she's certain.

CHAPTER FOUR

WAYNE

*I*t takes Wayne less than second after waking to realise how utterly shit he feels. He should never have had that last pint just before closing time, although, to be fair, it was probably the eight pints before it that contributed more to the way he's feeling this morning.

He blinks, trying to adjust to the brightness of the room. He must have forgotten to pull down the blackout blind last night, and he's paying for it now; the pale February light makes him feel even more nauseous. Gradually, though, his eyes adjust and he gets a proper view of his surroundings. That's when he realises the bed he's lying in isn't his. The sheets are white, not black. The headboard is pale pink velvet, not black leather. And there's a sleeping blonde in the bed beside him.

It takes him a moment to remember who she is. The memories are rather disjointed, but he remembers being in the back room of the Red Lion, playing pool with a couple of the lads, when a pretty blonde in tight jeans and a crop top came over and challenged him to a game. Never one to shirk a challenge, he agreed. He's usually pretty good at pool, but this girl – Polly – was something else. She beat him in three straight games and when he asked her what she'd like as her prize she smiled and whispered in his ear: 'Mr March.'

Him, in other words. She'd recognised him from his picture in the local charity calendar, 'Rural Pleasures'. He'd posed in his forge, muscles glinting from the heat of the furnace, hammer in hand and his anvil just about covering his modesty. Since the calendar went on sale, a few weeks before Christmas, his DMs have been blowing up his phone. Rachel Eydon, the landlady at the Red Lion, even has a copy open on March displayed on the bar; there's an orange sticker on it proudly stating 'Mr March drinks here'. It certainly hasn't hurt his pulling power. In fact, it seems as if every horse woman in the county wants to get in his pants, and who is he to disappoint them?

Wayne watches the blonde, Polly, sleeping peacefully on her side and really hopes he didn't disappoint her last night. He vaguely remembers them walking back to her place and getting naked as soon as they got through the door, but the details after that are more than a bit hazy. After that many beers, he hopes he could still perform. Fear grips him for a moment, but then he pushes it away. He's never had any trouble, or complaints, in that department, so he doubts he had any problems rising to the occasion.

As if sensing him watching her, Polly opens her eyes. She smiles when she sees him. 'Well, good morning, stud.'

Wayne grins. There was no problem with the ironwork last night then. 'Morning, yourself.'

Polly stretches, the movement causing the sheet to slip down, exposing a nipple. 'Can I get you some coffee, or something else?'

Makeup-less, with her attractively dishevelled hair cascading around her shoulders, she's even prettier than she seemed in the pub last night, thinks Wayne. He checks the time on his watch – he's got half an hour before he needs to get going to his first client of the day. Giving her a wolfish smile, he reaches out and pulls Polly towards him. 'Something else.'

Giggling, Polly slides her hands down his chest to his dick. 'Ready for action,' she says, stroking him. 'Perfect.'

Pulling her on top, Wayne lets her get to work, guiding him into her, and then riding him like she's trying to make up ground on the way to the finish line at the Derby. It's fast, hard and over quite soon. A perfect morning quickie to set him up for the day ahead.

He leaves Polly in bed and slips away to the shower. It's a neutral white suite with white subway tiles, but like the bedroom it's distinctly feminine; with scented candles on the vanity unit along with a massive collection of cosmetics, perfumes and creams. Wayne uses the fancy shower gel to get himself clean, and as the water from the rainfall showerhead cascades over him, he feels the worst of his hangover lifting. A quick stop on the way to his first job to grab a bacon sarnie and he'll be back to full form, he reckons.

Quickly, he dries off with one of the huge white fluffy towels from the heated towel rail, uses some of Polly's toothpaste on his finger to freshen up his mouth, and tames his black curls with a touch of water. He dresses back into his jeans, t-shirt and plaid shirt from last night, thankful that the outfit is fine for work today. Then he unlocks the bathroom as quietly as he can and creeps silently back into the bedroom.

Polly is asleep again. Wayne's relieved; it makes it easier for him to leave. There's no awkward 'will I see you again?' or 'what's your number?' questions to answer this way. Just a satisfied feeling and nice memories. Blowing a kiss towards her sleeping form, he softly closes the bedroom door and makes his way downstairs.

Stopping by the back door in the kitchen, he puts on his steel toe-capped work boots and laces them up. It's only as he opens the door that he notices the 'Rural Pleasures' charity calendar hanging from a picture hook beside it. His own face looks back at him, and he has to admit he does look good. He touches his fingers to his brow in a mock salute to his picture, then pulls the door open and leaves the cottage.

As he hurries down the lane towards the pub car park and his van, Wayne takes a quick glance at his DMs. There are twenty-three new messages since last night, all from women. Since the calendar went on sale, that's about average.

Reaching the van, he opens it and starts the engine. His favourite dance track is on the radio. The pale February sun is rising over the frost-coated hills, and there's enough time to get breakfast before his first client. Putting the van into gear, Wayne smiles to himself.

Man, he's living the dream.

CHAPTER FIVE

HATTIE

The frost is just starting to melt as they trot along the bridleway from the back of the Templeton Manor pastureland towards Melthorne Hill and the hundreds of acres of woodland that surrounds the Melthorne Estate. This is Hattie's favourite place to ride, and Mermaid's Gold seems to be enjoying it too. Her chestnut ears are pricked, and her rhythmical trot covers the ground and easily enables her to keep up with Daniel's much bigger horse, The Rogue, who at just over 17hh has an almost two hands height advantage over the diminutive mare.

'She's looking on good form,' says Daniel, as if reading Hattie's mind.

'I'm pleased with her fitness,' says Hattie. The event season starts in two weeks and she's put a lot of time and thought into the best fitness programme for the little mare in order to bring her to peak performance for their first competition of the year. 'Although we still need to work on our dressage.'

'I thought she was going well in that lesson you had with Willa last week,' says Daniel, taking a pull on the reins as a rather impatient Rogue breaks into canter. 'She looks a lot more settled and fluent in her work.'

Hattie smiles. Willa Alton, American dressage rider and neighbour of Robert Babbington, has been giving them weekly lessons over the winter. They get on well, and Willa is a patient and supportive trainer. 'Willa's helped a lot.' She gestures towards Daniel's horse. 'The Rogue looks like he's feeling good.'

'Yeah,' says Daniel, laughing as the horse puts in a little buck and snorts loudly. 'A little too good, perhaps, but I need to have him just right so we don't risk him doing the tendon again.'

Hattie knows Daniel's worried about The Rogue getting injured again. Last year, Daniel's hopes of winning Badminton Horse Trials ended abruptly on the cross-country course when The Rogue fell on the sodden and slippery ground and strained a tendon. It put the horse out of action for the rest of the competition season, but he was able to come back into work before Christmas. So far all the scans have shown that the injury has healed well. Hattie knows Daniel is keen to do everything he can to keep the large bay gelding sound and fit. As a result, he's entered several competitions in March and April. He won't run The Rogue at all of them, but it means he has options about which ones he'll use as a warmup to the big event in the first half of the season – the CCI5* Badminton Horse Trials in May.

'Have you decided which event you'll make your first run?' asks Hattie, steering the little mare around a large patch of boggy ground at the side of the path. 'I was thinking of taking Mermaid's Gold to Great Witchingham first, but given how she's feeling, I might run her a few weeks earlier at Tweseldown. I've got entries in for the Intermediate at both so we can get our eye in over a smaller track before doing some more CCI3* and stepping up to Advanced.'

'Good plan. She looks ready,' says Daniel. He seems thoughtful as they negotiate a gate from the public bridleway into the Melthorne Estate woodland and take the path that inclines up Melthorne Hill. 'I haven't decided about Rogue yet. On the one hand, it's a long time since he's been to an event so I think he could do with two or three runs to blow the cobwebs away before Badminton. But on the other hand, I don't want to overdo it and risk another injury.'

Hattie nods. It's a tricky balance with any horse; both too much and too little preparation can be hazardous, but when you're competing at a five-star event like Badminton Horse Trials the stakes are even higher. So far, every time she's asked Daniel about his plans he's been non-committal, but the event season is just around the corner now; he has to make a decision. 'Lady Pat says the early events have filled up quickly and they'll all go to ballot.'

'She's right,' says Daniel, asking a rather enthusiastic Rogue to steady his trot. 'That's why I've used a priority sticker on my entry into the Open Intermediate at Tweseldown to ease us back in. I just haven't decided whether to run him yet. He's being scanned again the week before to check the tendon is still healed and okay. If everything still looks good, and he feels right, then I'll take him.'

'Sounds good,' says Hattie. The Rogue snorts loudly as a pheasant flies up from the path a few metres ahead of them, and Hattie pats Mermaid's Gold on the neck as the mare continues in her rhythmic, ground-covering trot, unfazed by the pheasant's sudden movement or The Rogue's reaction. Hattie knows Daniel's worried about doing too much too soon with The Rogue, and that he still blames himself for their fall at Badminton last year, but the way the horse is looking now, he seems to be a picture of athletic equine good health. 'And you know the sandy going will be good at Tweseldown whatever the weather, so you don't need to worry about it getting too deep or sticky for him.'

'My thinking exactly,' says Daniel, giving the exuberant gelding a rub on his neck. 'What's your plan for the rest of the season?'

Hattie doesn't answer immediately. Her goal is to compete at Badminton. It's been her dream for as long as she can remember, ever since her mum took her to watch the legendary event back when she was just a little girl begging rides on other people's ponies. One of her earliest memories is of her young self, standing in front of the huge ditch at the infamous Vicarage Vee cross-country fence and announcing loudly to the other people walking the course that she could easily jump the fence on her pony. She didn't even own a pony. The one she was referring to belonged to the local farmer's son and whenever she rode him she'd fall off at least twice. She never let that put her off though – falling off is an occupational hazard for any event rider.

Her favourite picture from her childhood is of her and her mum smiling for the camera as they sit on the turf in front of the Vicarage Vee with the ditch stretching out behind them and the thick oak rail above. It's a little faded now, but when she moved to her cottage, Hattie put it into a new frame and in pride of place on the mantle over the fireplace. Looking at it reminds her everyday of what her mum had written on the back of the photograph: *Hattie says she'll win the Badminton trophy for me one day. I know she will*

Her mum might have lost her battle with cancer last year, but the promise still stands. Hattie doesn't want to break it but her partnership with Mermaid's Gold is still new and she refuses to rush the horse, so she smiles and gives a little shake of her head. 'Not yet, I still need to finalise the details with Lady Pat.'

'Wise,' says Daniel, nodding. 'And it's so nice that you've got such a keen supporter in Lady Pat. I could do with a few more myself.'

Hattie nods. It's easier to let Daniel think that Lady Pat is sponsoring her eventing costs than to tell him the actual truth. She will tell him when she's sure – just not yet. 'How's that going?'

Daniel shrugs. 'Nothing new at the moment, but then I'm a lot pickier about who I'll have as an owner these days.'

Hattie's glad he's more discerning. It was one of Daniel's

owners – Lexi Marchfield-Wright – who tried to take Mermaid's Gold from her last year and drove a wedge between her and Daniel before their relationship had even started. 'Have you heard anything from her?'

Daniel shakes his head. He doesn't need Hattie to say Lexi's name out loud to know exactly who she's referring to. 'No. Thankfully.'

'That's good.'

They ride on in silence for a long moment. The horses are keen as they power up Melthorne Hill. The going here under the trees is perfect – the ground untouched by frost and not overly damp either. The pale winter sun glints between the tree branches, casting strange shadows across the woodland floor. It's beautiful.

Daniel exhales hard, his breath pluming white into the frigid air. 'I need to bring in more money from somewhere. The costs of feed and bedding, and electric and everything, seem to keep going up.' His expression is tense. 'I was thinking about doing some more teaching and taking on more liveries. What do you think?'

She knows that Daniel's struggled for a long time to keep Templeton Manor from falling into complete disrepair and to fund the yard and horses. His tenacity is one of the things she admires about him. 'It makes sense. If you've got the time?'

'I'll just need to find it,' says Daniel, grimly. 'You know how it is.'

'Sure.' Everything does seem more expensive these days, even a basic grocery shop is far more than last year, but she's been unexpectedly cushioned from the stress of it after coming into a surprise inherence a few months ago, left to her by the father she never knew. If she's honest, she still hasn't processed what Lady Pat told her on the day she gifted Mermaid's Gold to her, that Lady Pat's late husband, Sir Harry, had been Hattie's father. It was the catalyst that spurred her on to finally open the trunk her mum had left her when she died. The letter inside confirmed that what Lady Pat told her was true, and that Sir Harry had invested money every year on Hattie's birthday on her behalf. She almost fainted when she looked at the account and saw how much was in it: over seven hundred thousand pounds. She still feels in shock over it, like it's not real, not hers. That's partly why she still hasn't told Daniel. It's a lot of money, enough to help him return the yard at Templeton Manor to its former Victorian glory and renovate the most dilapidated parts of the house. But it's too early in the relationship to commit to something like that. No matter what her heart is telling her, Hattie needs to be sensible. So she smiles and says, 'You'll find a way to make it all work. You were worried about Jenny coming in as a livery and that's working out brilliantly.'

'You're right,' says Daniel, his expression looking more relaxed. As if sensing a change in his rider's mood, The Rogue jigs and blows out hard and Daniel laughs. 'Fancy a canter?'

As the birds sing in the tree canopy overhead and a bold squirrel scurries across the path ahead of them, Mermaid's Gold and The Rogue canter along the bridlepath between the trees. Mermaid's Gold's stride eats up the ground, her chestnut ears are pricked forwards, and she feels happy and enthusiastic to be out in the world. The rush of cold air against Hattie's skin makes her cheeks tingle and her eyes run. She smiles, loving it.

Life doesn't get much better than this.

CHAPTER SIX

MEGAN

Megan hates being cooped up in the Doxford Millar shop all day. She'd much rather be working on her walk-to-canter transitions with Velvet Mimosa, her gorgeous black gelding who she bought as an unbacked two-year-old with every penny she had. Velvet is five now and progressing up the levels far faster than she could ever have imagined; they've qualified for the British Dressage regional finals in two weeks' time and she's beyond excited.

Velvet is the most precious creature in the world to her. He gives her life. That, and her dream of riding on the Olympic dressage team for Team GB one day are what keep her going even when she's knackered from working two jobs and sick of talking to yet another high-maintenance customer. When she climbs onto Velvet's back, everything is good in the world.

The bell over the door chimes, and Megan looks up from the display of new-season clutch bags that she's busy arranging on one of the plinths to see a heavily made-up middle-aged woman dressed in white jeans, a blue polka dot shirt and a blue blazer pushing her way through the door. The woman looks tired and is already laden down with several large shopping bags. Glancing towards her boss, Evelyn Piper, who is sitting on the stool behind the till, Megan waits to see if she'll stop flicking through the wholesale catalogue and serve their customer. Of course Evelyn doesn't move. After a long moment, she looks over at Megan, raises a perfectly waxed eyebrow and glances towards the customer.

Great, thinks Megan. Forcing a smile onto her face, she puts down the rather cute zebra-print clutch she'd been about to position on the display and approaches the new arrival. 'Good morning. How can I help you today?'

The woman looks at her with haughty disdain. 'I need a pair of size six ankle boots in leopard, and the Tiffany hat in peacock.'

'That's no problem at all,' says Megan, struggling to keep the smile on her face. She gestures to the plush turquoise sofas at the far end of the store. 'If you'd like to take a seat, I'll fetch them for you right away.'

As the woman plonks herself down onto a turquoise sofa, Megan goes through the door behind the counter and into the stockroom. Quickly, she finds the boots and hat the woman is looking to try, and then takes a bottle of prosecco from the wine fridge in the corner and pours a generous glassful. With the boxes balanced in one hand and the prosecco in the other, she goes back through the door onto the shop floor.

'Prosecco?' she says to the woman.

'Yes, good,' says the woman, taking the glass in her shimmery pink talons without a thank you and gulping half of it down in one mouthful.

Placing the boxes on the low table in front of the sofa, Megan fights to keep her smile in place. 'And these are the boots, and the Tiffany hat.'

The woman doesn't thank her or even respond, but she removes her shoes, takes the boots from the first box and tries to put them on.

Megan can tell right away that the woman's feet are at least a wide seven and there's no way the narrow ankle boots are going to fit, but she knows better than to interfere. She learnt that lesson the hard way. So instead she waits, a neutral expression on her face, while the woman huffs and puffs and curses under her breath as she tries to cram her obviously too-big foot into the boot.

'Oh, this is ridiculous,' says the now red-faced woman. 'Your sizing must be wrong. I'm a perfect size six in everything.'

'I'm so sorry about that,' says Megan, faking surprise. 'Perhaps you'd like to try the seven in a wider fit?'

'No, I would not,' says the woman, looking furious. 'My feet are very slender; they'd be lost in a wide fit. But I'll try a six and a half in the regular.'

'Of course,' says Megan, leaving the woman to try on the hat as she returns to the storeroom for a six and a half that, again, she knows won't fit. Why people don't just ask for the correct size, she has no idea; it's not like she's going to judge them for being a size seven or a wide fit. She's seen so many people buy too-tight shoes and hobble about like elderly penguins while trying to pretend that they're comfortable. It makes no sense. The boots here aren't cheap, and if you're going to spend all that money surely you should at least enjoy wearing them.

∾

Finally, it's eleven o'clock and time for her break. Leaving Evelyn on the shop floor, Megan heads through the stockroom and out into the small back office. There's a tiny kitchenette, with a sink, fridge, kettle and microwave, along with a small bank of lockers. Unlocking the one on the bottom right, Megan pulls out her bag and removes her phone so she can catch up on social media while she's drinking her coffee.

Weird. No one usually tries to get in touch when she's at work because they know she has to leave her phone in her locker, but she's had three missed calls and a message from Rosalie at the stables. Tapping the screen, she reads the message.

URGENT. Call me xx

Megan's heart rate accelerates. Has something happened to Velvet? Rosalie would only get in touch if something was very wrong. She presses Rosalie's number. Tries to hold the phone still, even though her hands are shaking.

It rings twice, then Rosalie answers. 'Where've you been?'

'I'm at work. My phone was in my locker.'

'Oh, yeah, of course.' Rosalie clears her throat. 'Look, I'm really sorry, but there's been a burglary here.'

Megan's mouth goes dry. She can barely get the words out. 'Did they take Velvet?'

'No, no, Velvet's fine. But they bashed down the back wall and cleaned out the tack room.'

'Oh my God,' says Megan, the relief she'd felt at Velvet being safe now replaced with a sick feeling in the pit of her stomach. 'They took my stuff?'

'They took everyone's stuff.' Rosalie lowers her voice. 'You can imagine the hissy fit Jem threw.'

'Did she blame you?' asks Megan, knowing that Jem isn't good at accepting personal responsibility.

'Of course,' says Rosalie. 'And then she did this crying Instagram thing and stomped off to who knows where. I've spent the whole morning dealing with the police and letting liveries know the bad news. I haven't even had time to turn out the horses yet.'

'Sounds like a nightmare.' Jem, the owner of the yard, is a drama queen on a good day; Megan can only imagine how she'd have reacted when the theft was discovered. And although Jem never seems to worry about money, there must have been more than forty grand's worth of saddlery in the tack room. Losing it would have to hurt.

'Yeah,' says Rosalie. 'Look, let me give you the crime reference number the police gave me; you'll need it for when you call your insurance company. I can send you the photos of the wall the burglars bashed down to get into the room as well. The door was still locked this morning.'

'Okay,' says Megan, the sick feeling churning in her stomach. She notes down the number, choosing not to tell Rosalie that Velvet's tack wasn't insured – that she wasn't able to afford the premiums when they went up last year and so she cancelled her policy. 'Thanks for letting me know.'

'No problem,' says Rosalie. She sounds a little distracted. 'Look, I'd better go. It looks like the maintenance guy has just turned up to rebuild the tack room wall and he's driven down to the gallops rather than into the yard car park. I'd better go and direct him.'

'Sure,' says Megan. 'I'll see you later for evening stables.'

'Great,' says Rosalie. 'Later.'

Megan stares at the screen of her phone until it goes dark. Now that she's off the call, the full implication of the theft is starting to hit her. Her tack is gone; she saved for nearly a year to be able to afford the saddle, and the bridle was specially made for Velvet, a combined birthday and Christmas present from her parents a couple of years ago. Now she's got the British Dressage regional finals in two weeks' time and no money to get herself replacement tack in time to compete. Going to the regionals was her chance, her big break to get noticed in the dressage world. It's everything that she's spent the last few years working towards, saving towards – putting up with the snobby customers and long hours and shitty jobs, just so that she can afford to train and compete. And now it's in jeopardy.

As the tears start to flow, she dabs at her eyes with a tissue, knowing that if she returns to the shop floor with red-rimmed eyes she'll get reprimanded by Evelyn for looking unsightly. But it does no good. In fact, it just makes her cry harder.

How the hell is she going to compete at the regional finals now?

CHAPTER SEVEN

JEM

It's almost nine o'clock, way past dinner time, but Jem doesn't feel hungry. This day has been the worst. Even brunch at Villa Rouge and the trip to Gucci hasn't cheered her up. She tried to console herself with a quick shag with the feed delivery guy, but he wasn't especially good. Now, all she can think about is those bastard thieves breaking into her tack room and stealing her stuff.

Jem shivers, and pulls her blanket from the White Company up to her chin. The telly is on, but she's not been paying it any attention. Instead she's just been lying here on her sofa, feeling awful. She feels violated knowing those criminals have been inside her lovely, pristine tack room with their grubby hands touching everything, taking everything, that she's worked for so very hard. She hasn't been able to stomach going out there again after this morning. It's just too upsetting.

And it's utterly unfair.

Why does everything bad have to happen to her?

On the table beside the sofa, her bloody phone keeps chiming away and it's totally doing her head in. The other thing doing her head in is Tyler, her boyfriend of six months, who despite being super keen to move in here with her, now seems to be becoming less and less attentive to her needs as the days go past. And what's the point of him being here if he isn't going to look after her? She needs devotion, and she really isn't getting it. 'Tyler?'

There's no answer.

Stretching behind her, she lifts her phone off the table, intending to message Tyler to find out where he is, but before she wakes the screen she hears a noise in the spare room. Shoving the phone into the pocket of her pyjama bottoms, she pads across the wooden floor to the spare room. The light is off, but there's a glow from the television screen.

Jem looks round the door and sees Tyler sitting – well, half-lying really – on his ridiculous gaming chair, Xbox controller in hand, frantically jabbing at it with his finger. Onscreen, there seems to be some sort of airborne battle taking place between a guy riding a dragon and another mutant character on an armour-wearing bird. She wonders how long he's been in here; she doesn't remember hearing him come home.

She clears her throat, and when that doesn't get his attention she says loudly, 'Hey.'

He doesn't answer. Just keeps jabbing away at the controller.

Stepping into the room, Jem leans down and pulls Tyler's headset off, not caring that she pulls out some of his shoulder-length brown hair along with it. 'I said hello.'

'What the...' He looks round angrily. Onscreen, the mutant character fires a purple missile at the dragon, and it's game over. Tyler curses. 'You killed me.'

'You kill *me*,' says Jem, pouting. 'You know I've had the most horrid day and you haven't checked to see if I'm okay for ages.'

Tyler exhales hard, then turns to look at her. 'I'm sorry. Are you okay?'

'No, not really,' says Jem, feeling tearful again. 'How can I be?'

'It's just stuff,' says Tyler, pushing his unruly hair from his face. 'You can buy more.'

'Just *stuff*?' says Jem, her voice getting louder. 'I've been violated, and my treasured possessions have been ripped from me, but you think I shouldn't care?'

'I just don't think it's that big of a deal,' says Tyler, shrugging as he restarts the game on his Xbox; onscreen, the dragon and their rider have seemingly been brought back to life. 'Just buy more tack. It'll be fine.'

Jem stares at him, open-mouthed. When they first got together, he was like this broody, sexy rock god who treated her like a princess, but lately all he seems to want to do is eat her food and play his online games. Maybe letting him move in was a mistake. She knows Mummy and Daddy don't approve; they told her often enough that he was a freeloader who was only with her for an easy ride. But she told them they had it wrong, that Tyler loves her and, anyway, it was her life, her decision. Now, if she throws him out, she'll have to admit that she was wrong, and she *really* doesn't like to be wrong.

'Well, I'm going to bed.' She gives him a come-hither look. 'Are you going to join me?'

'Yeah, later, okay,' says Tyler, pulling his headset back into place. 'I just need to level up, and it might take a while seeing as you just got me killed.'

Jem sighs. The sting of rejection hurts and she turns away before he can see the tears forming in her eyes. 'Fine.'

It's not fine, though. It seems like every night he stays up playing online for hours, leaving her alone, and often horny, in bed. It's been several months since they last had a proper marathon shag. All she gets now is the occasional quickie and that's really not enough. So in between times, she has to make do with slumming it and shagging the help, but that's often unsatisfactory too.

She pads down the wooden-floored hallway to the bedroom and slams the door shut behind her. Usually her beautiful bedroom, designed at great expense by one of the best interior decorators in the country, brings her joy, the muted off-whites and greys soothing her from the stress of the day and acting like a comforting sanctuary. But not tonight. All she sees now are the imperfections: a chip in the skirting board paintwork, the white sheepskin rug that needs a hoover, and the pile of dirty clothes left in the corner by Tyler's side of the bed.

Trying to divert her focus from the irritations, she flops down onto the super king-sized bed, and pulls out her phone. That's when she's sees her notifications.

Oh. My. God.

Her Instagram is going crazy.

Over 1,200 likes. Almost 700 comments.

With all thoughts of Tyler forgotten, Jem opens the app and scrolls through what people are saying.

Hang in there babes. You got this xxx
So sorry this happened <sad face>
Sending hugs
Bastards. I'll find them for you.
Stay strong horse girl

People are so kind, thinks Jem, as she keeps scrolling. There are so many offers of support and people saying that they're thinking of her. Some are her followers, but others are totally new to her grid. Still, they obviously realise how hard she works and how unfair this is. For a moment she thinks about Tyler's lack of concern, and scowls, then she goes back to scrolling through the comments. At least some people recognise the horrific trauma she's been subjected to today.

Then she sees her DMs. There are over fifty of them.

Toggling to her inbox, Jem reads the messages. Her heart starts to race. She can't believe it. People are offering her stuff – free stuff. Saddle cloths from a local saddlery company, white dressage bandages from a well-known brand, a dressage saddle from a popular German saddler, four bridles from a boutique saddlery in the North, and the list goes on. All they want is for her to post about the item they've given her on her social media.

It's happened. It's finally happened. She's gone viral.

This is her moment, her invitation to join the big leagues.

Jem Baulman-Carter – equestrian influencer.

Smiling, she leans back against her padded grey headboard and watches as the likes and comments on her crying video continue to rise. Her inbox pings as the DMs flood in – more people offering her more free stuff. Tyler might prefer playing his stupid Xbox to being with her, but she has fans now. Proper fans who care about her. Fans who want to help her and give her stuff.

As she starts replying to the DMs, she begins to think that perhaps the pain and shock of the break-in wasn't so bad, really.

After all, now she's practically famous.

CHAPTER EIGHT

HATTIE

Hattie's looking forward to girls' night. It's been a few weeks since she last saw Liberty and Lady Pat, and so a catch up is very much overdue. In the kitchen-diner of her rented cottage, Hattie lays the table. She's glad the cottage came furnished; she's never had her own place before, always living in staff accommodation at the yards she's worked or places that she's done house sitting. It's been a new experience for her, living alone, but she's discovered she really quite likes the calm and quiet.

As if on cue, Poppet flies across the flagstone floor, chasing a ball. Snatching it up, he bites down on it, the ball emitting a loud squeak. Tail wagging furiously, Poppet bites the ball over and over: squeak-squeak-squeak-squeak. Hattie laughs. So much for calm and quiet.

Moments later, the back door opens and Lady Pat appears. Tall, handsome in a rather regal way, and ever practical, beneath her usual Barbour she's wearing an emerald-green jumper, a black velvet scarf, black trousers and sturdy winter boots.

'Evening, Hattie. It's jolly cold out there tonight.'

'Yes, the temperature has really dropped,' says Hattie, smiling.

Lady Pat never knocks. It used to unnerve Hattie when she first met her but she's grown quite used to it now, and all her other eccentric quirks. 'It'll be another sharp frost, I reckon.'

'No doubt.' Lady Pat leans down to give Poppet a stroke as he races over to greet her, the ball in his mouth still squeaking. 'You're very proud of all those squeaks, aren't you, little man?' She looks back up at Hattie. 'Isn't he such fun?'

'Always,' says Hattie, nodding. It's funny, Lady Pat doesn't suffer fools, but she has endless patience with dogs and other animals, even when they're getting themselves into trouble.

There's a knock on the front door. Poppet drops his ball and hurtles towards it. Hattie follows behind him and takes hold of his collar before opening the door, knowing that otherwise he'll immediately run outside the moment it's open wide enough.

'Hey, girl.'

Hattie grins at her friend Liberty, who is standing outside holding a bunch of white roses. 'Come in.'

Liberty steps inside and, after the door is safely closed, they hug hello while Poppet bounces around them, wanting to be part of the embrace too.

When they break apart, Liberty gives her the roses. 'Here you are, a little thank you for dinner.'

'They're beautiful,' says Hattie, taking the flowers. 'And dinner is very basic.'

'It smells great,' says Liberty, bending down to make a fuss of Poppet. 'Doesn't it, sweetie? I bet you want some too, don't you?'

'He's not having any,' says Hattie, carrying the flowers over to the kitchen. 'He's been trying to beg scraps ever since I started cooking.'

'Just as he should,' says Lady Pat, approvingly. 'It's the dog's way.'

'True.' Hattie laughs.

'You've made this place so nice,' says Liberty, slipping off her snow boots on the doormat, and then taking off her ankle-length leopard-print fluffy coat and hanging it with the other coats on the rack by the door. She's wearing a long, black jersey dress and a big camel-coloured chunky knit scarf and looks as chic and quirky as usual. 'It's really homely now.'

'Thanks.' Hattie puts the flowers into a vase, and takes a bottle of wine out of the fridge. She pours a generous amount into three glasses. 'It's starting to feel more like mine now.'

'Lovely, but are you here much?' says Liberty with a wink.

Hattie smiles, and hands a glass of wine to Liberty and then Lady Pat. 'Three or four nights a week. It's fun hanging out with Daniel and the gang over at Templeton Manor, but I like my own space too.'

'Jolly good,' says Lady Pat. 'You don't want to move too fast. Keep him keen, and all that.'

'My thoughts exactly,' says Hattie, taking a sip of wine.

Liberty cocks her head to the side. 'Oh I don't know…'

Hattie laughs. 'How are things with JaXX?'

Liberty beams. 'Brilliant, actually. Although I haven't moved in.' She glances at Lady Pat. 'I'm keeping him keen.'

Lady Pat nods approvingly, then bends down and picks up the squeaky ball that Poppet has just dropped at her feet. She looks at the puppy. 'You want me to throw this, do you?'

'We've talked about moving in together at High Drayton,' says Liberty. 'And I'd love to be with him full-time, but it'd be a real wrench to leave Badger's End.'

'I bet,' says Hattie, as she gets the lasagne out of the oven and carries it across to the table. Liberty's home, Badger's End, is a gorgeous period cottage that neighbours Robert Babbington's land. Liberty runs her luxury candle business from the kitchen and has turned the garden into a botanical paradise of home-grown vegetables and intoxicating scents for use in her candles. 'But you wouldn't have to sell; I'm sure you could easily rent out the cottage.'

'True,' says Liberty. 'I'd have to convert some of JaXX's garden to grow my flowers and veggies, though.'

'I'm sure you'll find some room for that,' says Hattie, smiling as Poppet scurries after the ball thrown by Lady Pat. JaXX owns a whole estate; there are acres of space for Liberty to recreate the Badger's End garden on a much larger scale.

'Clever boy,' says Lady Pat loudly as she makes a fuss of Poppet. 'He's good at bringing the ball back, isn't he?'

'Very good,' agrees Liberty.

'Okay, grab a seat.' Hattie gestures towards the table as she goes back to the oven for the freshly baked garlic breadsticks, and grabs the salad she prepared earlier from the fridge. 'And start helping yourselves.'

There's a brief lull in the conversation while they load their plates with vegan lasagne, breadsticks and salad. Hattie tops up their wine and gives Poppet a bit of breadstick, unable to handle any more of his wide-eyed and mournful-faced begging.

'I'm sure you'll find a way to make it work,' says Hattie, looking at Liberty. 'You two are great together.'

'Thanks, I hope so,' says Liberty, taking another mouthful of lasagne and pointing to her plate with her fork. 'This is amazing, by the way.'

'It is rather splendid,' agrees Lady Pat, taking another mouthful and tossing a bit of breadstick to Poppet, who jumps into the air and catches it before gobbling it down happily. 'Anyway, enough of this talk about men. Tell me, what's your plan with Mermaid's Gold this year?'

Hattie thinks for a moment. She's been musing over the British Eventing fixture list for hours, planning her campaign, but talking her ideas through with Lady Pat is always helpful. 'Ultimately, my goal is Badminton, but there's a long way to go in order for us to qualify, and it's important I get more experience. I know Mermaid's Gold has done more than me, but I need to be up to the job.'

'True,' says Lady Pat. 'And I have no doubt you will be.'

'For sure,' says Liberty, nodding.

'Thanks,' says Hattie. 'Basically, I think the best plan is to get more Intermediate and CCI3* experience this year, with a step up to Advanced and perhaps a long-format CCI3* at the end of the year if we're ready.'

Lady Pat looks thoughtful. 'And talk me through the longer-term plan.'

'Okay,' says Hattie, trying not to feel like she's being assessed. She knows this analytical manner is just Lady Pat's way. When Mermaid's Gold turned up at Clover Hill House while she was house sitting, and Lady Pat suggested Hattie use her horse whispering methods to help the traumatised horse to gain back her trust in humans, Hattie never imagined that she would be in this position. But now that she is, she's determined not to blow it. 'Next year I'd hope to complete qualification for a CCI4*, and aim for Blenheim Horse Trials in the autumn. The following year, if we were qualified and felt ready, we could aim for Badminton CCI5*.'

Lady Pat is silent for a moment, then nods. 'I like that plan. It will depend on qualification though: there are a lot of Minimum Eligibility Requirements.'

'Yes, and I don't meet many of those MERs yet,' says Hattie. 'But that's okay. Like I said, I need more mileage over the bigger fences. I don't want to rush too quickly and not have the experience to get safely round.'

'Wise.' Lady Pat again looks thoughtful. 'So which specific events are you thinking for this year?'

'I'm going to start at Tweseldown in a couple of weeks; the ground is always good there, and Mermaid's Gold is fit and ready to get going.' Hattie thinks through the list she wrote out the other day. 'Next, I'm thinking Burnham Market in mid-April, then Rockingham Castle International in late May, and something else before heading to Aston Le Walls at the end of July, possibly for the Advanced. Then, if we've got the qualification, aiming for Osberton International in the autumn to do our first CCI3*Long.'

Lady Pat considers this while eating the last of her lasagne. 'I think that will work. They're all good galloping courses that should suit the mare well, and if you end the season with a long-format run you'll be putting less pressure on yourself for next year.'

'Exactly,' says Hattie, pleased that Lady Pat agrees with her plan.

'And how are Daniel's Badminton preparations going?' asks Lady Pat, mopping up some of the sauce from the lasagne with a breadstick.

'The Rogue is looking great, and he's very full of himself, which is a good sign.'

'And the scans are clear still?' asks Lady Pat.

'The vet is very happy with them.'

'That's excellent news. It'll be good to see Daniel back on form with that horse. It was such bad luck last year. Hopefully this time things will be better.'

Hattie nods. 'Yes, I hope so.'

'We should do a toast to the new season,' says Liberty, raising her glass. 'To success and happiness.'

They clink their glasses together, and repeat the toast.

Hattie feels the nerves flutter like skittish butterflies in her stomach. She takes a gulp of wine, but that only serves to make them flutter more. She needs to do well this season to work towards qualification for Badminton.

She has to fulfil the promise she made to her mum.

CHAPTER NINE

WAYNE

*J*em Baulman-Carter is his last client of the day. He pulls into her yard at four thirty on the dot, but there's no sign of Jem or either of her grooms. Dammit, thinks Wayne, as he parks the van in his usual spot at one end of the yard and climbs out. If they don't get the horses ready for him soon, he's going to be late for footy tonight, and he promised the lads he'd be part of the Red Lion starting line-up in the five-a-side match against the Dog and Duck pub team, their most local rivals in the league.

'Anyone about?' calls Wayne, rubbing his hands together to fight off the cold as he scans the yard. He was hoping for a mug of tea while he worked, but with this delay there's not going to be time for a tea break. 'Rosalie? Peter?'

'Sorry, they've taken the last two horses out for a long hack in the woods,' says Jem, appearing from inside a nearby stable. 'But I can help you.'

'Great,' says Wayne. 'Who've we got today?'

'Just four,' says Jem. 'Watermelon, Bugsy, Hollington and Velvet.'

'Cool,' says Wayne. Opening the back of his van, he starts

getting his equipment for shoeing the horses ready, lifting out the portable anvil and his tools.

'Before you get started, could you help me out with something in the barn?' asks Jem, smiling.

'Sure,' says Wayne, although to be honest he could do without any more delays. He puts his tools down beside the anvil and follows her across the neatly swept yard to the large barn. Jem unbolts the door and he follows her inside.

Jem closes the door behind them, then turns to face him. There's an expression on her face that he can't read.

'So what can I help you with?' asks Wayne.

Smiling, Jem steps towards him. Reaching out, she slides her fingers under the buckle of his leather farrier chaps, and pulls him to her.

'Hello,' says Wayne, unsure about this sudden change in her. 'What—?'

Jem silences him with a kiss. Her hands are in his hair now. Her tongue is ramming itself into his mouth. For a moment he thinks he's going to choke, she's so rough. Then she pulls away from his mouth, nibbling her way across his jaw to his earlobe.

'Fuck me,' Jem whispers into his ear. 'Bend me over the hay and take me from behind.'

Jesus. He wasn't expecting this. Jem's always been civil but fairly frosty whenever he's been here before. He always got the impression she thought she was too fancy to look at the likes of him. But now she's the opposite. She must *really* like the calendar. 'Should we really be—'

'I need you,' she says, undoing the buckle on his chaps, pulling down the zipper of his jeans and taking hold of him. 'Fuck me.'

He feels himself harden in her grip. This is better than the mug of tea he'd been hoping for. Turning her away from him, Wayne leans her forward over the nearest stack of haybales.

Jem pulls down her breeches and opens her legs, then looks over her shoulder at him. 'Do as you're told, and fuck me, Wayne.'

He pushes himself into her. She's wet and welcoming, and that, along with the unexpectedness of the situation and her enthusiastic moans, has him peaking sooner than usual. He grabs her hips and thrusts harder, faster. Jem bucks beneath him, her fingers clenching the hay, clearly enjoying herself. They cum together, sweating and breathless.

Wayne's still getting his breath back when Jem turns back around.

Pulling up her breeches, Jem raises her eyebrow. 'Well that was… fast.' She gestures to his jeans and chaps, which are still around his ankles. 'Sort yourself out, and then you'd better get on with shoeing. I don't want to be waiting around all night for you to finish the job; I've got things to do.'

'Alright, but you were the one who—'

'Just hurry up, okay,' says Jem dismissively as she struts towards the door.

With his jeans still around his ankles, Wayne stares after her, and wonders what the hell that was all about.

~

Two hours later and Wayne has finished shoeing the horses. The air has a touch of frost to it, and it's completely dark now. He never did get that tea, but at least he's managed to work double quick, so if he can just get his money he should be free and clear to make the footy in time before kick-off. Problem is, there doesn't seem to be anyone left in the yard. Untying Bugsy, a big, chestnut warmblood gelding, he leads the horse back to his stable and removes the headcollar. 'There you go, chap.'

The horse immediately gets to work on the hay net hanging in the corner of the stable, and Wayne lets himself out and bolts the door behind him. Going back to his van, he packs away his anvil and tools and is soon ready to get going, but there's still no sign of anyone.

Sighing, he gets his diary out of the van, and sets off across the floodlit yard, looking for Jem or one of the grooms. 'I'm finished,' he says into the silence. 'Anybody about?'

There's no answer. He hasn't seen Jem since she walked out on him in the barn, but not long ago both Peter and Rosalie, Jem's two grooms, were bustling about, topping up water buckets, putting full hay nets into the stables and feeding the horses dinner. He frowns; maybe they've finished for the day and forgotten about him.

Wayne checks the time on his watch. It's getting closer to quarter to seven, and with kick-off at seven thirty he needs to be out of here in the next ten minutes if he's going to make it back home to grab his kit and then get over to the five-a-side pitch in time. Continuing across the yard, he sees a light on behind the almost-closed door of the tack room.

Opening the door, he finds Peter, Jem's tall, willowy groom, and a curvy, petite brunette with the cutest freckles, talking in hushed voices. They stop talking when they see him, and Wayne gets the distinct impression that he's interrupting something. Still, the clock's ticking and he needs to get going. 'Erm, hi there. I'm all done out here, I just need to book you guys in for next time and collect my money, but there's no sign of Jem.'

'Sorry about that,' says Peter, hurriedly putting down the tack-cleaning sponge he's holding and moving towards the door. 'Jem's probably already inside for the night, you know how she is. I didn't realise it was that late already. Let me go and grab your money from the kitchen.'

'Thanks,' says Wayne. 'Appreciate that.'

Peter disappears out onto the yard, leaving Wayne and the brunette in the tack room. Wayne heard about the break-in at the yard when he was in the pub last night. It's not the first he's heard of in the local area, and it seems the thieves are getting bolder. To dismantle a wall to get into a tack room, especially in a yard with all the security and CCTV that this one has, takes careful planning and a lot of bravado. He can see that the back wall has now been reinstalled, but the place is fairly free of tack – there are only a couple of dressage saddles and bridles on the wooden tack-cleaning saddle horse by the sink, and the saddle brackets and bridle hooks around the walls are all empty.

'Awful about the burglary,' says Wayne. 'There are some really shitty people around.'

'Yeah,' says the brunette, her voice subdued.

Wayne frowns. 'Hey, are you okay?'

The brunette nods, but it's clear from her red-rimmed eyes and puffy face that she's been crying. 'I'm fine.'

'Are you sure?' asks Wayne.

'It's just, the break-in…' says the brunette, clearly trying to hold back more tears. 'My tack was taken and it wasn't insured.'

'I'm sorry,' says Wayne. 'Can you claim off Jem's yard insurance?'

'Apparently not,' says the brunette, her voice quivering. 'And I can't afford to buy a saddle right now. Velvet is tricky to fit. The last one had to be customised and that costs even more so… I'm meant to be riding in the regional finals in ten days' time but I think I'm going to have to withdraw.'

'That really sucks,' says Wayne, realising this pretty brunette must be Velvet Mimosa's owner. 'If it helps, you can delay paying me for your horse's shoes until I'm here next time.'

'Really? That's so kind.' She gives him a smile. 'Thank you.'

'It's not a problem,' says Wayne. And, although he's usually highly reluctant for clients not to pay immediately after he's shod their horses, this time he's fine about it.

Seeing the pretty brunette smile is payment enough.

CHAPTER TEN

HATTIE

*I*t's been a good day. Driving home from the Weslingbury craft fair, held in the grounds of beautiful Weslingbury House, Hattie and Liberty are in high spirits. Even the weather, which has been getting steadily worse all day, hasn't dampened them – although now, with the temperature dropping rapidly, thick, freezing fog is making the driving conditions rather difficult.

'I think that's the best craft fair I've done,' says Liberty, switching on the wipers. 'We sold out of all the small candles and most of the melts.'

'And I only packed a few of the large candles back into the car,' says Hattie. 'They loved them.'

Liberty smiles. 'Dinner's on me tonight. What do you fancy? Curry, pizza?'

'Pizza,' says Hattie. 'With dippers.'

'Perfect,' says Liberty, as she indicates left and turns off the main road and onto a smaller lane.

'Gosh it's dark down here,' says Hattie, peering out through the windscreen.

'Yeah,' says Liberty, flicking the headlights onto full beam and then back to dipped as she realises all the full beams do in the fog is reflect the light back at them. She drives slowly along the single-track lane, trying to avoid the potholes. 'This seems more like a track than a road.'

'Are you sure this is the way we came?' asks Hattie, looking out of the window, trying to get a sense of the surroundings, but it's impossible.

'I think so,' says Liberty, but she doesn't sound certain. She taps the satnav and enlarges the map. 'Yes, it thinks we're going the right way.'

'Okay,' says Hattie.

They follow the winding lane. On either side of them are high banks leading up to stone walls. If a car comes from the other direction, there's no way of passing. Hattie hopes they don't meet anyone.

Liberty leans forward, and puts the windscreen wipers on faster as she tries to see through the fog. 'I hate this.'

'Me too.' Their buoyant mood from earlier has disappeared. It seems even colder, and eerie, out here in the fog with no sense of where they actually are. The satnav says they've got two miles to go and then it looks as if they need to turn onto a bigger A-road. Hattie can't wait for them to reach it.

They chug steadily along the lane at no faster than twenty miles an hour. There's less than half a mile to go before they meet the main road when it happens. Headlights, bright and dazzling, appear around the sharp bend up ahead. They're angled high, belonging to a four-by-four probably, and they're approaching fast.

'Oh my God,' says Liberty, braking hard. 'What are they...?'

The oncoming car isn't slowing down. Liberty flashes her lights and pulls as far into the edge of the lane as she can. Hattie takes a sharp inhale. She can't see how the car isn't going to hit them.

At the last moment, the driver of the oncoming vehicle seems to realise the road is too narrow to pass, but they're travelling too fast to stop. As the larger car looms out of the fog, it almost seems to rear up as its driver yanks the steering wheel and goes up the bank at such a dramatic angle that Hattie fears it'll flip over and crush them.

Somehow it doesn't, though, and the four-by-four continues on, speeding away down the lane. Hattie exhales loudly. 'What the... how did they...?'

'That was close,' says Liberty. 'Too close.'

'Let's get off this lane,' says Hattie, hugging her arms around her.

'Yep,' says Liberty, accelerating the car forward again. 'Not too far now.'

They continue in silence, and Hattie gradually feels her heart rate returning to normal.

'What's that?' says Liberty, peering out into the foggy lane. 'On the other side of the road.'

Hattie looks at where Liberty is pointing. 'It looks like something's there. It's moving. You'd better stop.'

Liberty brings the car to a halt and Hattie jumps out. The cold air nips at her skin. The fog feels like a cold, damp cloth around her throat. She rushes towards the place where they spotted the movement. 'Oh no... you poor little...'

Hattie turns towards the car and gestures for Liberty to join her.

'What is it?' asks Liberty, as she gets out of the car.

'A deer,' says Hattie, crouching down near the animal. 'I think it's been hit.'

'Probably by those idiots who nearly crashed into us,' says Liberty. 'What shall we do?'

The deer is pretty large. Hattie thinks it's probably a female roe, but she isn't a hundred percent sure. What she is sure of is that the animal needs veterinary attention. It doesn't look able to get up and there's a bloody gash on one of its front legs. It's alert though, and as she gets closer it starts struggling to stand. 'We need to get it to a wildlife hospital.'

Liberty looks worried. 'How?'

Standing up and taking a few steps back until the deer stops struggling, Hattie says, 'Can you put the candles and stuff from the craft fair on the back seat? Then we can put the deer in the boot; that'll be safest.'

'Okay, just give me a minute.'

As Liberty clears the boot of the car, Hattie takes off her Puffa coat and approaches the deer. She doesn't know a huge amount about deer, but she knows from her horse whispering training that they have the same prey animal instincts as a horse, only as they're wild they're far more sensitive and flighty. If you want to get a wild, injured horse to go somewhere it doesn't want to go, blindfolding it is a measure of last resort. If her getting close to the deer is going to stress it, perhaps some kind of makeshift blindfold will help.

Her coat is too bulky, but the sweatshirt she's wearing underneath could work. Removing the sweatshirt, Hattie puts her coat on over the thin t-shirt she's left with and starts to approach the deer again.

'Okay, the boot's clear,' says Liberty. 'We should get the deer moved. Another car could come along any time.'

'Agreed,' says Hattie. She needs to get this done.

As she gets closer to the deer, it starts thrashing around again, but it isn't able to get up. Hattie keeps walking, and holds the sweatshirt ready to put over the terrified animal. It cries out, scared.

'It's okay. We're going to help you,' says Hattie, keeping her voice low and calm.

The deer struggles harder to get up.

Hattie pauses. She's not sure how to pick up the deer. She doesn't want to hurt it, but it's pretty big – at least the size of a large Labrador – and so she'll need to have a firm grip in order to carry it over to the car.

'Do you need me to help?' asks Liberty.

Hattie shakes her head. She can't delay; a car could hurtle down the lane at any moment and the deer needs a vet. Taking a deep breath, she bends down and puts the sweatshirt over the deer's eyes. It cries out, but Hattie can't let that put her off. Deciding to hold the animal as if it were a young foal, she slides her left hand around the front of its chest and her right hand around its haunches, and lifts it up.

The deer cries again, but doesn't struggle.

Hattie carries the animal across to the car. She tries to keep her breathing slow and steady, knowing that the deer will pick up on any signs of stress, and talks calmly to it. 'It's okay, little one, we'll get you to the hospital, it'll all be okay.'

'I've spread a blanket out for it,' says Liberty, as Hattie reaches the car.

'Great,' says Hattie. The deer is calm at the moment, but it's quite heavy and she'll need to get it into the boot without hurting it.

Slowly, she lifts it into the boot, and then gradually lowers it down onto the blue towel that Liberty has put there. The deer doesn't struggle, and Hattie's thankful for that. She talks to the deer, to help herself stay calm more than for the animal. 'Good girl, well done, it's okay.'

With the deer safely on the blanket, Hattie releases her grip and then slowly removes her sweatshirt from over the animal's eyes. That's when things start to go wrong.

Terrified, the deer cries out again and starts to thrash around. Hattie steps back, trying to get clear, but she's too close, too slow. The deer strikes out. There's a crack as one of the deer's hooves hits Hattie's wrist. Pain ricochets through her.

'Oh my God, are you okay?' asks Liberty.

With her uninjured hand, Hattie reaches up and shuts the

boot. The deer should be okay now; the darkness of the closed boot should help it become calmer. She looks at Liberty. 'My wrist and my shoulder… they really hurt.'

Liberty's looking at Hattie's shoulder in horror. 'Your shoulder…?'

Glancing down, Hattie sees that it's hanging at a weird angle. She feels a wave of nausea flood through her. 'I think it's dislocated.'

'You need to go to A&E,' says Liberty. 'Get in the car, I'll take you to—'

Hattie shakes her head, determined. 'The deer needs a vet first. We'll go to the wildlife hospital in Long Casden, they take casualties 24/7, and then I'll go to hospital.'

CHAPTER ELEVEN

MEGAN

It took twenty-two minutes of waiting in a queue listening to instrumental versions of 80s hits before Megan's call to the credit card company was answered by a human, and less than two minutes for that human to tell her that they couldn't increase her credit limit. Her bank had already said the same about her overdraft. So now here she is, parking outside her parents' house, psyching herself up to ask them for a loan so she can buy Velvet a new saddle and bridle.

Through the window, and the rain, Megan gazes over the neatly clipped miniature hedge and across the front lawn to her childhood home. It's a classic chocolate box thatched cottage, with white plaster walls, red and pink roses in the flowerbeds, and a stone pathway leading from the white wooden gate across the grass to the red front door. Unlike the last time she visited, there's scaffolding around the house. Megan wonders why; her parents haven't mentioned that they're having work done.

They bought the cottage six months before Megan was born, and it's the only place she lived until she moved out into a tiny studio flat in the town when she was 22 years old. Every time she comes back, Megan wonders whether moving out was a mistake, but then she goes into the room that had been her bedroom and sees her mum's wonderful brass sculptures, and knows it was the right thing to do. Her mum has waited all these years to be able to do her art at home; it's right that she has that dedicated space now. Megan just has to get on with adulting.

She climbs quickly out of the car and trots up the path to the front door. She's barely had time to use the old, brass door-knocker when the door is pulled open.

'Come inside, love, before you're drenched,' says her dad, smiling. He's wearing jeans, a t-shirt and his favourite baggy beige cardigan. He gestures at her to enter. 'Hurry up, don't dither.'

'Hi, Dad,' says Megan, laughing as she steps over the threshold and into the living room. It's only once her dad has shut the door that she notices a strange, mouldy smell that isn't usually there. Over in the dining room, a couple of red buckets are positioned by the far corner. Turning to her mum, Megan gestures towards the buckets. 'What are they for?'

'The roof failed,' says her mum, removing her work apron from over her jeans and sweatshirt, folding it neatly and placing it onto the arm of the sofa. 'We'd hoped it'd hold out for another year, but the storms last month finished it off. We had rain coming through the ceiling into our bedroom, and that corner of the dining room is really quite damp now, so we couldn't put it off any longer.'

'That's what the scaffolding's for, love,' says her dad. 'The thatchers are starting next week and hope to be done within a month.'

'Sounds expensive,' says Megan, her heart sinking.

'It is,' says her mum, blowing out hard. 'Just over £15,000, according to the estimate, although there's a chance the timbers in the back corner are damaged so if they need replacing…'

'Let's just say we'll not be taking any fancy holidays anytime soon,' says her dad, trying to make light of it. 'At least not until your mum's sold a few more of her bigger sculptures.'

'Might need to sell a few hundred.' Her mum laughs. 'Come on through to the kitchen; your dad was just making some tea.'

Megan smiles and follows her parents through to the kitchen. It's warmer in here, thanks to the red Aga, and she can smell freshly baked bread. The kitchen is largely the same as it's been since she was born; the wooden cabinets have had a new coat of pale green paint, and the handles have been updated, but her parents' motto is 'make and make do' – nothing gets replaced until it's no longer serviceable.

It's great to be home, but despite her parents' joking, Megan can see the worry in their eyes. They've always been thrifty, and they have some modest savings, but the new roof will wipe them out and then some. There's no way she can ask to borrow money for a saddle now.

As her dad takes the cosy off the teapot and pours strong brewed tea into three large misshapen pottery mugs, Megan puts her hand on her mum's arm and gives it a squeeze. 'I'm really sorry about the roof. I wish I could help.'

'We're fine,' says her mum, covering Megan's hand with her own.

'Yes, don't worry, love,' says her dad. 'Things always work out in the end.'

Megan hopes he's right.

She sits down at the whitewashed pine kitchen table as her dad puts the mugs of tea, along with the blue-and-white striped biscuit barrel, down on the mat in the centre, and then fetches the milk and sugar.

'So how's your job going?' asks Mum, pouring milk into each of the mugs.

'It's okay,' says Megan, forcing a smile.

'And the dressage training?' asks her dad, putting two sugars into his tea and stirring.

'It's good. Velvet is a star, as always,' says Megan, fighting to hold the smile in place.

'Excellent,' says her dad. 'I have every faith in the pair of you. You're going to wow those judges at the regional finals.'

Megan takes a sip of her tea. She can't trust her voice to sound normal, and she doesn't want her parents to see that something's wrong. They've always scrimped and saved to let her indulge in her passion for horses – Dad doing regular overtime at his job as a postman, and Mum taking on private pupils on top of her high school art teacher job to bring in enough to fund riding lessons, and then later, a pony. They've earned their retirement, and she's an adult now. She'll just have to figure things out on her own.

CHAPTER TWELVE

HATTIE

Having taken the deer to Long Casden Wildlife Hospital, Liberty drove Hattie to Leightonshire Hospitals NHS Trust. Hattie had her dislocated shoulder put back into place just after midnight and has been waiting to hear the results of the X-ray on her wrist for the past two hours. It's almost four o'clock in the morning, but the accident and emergency department is still busy and the staff are doing an amazing job seeing people as soon as they can. Tiredness is starting to get to Hattie, though. She's had zero sleep, is in pain, and *really* wants a chocolate bar but has been resisting as the nurse told her not to eat anything in case they needed to operate.

Hattie's just messaging Liberty, who's out in the waiting room, when a doctor hurries into the cubicle. The young woman is probably just a few years older than Hattie, but there are dark shadows under her eyes.

'Harriet Kimble?' says the doctor, consulting the notes on her handheld tablet.

'Yes, that's me,' says Hattie, sitting up on the trolley bed and swinging her legs around so she's facing the doctor.

'So you've got a rather nasty break, here and here,' says the doc, holding out her tablet and pointing to a couple of places on the X-ray. She taps the second spot. 'This one has displaced the bone alignment.'

'That'll be why it hurts so much then,' says Hattie, grimacing.

'Indeed. We'll need to get it back in line so it heals correctly,' says the doc, putting the tablet down on the cabinet at the side of the cubicle. 'So I'm going to manually manipulate it back into position, and then we'll put you in a cast which you'll need to keep on for six to eight weeks.'

Hattie's heart sinks. She thinks of her plans. Six to eight weeks in a cast will completely mess up her spring season events with Mermaid's Gold. 'Is there any way to get it to heal faster?'

'Not that I know of; it's just rest and time I'm afraid,' says the doc, taking hold of the injured hand. 'Now, deep breath. This is probably going to hurt.'

CHAPTER THIRTEEN

JEM

She wakes at five o'clock feeling horny as hell. The bedroom is in darkness aside from the soft glow of the display on her digital radio. Beside her, Tyler is snoring softly. Turning onto her side to face him, she sees he's sleeping with his back towards her. She'd prefer him to spoon her, but he never does. He'd probably spoon his damn games console if he could, though, she thinks bitterly. He'd still been playing his online game in the spare room when she turned in around quarter to eleven. She wonders what time he came to bed; she suspects it would have been well after midnight.

She's annoyed with him, but she can't deny the throb between her legs. Moving closer to Tyler, Jem runs her hand over his shoulders and down his side. Kisses him between the shoulder blades. 'Are you asleep?' she says, in her sexiest voice.

There's no answer.

Jem pokes Tyler in the ribs with her finger, and says louder, 'Are you sleeping?'

He mumbles something incoherent.

Jem curses. She gives his shoulder a little shake and, with all traces of her sexy voice gone, says, 'Wake up.'

Tyler mumbles again, and turns over to face her, but his eyes are closed and he's obviously still asleep.

Running her hand across his stomach and down into his boxers, Jem takes hold of his dick. He murmurs something, and licks his lips. Jem grips him a little tighter. Moves her hand faster. Tries to get a reaction.

Tyler gurgles, and lets out a loud snore.

It's not the reaction she was looking for.

Swearing, Jem lets go of Tyler.

It's not fair. She pays all the bills and he barely lifts a finger to help around the house while living here with her rent free. The least she should get out of it is having her needs met once in a while. Of course, she could sort herself out on her own, but why should she? She doesn't ask much of Tyler, but surely satisfying her shouldn't be too much of an ask. Before he moved in, she'd just go across to the staff accommodation and screw Peter if she needed attention, but if she does that right now she might bump into Rosalie getting ready for morning stables. Jem doesn't want to have to deal with her disapproving looks.

So she stays in bed and watches Tyler sleeping. Maybe she should dump him. The problem is, he's really hot, and with his hair all dishevelled it only adds to his sexiness. And he still has those cheekbones and a chiselled jaw to die for. Plus he looks good beside her when they go out; they turn heads and she does love that.

Jem sighs. Also, if she dumps him her parents will be proven right, and she can't let them win. No, she needs an alternative plan, something that will cause Tyler to become more attentive to her in every way.

An idea comes to mind.

She needs to make Tyler really jealous.

CHAPTER FOURTEEN

MEGAN

Megan half-halts as she sets Velvet up for the long diagonal of the Olympic-sized indoor arena, then eases the tension on the rein and gives the aid for medium trot. Ever responsive, Velvet opens up his stride and powers across the arena. To Megan, it feels as if they're floating on air.

It's in moments like this that her worries about money and the frustrations of working at the Doxford Millar store melt away. There's just her and Velvet, and their ever-developing partnership. The feeling of being in sync with her wonderful boy makes everything worthwhile.

Transitioning from the medium trot to a working trot before they reach the end of the diagonal, Megan lets the reins slip through her fingers and encourages Velvet to stretch out his neck. She rides a few large circles in rising trot, something that is a little bit of a challenge riding bareback without a saddle, and then brings him to a halt.

Sliding from his back, she pats Velvet's neck and pulls a mint-and-herb treat from the pocket of her breeches, feeding it to him. He munches it happily, and then raises his top lip in appreciation. Megan laughs.

'You really shouldn't spoil that horse,' says Jem from behind her.

Turning, Megan sees Jem and her talented chestnut youngster, Star Child, walking in a circle nearby. 'He loves them, and one won't hurt.'

'One is one too many,' says Jem, wrinkling up her nose. 'No wonder the creature's getting fat.'

'He's not fat,' says Megan, indignantly, giving Velvet's neck another stroke. He is perfect just as he is.

Jem shrugs. 'If you say so.'

Megan turns back to Velvet and gives him another treat, just to show Jem that she'll do what she wants with her own horse. Velvet loves people and enjoys his work, which is more than can be said for Star Child who, from the way he's stomping his forelegs every few strides and grinding his teeth against the fancy gold bit in his mouth, is distinctly unhappy.

Loosening off Velvet's noseband, Megan walks him in a circle then stops. Jem has halted an increasingly tense-looking Star Child a few metres ahead and is looking at her with a strange expression on her face.

'You okay?' asks Megan, giving Velvet's neck another rub as he nuzzles her pocket in hope of some more treats.

'You know you can't compete at the regionals bareback, right?' says Jem.

Megan feels her happiness deflate like a punctured balloon. 'Of course, but I can't afford a saddle at the moment so…'

Star Child throws his head up and walks forward. Jem wrestles the horse back to a halt, then, in a tone as if she's talking to a small child, says to Megan, 'Just put it on a credit card or something. It's bad for that horse's back to have you bumping around on him like a sack of potatoes all the time. I mean, you're not getting any lighter either, are you?'

Megan bites her lip before she says something she'll regret. She knows how Jem is: blunt and unself-aware when it comes to the things she says to others, but highly sensitive to anything said to her. 'I don't have any credit left.'

Jem screws up her nose as if she can't imagine not having credit. 'Well, apply for another card then.'

She probably can't imagine what it's like to be maxed out on what you can borrow, thinks Megan. Not when she was born into luxury and privilege. 'I can't.'

Jem frowns, and puts more pressure on the reins, forcing Star Child to overbend his neck. The powerful gelding lifts a foreleg and starts to paw at the ground, scraping the synthetic sand arena surface into a pile beneath him. 'Well, if you want to go to the regionals you'll have to think of something. You absolutely can't ride like that.' She waves her hand at Megan, as if she's a bad smell.

'Maybe I...' Megan pauses, cautiously, as she fiddles with a piece of Velvet's mane. Steam from his body rises up into the cold evening air; he needs to get back to his stable and his rugs before he starts to get cold. But, although Megan really hates to ask Jem for a favour, she can't see any other option. And seeing as Jem has been sent at least fifteen saddles since her Instagram video went viral, and she has fewer horses than that, it's not like she needs to use them all. 'Perhaps I could borrow one of the saddles you've been sent?'

Star Child blows out vigorously and tosses his head. Jem hardens her expression. 'I'm sorry, but I can't let you have one.'

'You can't let me borrow one for a day?' says Megan, confused. 'But I thought they'd be gifted to—'

'I'm going to sell the spare saddles so they need to be unused. The money will help me to get through the trauma caused by the break-in.' Jem gives a little shake of her head and her expression becomes more haunted. 'I know it's hard for someone like you to understand, but at my level you feel things so much more deeply. The hurt, and the violation, is so very acute.'

Megan stares at Jem. She knows Jem is self-centred, but this condescending selfishness is bad even by her standards. Megan can't think of how to respond without getting angry, so she bites her lip and says nothing. Much as she hates not standing up for herself, she can't afford for Jem to throw her and Velvet out of the yard on top of everything else that's happened. So she takes Velvet's reins over his head, and leads him across the arena to the door and out into the dark, chilly evening.

∽

As Velvet eats his dinner, Megan sits in the tack room and uses her phone to check the items she listed on Vinted – a couple of pairs of nice shoes, a dress she's never worn, and a designer handbag that she'd bought on her twenty-first birthday as a special treat. They've all sold, which is great news, but the bad news is that she still can't afford a saddle. She can buy a pair of stirrups perhaps, and maybe some stirrup leathers and a girth, but not the actual saddle to put them on. It's hopeless. She's worked multiple jobs just to be able to afford to train and compete, and now, just as their efforts are starting to pay off, she's lost her big chance to compete in the regionals and, maybe, make it to the national championships.

Tears prick at Megan's eyes, and she blinks them away. She clenches her fingers tighter around her phone. She can't blow this chance to ride in the regionals. She has to find a way to get a saddle.

Shaking her head, she puts her phone back into the pocket of her quilted jacket, and walks over to the sink. It's already pretty late and she needs to clean her bridle and then get home and make dinner – beans on toast again – so she can get to bed at a decent time, and then get up early again to open the shop tomorrow morning.

Filling the sink with warm water, she dampens her tack sponge and starts to wipe over her bridle. That's when she notices the 'Rural Pleasures' calendar that's been pinned up on the wall behind the kettle. It's already open on March, even though they're still a few days off the new month. Looking quickly away from the date of the regionals that have been circled in red, Megan glances at the feature photo.

'Jesus,' she says, doing a double take.

There, naked aside from his leather chaps and a strategically placed anvil, and looking unmistakably hot, is their farrier, Wayne.

Megan stares at his picture for a long moment, then lifts up the page and flicks through the other photos. Each is of a good-looking guy posing in their place of work – Wayne in his forge, a farmer astride his tractor, a market gardener with his wheelbarrow full of plants covering himself, the local baker wearing just his apron, and so on. She remembers hearing something at work about how successful the calendar has been, and that the charity has made a record-breaking profit since it switched from the country landscape scenes of the previous calendars to this new sexy rural guys approach.

She narrows her eyes, remembering a documentary she saw on the telly a few months ago about a website, or app, that lets you post spicy pictures online viewable only by those who pay to subscribe to your feed, like a pay-per-view version of Instagram.

Pulling out her phone again, she searches for the site: OnlyFans.

Maybe there is another way she could make some money fast.

CHAPTER FIFTEEN

HATTIE

The event season has started and the going at Tweseldown Horse Trials is as good as ever. The sandy, well-drained ground has prevented the course from getting too boggy despite the days of incessant rain they've had recently. With Hattie out of action with her wrist in plaster, they've only travelled two horses here to compete. Daniel has brought The Rogue to do the Open Intermediate, and Jenny the vet has brought Dinky, her pint-sized event horse, to run in the Intermediate.

Both horses did good efforts in the dressage, with The Rogue putting in a cheeky little buck in the walk-canter transition but otherwise being very restrained, and both jumped clear in the show jumping. They're getting ready to go cross-country now, with Jenny due on the course a few minutes ahead of Daniel. Hattie's thankful that, so far, the rain has held off today. She hopes it'll stay away until after both horses have jumped.

'I'm heading down now,' says Jenny, leading Dinky alongside the lorry ramp so she can use it as a mounting block.

Jenny's wearing her pink-and-white cross-country colours, and Dinky has his matching overgirth and boots. As she prepares to get on, Eddie hurries over and holds the off-side stirrup to stop the saddle slipping as Jenny mounts.

Today they've agreed that Eddie will go down to the cross-country with Jenny. Normally he'd be with Daniel and The Rogue, but on seeing how nervous Jenny was looking about a couple of the larger fences, Daniel said he'd be fine to sort The Rogue out and would come down a bit later with Hattie. Eddie gives Hattie a wave. 'See you at the start.'

'Good luck,' says Hattie. She can see how nervous the usually chilled Eddie is for his girlfriend. They are such a sweet couple. 'I'll bring the dogs with me.'

'Thanks,' says Eddie, turning and hurrying after Jenny as she sets off across the lorry park towards the cross-country course at a purposeful walk.

'Have a great run,' calls Daniel. He's crouched beside The Rogue, applying tape around the straps of the big gelding's protective leg boots. If one of the straps was to snap when they're out on the course, the tape should hold the boot in place and give them enough time to pull up safely.

'Is there anything I can do?' asks Hattie.

'No, I'm good, thanks,' says Daniel without looking round. 'Nearly done.'

Hattie doesn't reply. She knows that there's not much she can do with her stupid broken wrist; it's so frustrating. That's why she's in such a bad mood, although she's trying her best to hide it. After all, it's not Daniel and Jenny's fault that they get to ride when she can't, but as they walked round the cross-country course earlier, Hattie knew how much Mermaid's Gold would have loved both the sandy going and the big timber fences that favour bold horses. It isn't going to happen, though. Hattie still has many weeks in plaster ahead of her.

She hasn't told Daniel because she knows he'd have tried to dissuade her, but she'd tried to ride one-handed earlier this week. Mermaid's Gold is a sweetheart to hack, and so Hattie hoped they could go out along the bridleways for a bit each day to help keep the mare's fitness, and her own, up to a good level. But it wasn't meant to be. Hattie winces at the memory of the searing pain in her wrist as she tried riding around the arena, and how any sudden movement jolted her still-sore shoulder. Mermaid's Gold is a good girl, but riding at the moment just isn't realistic. Neither is the idea that someone else could ride the mare to keep her ticking over while Hattie recovers. Mermaid's Gold has made it very clear to anyone who has tried to carry tack towards her that the only rider she'll allow is Hattie. So, as a result, Hattie's made the decision to turn the mare out in the field for a few weeks. It means writing off the first part of the season, and she's yet to work out what that means for her qualification plan, but there's nothing she can do about it. She just hopes her damn wrist and shoulder heal quickly.

'You okay?' asks Daniel, standing up after having finished taping the gelding's boots. He looks concerned.

'Yeah.' Hattie forces a smile. She doesn't want to bring the mood down for him and Jenny, and he needs to be focused on the course and giving The Rogue a great round, not on her moping about. 'I was just thinking about that combination at fence nine and how I'd ride it on Mermaid.'

'Straight through the middle,' says Daniel with a grin. 'Fastest route for that little mare, every time.'

Hattie's smile becomes genuine rather than forced. Daniel's right, of course, Mermaid's Gold favours the quickest route through her fences; she's not a fan of dithering around. 'Very true.'

As Daniel unties The Rogue and leads him round before mounting, Hattie goes into the living area of the lorry to fetch Eddie's collie, McQueen, and Poppet. Jenny decided to leave Popsy, Poppet's spaniel sister, back at Templeton Manor in Bunty's care today, thinking trying to keep watch on the young puppy might make it difficult for her to fully concentrate on the job in hand.

As she steps through the door into the living space, Hattie thinks Jenny had the right idea. The dogs, or rather Poppet, have been busy. There are hundreds of tiny pieces of white tissue strewn around the lino floor of the small kitchenette and across the bunk seating around the collapsible table. Poppet himself is sitting with a half-chewed cardboard tissue box in his mouth, which is now empty. Hattie shakes her head. 'What have you been up to?'

McQueen looks up from his bed in the corner, a long-suffering look on his face. Poppet tilts his head to one side and gives her his cutest butter-wouldn't-melt expression. She laughs. 'Don't worry, McQueen, I know exactly who did this, don't I, Poppet?'

The little dog lifts up his ears.

'You okay in there?' asks Daniel. 'I'm going to get on now.'

'Yes, all good,' replies Hattie. The tissue situation can wait until after the cross-country. Thankfully Daniel's basic but dependable Bedford horsebox doesn't require the same level of cleanliness as the white-leather upholstered lorry he used last year, owned by his now ex-owners, Dexter and Lexi Marchfield-Wright.

Taking the lead and the coupling strap from the table, she clips one end of the coupling strap to McQueen's harness, and the other to Poppet's harness, then fixes the lead to the centre ring. Luckily, Poppet idolises McQueen. He's very happy to be coupled to the three-legged older dog, and McQueen is tolerant of the bouncy, excitable puppy, enabling Hattie to have them both on just the one lead in her good hand.

'I'm on,' says Daniel.

'Great.' Harriet opens the door and manoeuvres the dogs down the steps. Eddie has already taken the spares bucket down to the cross-country warmup, so all she needs to do is lock the living door. 'We're all set.'

～

Watching the cross-country is more nerve-wracking than if she was riding herself. It's not because she doesn't have faith in Daniel and The Rogue, because she absolutely does, but more that she so wants things to go well for them this year. As much as she's disappointed that her own plans have been thwarted due to having broken her wrist, Daniel had such an awful time last year that he really deserves a good season. But, of course, that isn't the way things work. Eventing is a dangerous sport, and although you do everything you can to limit the risk, it's a rare day when everything goes fully to plan. Nothing is ever guaranteed, no matter how thorough your preparation.

As Daniel trots and canters The Rogue around the warmup area, Hattie sees that Jenny and Dinky have been called down to the start. She watches as Eddie does a final check of the girth and the rest of the horse's tack, and then gives Jenny the nod.

Moments later, Jenny is beckoned into the start box by the starter, a tall, distinguished-looking man in cords, a battered Barbour jacket and a tweed cap. Hattie can't hear the countdown because she's standing too far away, but she sees the diminutive Dinky spring out of the box and canter towards the first fence, flying over with ease and galloping on towards the second. Leaving the spares kit next to the start box for Hattie and Daniel, Eddie sets off at a run along the white boundary rope that keeps spectators off the course, so that he can get up to higher ground and a better vantage point over the course.

The loudspeaker on the other side of the warmup area crackles into life, and the plummy commentator says, 'And our new starter, number 386, Jenny Jackson riding her own, Dinky, are over fences one and two and heading towards the Paradise Palisade at three.'

With Jenny now out of sight into the wooded area of the course, Hattie turns back to see how Daniel's warmup is going. She watches as The Rogue jumps the cross-country practice fences well. Daniel pats the horse's neck and then brings him back to walk, turning towards Hattie.

'He's looking good,' says Hattie.

'He feels it too,' says Daniel, checking the time on his watch. 'I think he's ready. Let's head over to the start.'

Hattie follows as Daniel walks the gelding towards the collecting ring. He halts and she does a quick check of his equipment, then he walks the horse in a large circle. As he comes back towards the start, the starter waves him over.

Hattie feels her stomach flip, her nerves getting worse. She tries to ignore them, and says to Daniel. 'Good luck, and have fun.'

'Thanks,' replies Daniel. He sounds more nervous than she expected him to be, but then he knows that this isn't just any run; how they perform today will be of interest to the team selectors and the equestrian media alike. They'll all be wondering if Daniel and The Rogue are back on form, or if the horse's injury and time out has dented his confidence. Hattie suspects Daniel is wondering that too.

Waiting beside the spares kit, Hattie watches as the starter raises his hand to give Daniel the ten-second warning. Finishing his circle, Daniel rides The Rogue towards the start box.

The starter, stopwatch in hand, continues the countdown. 'Three, two, one... good luck.'

The Rogue leaps from the box and sets out at a strong canter towards the first fence, a kind but full-height log pile. Springing over the jump easily, The Rogue puts in a cheeky buck on landing and gallops on towards the second fence, a large log with a drop on landing that will take him into the wooded section of the course. Hattie, heart-in-her-mouth, watches as the big gelding pops the fence like it's nothing and disappears into the woods.

Leaving the spares kit where it is, she sprints along the boundary rope towards the raised ground with the dogs bounding along beside her. She listens to the commentary over the loudspeaker as she runs.

'... Jenny Jackson and Dinky are over the combination at seventeen and take a flyer over the ditch-hedge at eighteen. And our new starter on the course, number 429, Daniel Templeton-Smith riding his own The Rogue are over fence four and heading towards the water at five.'

Hattie runs faster, ignoring the ache that's intensifying in her wrist from the movement. Poppet races along next to McQueen, and Hattie's glad that the older dog is helping her to keep the puppy straight as she runs. If she can get to the top of the hill in time, she'll be able to see Daniel at the water. Up ahead, she can see that Eddie is already there at the vantage point. There are just a few metres to go.

She makes it just in time. Down below them, across the course, she can see the glade between the trees where the water fence is situated. Her heart is racing, as much from the run as from nerves. Poppet jumps up at Eddie, delighted to see him. Eddie turns to stroke Poppet and McQueen. He looks at Hattie. 'He should be there any moment.'

'How did it jump for Jenny?' asks Hattie.

'Okay,' says Eddie, stroking McQueen's head. 'She took the long route.'

'Cool.' There are two different routes that riders can choose from at the water. The long route involves four jumping efforts: a fence before the water, then a stride between that and a small log to jump over and down into the water, a few strides through the water, then up a step, a stride and then a right-handed turn around to another fence before looping back left and on around the course. The direct route is much faster, but the jumping efforts are bigger and require boldness: a big log down into the water, two strides and up a big step followed by a bounce, where the horse lands and immediately jumps again without taking a stride, over another large log.

As she watches, Daniel and The Rogue come into view. She can tell from the way he's approaching the water that he's intending to go the direct, faster route. It's what they discussed when they'd walked the course. The Rogue is a bold, experienced horse so the direct route should suit him well.

Hattie sees Daniel steady the horse's gallop to a shorter, bouncer stride. She holds her breath as he nears the log into water.

The Rogue never falters. He pops over the log like it's nothing, then powers confidently through the water, jumps up the step and bounces over the other log with ease. Hattie cheers. Eddie claps his hands. They both grin. Poppet jumps up at Hattie, his front paws scrabbling at her thighs for attention. Laughing, she strokes his head, then gently pushes him down.

Through the loudspeaker on the top of the hill, the commentator says, 'And Daniel Templeton-Smith and The Rogue show everyone how it should be done, negotiating the water at five in copybook style.'

As Daniel disappears back into the woodland, Hattie and Eddie watch Jenny and Dinky come back into view at the side of the racecourse. She jumps well through the corners, and Dinky does a huge leap over the Trakehner – a huge water-filled ditch with a maximum-height rail suspended diagonally across it.

'See you back at the finish,' says Eddie, turning and running down the hill towards the end of the course as Jenny gallops closer.

'Daniel Templeton-Smith is over fence twelve and is heading out towards the sunken road,' says the commentator over the loudspeaker. 'Jenny Jackson and Dinky have two fences to go, and we have a new starter about to get underway on the course –

Westworlder, owned by Mrs Clifford and ridden by Greta Wolfe.'

Hattie watches Jenny and Dinky jump the last two fences and gallop through the finish. Moments later, German team rider and Olympic medallist Greta Wolfe canters through the start on Westworlder. Daniel's still out on the section of the course that isn't viewable from up on the hill, and Hattie waits impatiently for news on his progress from the commentator. But nothing comes. The commentary is silent.

She clenches her fists and tells herself not to worry. But the nerves flare inside her like hundreds of papery butterfly wings thrashing around in her chest. Beside her, Poppet starts to whine. McQueen looks up at her, a worried expression on his face.

Where is Daniel?

The loudspeaker crackles and lets out a burst of static, but no commentary.

Hattie clenches her jaw as a wave of nausea hits her.

Then Daniel and The Rogue gallop into view. They jump through the corners smoothly, leap over the Trakehner with ease, and gallop on towards the last two fences and the finish. The Rogue is covering the ground well and still looks fresh. As relief floods through her, Hattie sets off down the hill at the run, heading towards the finish.

'Come on,' she says to the dogs.

They're happy to oblige. As she runs, Hattie watches The Rogue make light work of the final fences and storm through the finish flags.

She hears the commentary coming over the loudspeaker near the finish. 'And Daniel Templeton-Smith and The Rogue are home and clear after a copybook round that, by our reckoning here in the commentary box, is well within the time.'

Daniel lets The Rogue run on along the track, letting him come gradually to a trot and then a walk. Then he's leaning forward and patting him, before jumping off to take the pressure off the horse's back and loosen his girths.

'Well done. That looked brilliant,' says Hattie, grinning, as she reaches him. McQueen and Poppet, his energy a little zapped from the sprinting, are happy to slow to a walk.

'He was amazing,' says Daniel, his delight at the way the horse has gone is clear in his expression and his tone. He rubs the horse's neck as they keep walking. 'He flew everything like it was easy. He's such a superstar.'

The Rogue blows out, as if to say he knows that he's a superstar.

After collecting the spares bucket from near the start box, they walk The Rogue back across the warmup field towards the lorry park, checking for injuries as they go, and making sure the gelding is sound and well. They keep the horse moving as he gets his breath back, making sure he doesn't cool down too quickly and get a chill in the damp weather.

Once his breathing is back to normal, Hattie fetches the packet of ginger biscuits –Rogue's favourite treat – from the spares bucket and hands it to Daniel. Daniel loosens the gelding's noseband and, breaking a biscuit into sections, gives the horse a piece.

The Rogue takes the biscuit, and as he's crunching it, immediately nudges Daniel's hand with his nose for another piece.

Daniel laughs. There are tears in his eyes as he rubs the horse's neck again. 'He's back.'

'He definitely is,' says Hattie, putting her arm around Daniel and giving The Rogue a pat. 'You both are.'

CHAPTER SIXTEEN

MEGAN

*I*t's only six days until the regional finals. If Megan is going to do this, she needs to do it now while her boss is at lunch and the store is quiet – it's the perfect time.

Closing the door to the storeroom behind her, Megan strips down to her black lacy underwear and then zips on a pair of Doxford Millar's signature-heeled knee-high boots in leopard print. After moving the boxes stacked in front of the floor-to-ceiling mirror, she sits down with her back to the mirror, pulls her knees towards her chest and crosses her feet. Then she puts on the popular *Felicity* hat in a light shade of camel, and angles it so that when she looks down, only her nose and lips are visible. Her image, reflected in the mirror, shows her dark brown hair cascading in waves around her shoulders.

She takes a few pictures of the full effect, then applies some bright red lipstick and fluffs up her hair before changing position onto her hands and knees to snap some photos with more obvious cleavage. It's tricky getting the shots right when it's just her here, but after a few attempts she gets the hang of things and manages to get a couple of over-the-shoulder pictures too.

Sitting on the floor, she opens the OnlyFans app and logs into the account that she created on the site earlier. She hasn't uploaded any pictures yet. First she crops one of the pictures so only her cleavage, shoulders, lower face, hat and hair are visible, and makes it her profile picture. The photo appears beside her username, @naughtyhorsegirlX, and she smiles. It's a cute picture; a little racy, but not too explicit. The best part is it's impossible to tell her identity.

Next she uploads one of the photos of her sitting with her back against the mirror. It's a little spicier, but still fairly modest. She makes it freely available to anyone viewing her page. Next she sets a subscriber price of ten dollars for people to sign up to view her exclusive content, and then uploads two photos accessible to subscribers only – one black-and-white of her on all fours, and one in colour of her glancing over her shoulder as she kneels in front of the mirror.

It's not obvious who or where she is in the picture, but it still feels like she's letting strangers into her private world. She pauses, thinking; does she really want to do this? She could withdraw from the regionals and hope that she can qualify another year once she's saved up the money for a new saddle.

Her finger hovers over the button that will make the pictures go live. Yes or no?

That's when she hears the bell go.

Her heart rate accelerates. Someone is at the front door. She's run out of time.

Without thinking any more, Megan presses the button to make the photos live. Leaping onto her feet, she takes off the hat and quickly pulls her navy tunic dress over her head. She pushes the stack of boxes back in front of the mirror, then hurries to the staff area.

The bell rings again. And, after a brief pause, yet again for a third time.

Whoever is waiting is getting impatient.

Shoving her phone back into her locker, Megan smooths

down the front of her dress and rushes out of the staff area, through the store to the door.

Evelyn, her boss, looks furious, her resting bitch face deployed to full effect. Still, Megan's just relieved her boss didn't take her shop keys with her when she went for lunch. If Evelyn had found her in the storeroom on all fours in her underwear, things would have been far more awkward.

With a nervous smile, Megan unlocks the door and opens it quickly. 'Evelyn, I'm so sorry, I just—'

'Why was the door locked?' demands Evelyn, scowling. 'We never lock up during opening hours, especially not during lunch time, I've told you that many times.'

Megan feels her cheeks flush red. She can hardly tell Evelyn the truth. 'Erm... I needed to go to the loo and I didn't want to leave the cash register unattended.'

Evelyn eyes her with disapproval. 'I was only gone half an hour; surely you could've held it? We don't pay you to skive off to the loo all the time.'

'It was urgent,' says Megan, looking down at her feet and hoping that Evelyn doesn't notice the leopard boots that she's still wearing. 'I'm really sorry. I think I must have eaten a dodgy prawn last night and—'

'I don't need the details,' Evelyn says, grimacing. 'Just don't make a habit of it. I need you to pull your weight around here, yes? I can't do everything myself.'

Keeping her eyes downcast, Megan nods. Evelyn does very little. She's the one who does at least 75% of the work here. But Megan doesn't say that. She needs this job too much. 'Of course.'

'Good,' says Evelyn. 'You can get back to work on that stocktake now. I'll look after the customers.'

Megan forces herself not to react. It's gone two o'clock now – the lunchtime trade has finished and things on the shop floor always sink into a lull between now and when the schools finish. In saying she'll look after the customers, what Evelyn really means is that she'll sit at the till reading her book, something Megan never gets to do. It pisses her off, but Evelyn's the boss. So she smiles sweetly and says, 'No problem.'

∼

Megan stares at her notifications. She can't believe what she's seeing. In the few hours between her boss returning from lunch at two o'clock and her clocking-off time of six o'clock, she's had over three hundred notifications from OnlyFans.

People have been subscribing to her page. Two hundred and forty-six people have subscribed, to be precise. That's nearly two and a half thousand dollars she's made in just the last four hours, more than enough to buy Velvet a new saddle.

And it's not just that people have subscribed. She's had loads of direct messages asking for exclusive content – one-off pictures and videos shot specifically for that person. Some of the things they're asking her to do are rather cringe, but the money they're offering... well, it's pretty tempting.

She leaves the shop and walks back through the town towards her flat in a daze. It's drizzling, but Megan barely feels the damp and cold. It seems unreal; she's earned more money in the last few hours than she usually makes in a month.

Pulling her hood up, she scrolls through the direct messages as she walks. It's clear that the boots are a big hit. Most of the exclusive content requests involve wearing boots and not much else. Only a few DMs mention the hat.

It seems like a strange way to make money, sending pictures to strangers, but right now it's a lot more preferable to serving demanding, high-maintenance snooty customers in the shop. And a lot more lucrative too.

Reaching her flat, she puts her key into the lock of the foyer door, and makes a decision. She's going to set a high price for her exclusive content and go back to each person who has direct-messaged her with her fee. They can take it or leave it, but if she's going to be doing more risqué pictures she's sure as hell going to be paid a lot for them.

She pushes open the door and steps across the foyer to the pigeonholes for post. There's a stack of bills in hers but, for the first time in as long as she can remember, she doesn't immediately worry about how to pay them. Pushing the bills into her bag, Megan turns and heads up the stairs to her second-floor flat.

Once she's ridden Velvet and put him to bed this evening, she's going to treat herself to a fancy takeaway from the nice Thai place, and a good bottle of wine. Tomorrow, she'll shoot some exclusive photos and videos; she's got a few different Doxford Millar boots, all seconds or boots that arrived damaged so couldn't be sold, bought with her store discount, so she should be able to do some pictures for subscribers too. And then she's going to go saddle shopping.

Megan smiles to herself. Velvet deserves the best and even if only a few of the people after exclusive content pay up, he'll totally be able to have it.

CHAPTER SEVENTEEN

JEM

'Have you seen my Insta?' says Jem, holding her phone out across the island unit towards Tyler so he can see the number of likes and comments on her latest post. 'They love me.'

'Yeah, great.' Tyler takes another mouthful of the tuna salad he's eating and doesn't look up once from his own phone.

Jem frowns. They're supposed to be having lunch together. She planned her riding schedule to make it happen, and yet Tyler can't even be bothered to look at her Insta or hold a conversation with her. It's not fair. She's so busy schooling the horses and making sure the lazy grooms are doing their work properly, but Tyler just doesn't appreciate that. It's as if no one cares how hard she's working; they just take her for granted. She hardens her tone. 'You're not looking at it.'

Tyler looks up. 'Sorry, I've had a message about some potential gigs for the band. You remember that guy who came to see us play at the hockey club and said he did event promo? Well, he's offering a few paid gigs next month.'

Jem's frown deepens. She doesn't remember, but that's irrelevant. She's trying to talk about *her* Instagram success, not his stupid band. It's so typical of Tyler to just think of himself. 'Okay, but my Insta is off the chart. I've got thirty thousand new followers this month, and so many offers to be a brand ambassador.'

Tyler looks at her, saying nothing. Then he shakes his head. 'I guess the burglary ended up being a positive.'

'A positive?' says Jem, her voice getting louder. 'I was *violated*. My personal possessions were *stolen*. It was *horrifying*. I'm still *traumatised*.'

Tyler shrugs and takes another mouthful of tuna salad.

Jem clenches her fingers tighter around her fork. She hates the way tuna smells, and he knows it. She offered to prepare some feta for him when she did her own, but no, he opened a can of tuna and dumped it onto the salad she put together. It's so typical of him. And how dare he belittle her trauma? She's going to need months of therapy because of the theft. 'I just don't understand how you can—'

'Okay, okay,' says Tyler. Getting off the stool, he walks over to the bin and tips the rest of his salad into it. 'My bad.'

'Where are you going?' says Jem. 'We haven't finished lunch yet.'

'I have,' says Tyler, grim-faced, as he rinses off his plate.

Jem exhales hard. 'But I thought we were going to spend some time together? You know I've got a busy period coming up – loads of key competitions and training clinics.'

'Aren't I lucky that you made a gap in your schedule for me,' says Tyler, the sarcasm clear in his tone.

Well, yes you are, thinks Jem. 'Don't be like that. You know I want to be with you.'

The words sound fake even to her, but Tyler doesn't seem to notice.

'So tell me about these competitions,' he says, taking a seat opposite her at the island.

'Well, in a few days I'll be off to the regional finals,' says Jem, with pride. 'Downton X, Zayanne and Star Child are all competing. I'm confident I'll get at least one win, but they should all place. Then, after that, there'll be the nationals in April, and of course we're already into qualifying season for the summer championships and I'd like all the horses to qualify for the summer regionals at least.'

'Sounds good,' says Tyler, nodding as if he actually understands the qualification process for the championships. 'Anyone else going from round here?'

'A few people,' says Jem, trying to feel happy that he's finally taking an interest in her riding. 'If she can afford a saddle in time, then Megan will take that funny little horse of hers to the regionals. And—'

'Couldn't you lend her one of your saddles?' asks Tyler.

'No,' says Jem, her tone making it very clear what she thinks of his stupid suggestion. 'Those saddles were given to *me*, they're not for Megan. She can bloody well get her own.'

He frowns. 'But if you're not using them all, it seems fair to—'

'I said no, and that's the end of it,' says Jem, wondering why Tyler is suddenly so keen for Megan to be able to compete. Does he fancy her or something? Is that why he's been less than interested in shagging recently?

'All right, steady,' says Tyler, holding his hands up. 'Who else is going?'

Jem thinks for a moment. 'Well, I expect Alexander Bovey and his team will go for the whole thing – he's got six horses qualified – and Lucy Gray and Susi Doppler-Mung are always strong local contenders.'

'Hmm, that Susi Doppler-Mung is the hot one, yeah? Didn't she do that modelling campaign for Calvin Klein back in the day?'

'She's ancient, nearly fifty,' says Jem, dismissively. 'But, yes, she used to be a model.'

'She's still hot,' says Tyler.

Jem rolls her eyes. 'If you say so.'

Tyler's gaze flicks back to his phone. 'So will you come and see me in action at these gigs?' he asks. 'You haven't come along to watch us for a while.'

Jem looks at him and tries not to let her irritation show that, again, he's brought the conversation back to him. He isn't the centre of the universe; he really should realise that. And his stupid band is never going to make it. He's twenty-seven years old, and if he was going to hit the big time, he'd have done it already. But seeing as she can't dump him without proving her parents were right about him being a bad choice of boyfriend, she forces a smile and says rather too sweetly, 'If I can.'

'Great,' says Tyler, as enthusiastically as a spaniel welcoming its owner home. 'I'll message you the dates.'

'Lovely,' says Jem, trying hard not to sigh.

As Tyler leaves the room, she shakes her head.

Fuck this shit. She's a dressage rider, a serious competitor, and now an Instagram influencer. She really shouldn't have to deal with this gig nonsense; it's so utterly unimportant. Her boyfriend should dote on her, worship her even. He should be doing things for *her*. Nothing should be too much trouble.

CHAPTER EIGHTEEN

HATTIE

Since Daniel and The Rogue won the Open Intermediate at Tweseldown Horse Trials, and Jenny and Dinky came fourth in their Intermediate section, the mood in the yard is even more positive about this year's event season.

Today, Daniel is working on his dressage with The Rogue. He's been having more dressage lessons with Willa since the Tweseldown run, focused on getting his and Rogue's dressage as good as it possibly can be before Badminton Horse Trials. Hattie watches from the side of the arena as they practise some of the more complex sideways movements from the test they'll ride at Badminton.

'That's good,' says Willa, from where she's standing in the middle of the arena. 'Now a little more collection, and then come across the short diagonal in half pass.'

Daniel does as she instructs, collecting the trot and setting up the half pass as they come out of the corner. The Rogue responds, moving sideways and forwards across the short diagonal.

'Nice, good,' says Willa. 'He's maintaining his rhythm much better now. Just allow him to take you forward a little more; don't lose the personality.'

Daniel relaxes his reins a fraction and the horse lifts more in front, his stride showing the full extent of his flamboyant paces. It's impressive, thinks Hattie, how Willa is able to spot what tiny adjustments will make a big difference. Dressage really is an art.

As Daniel and The Rogue take a break, walking around Willa on a long rein as they debrief on the half pass, Hattie heads out towards the fields. Mermaid's Gold is in the furthest paddock, grazing alongside Daniel's newest horse, Slinky, an ex-racehorse bought by one of his long-term owners, Tyler Jacobs. Highly sensitive and reactive when she arrived a couple of weeks ago, Slinky is already filling out and becoming more chilled.

As Hattie approaches the gate, Mermaid's Gold throws her head up, whinnying.

'Hey, girl,' says Hattie.

The chestnut mare, her purple New Zealand waterproof rug covered in mud, trots across the field towards her with Slinky following close behind.

Opening the gate, Hattie lets herself into the field and stands, waiting for the horses to reach her. Mermaid's Gold halts beside her, immediately nuzzling her pockets for Polos. Slinky, still a little wary, stops a couple of strides back and watches.

'How are you doing, girl?' says Hattie, rubbing the chestnut mare's forehead and laughing as Mermaid tries to push her upper lip into her pocket to take the packet of mints. 'You can't be hungry; look at all this grass you've got.'

Hattie feeds Mermaid a Polo and smiles as the horse crunches her treat happily. It's true about the grass – all the recent rain, followed by a week of warmer weather, means spring has truly sprung. As well as the grass coming through, the better weather has helped dry up the waterlogged ground and the going is nearing perfect.

If Hattie hadn't broken her wrist, they'd be running in another Intermediate and then starting preparations for Burnham Market

CCI3*. As it is, she's still weeks from being able to compete. She sighs, and feeds Mermaid another Polo.

It's not that she regrets stopping to rescue the injured deer; if they'd left the animal on the road it would have died in pain, and that would have been awful. As it was, she called the wildlife hospital the other day and they told her that the deer had suffered a broken leg but that they'd been able to operate successfully and, once fully healed, it should be able to return to the wild. Hattie is happy that she and Liberty played a part in that, but it doesn't stop the frustration of not being able to ride or compete.

Mermaid's Gold licks her palm as if to tell her it's okay, they'll have their chance.

Hattie really hopes so.

CHAPTER NINETEEN

MEGAN

*A*s they trot down the centre line, Velvet feels like a million dollars wearing his new tack. The saddle alone cost her well over a thousand pounds, but it fits Velvet's conformation perfectly and it's super comfortable for her. She had enough money left over to buy herself a new black dressage jacket, white suede-seated breeches, and a pair of the most luxurious long leather riding boots. She was even able to hire a plusher horsebox to transport Velvet here from the yard, with extra room for him and nice padded partitions in the stall for him to lean against for balance if needed.

It takes everything for Megan not to pinch herself. She can hardly believe that she's actually here, at the regional dressage finals, competing in the Elementary Silver Regional Final. The test is Elementary 59 and she's learnt every prescribed movement by heart. Now she has to remember them in order and ride Velvet to the best of her ability.

Despite the frost on the ground outside, and her and Velvet's breath rising from their mouths like smoke as they breathe out, even in the indoor arena, Megan doesn't feel cold. She tries not to think about the people watching them from the viewing gallery, and the judges scoring every movement they complete, and the instrumental versions of pop hits playing over the loudspeaker system, and focuses instead on her riding.

In the centre of the arena, Megan asks Velvet to halt. Taking her reins into her left hand, she salutes to the judges seated in the boxes behind the arena markers at C, E and M. As she takes her reins back into both hands, she inhales a long breath and makes sure not to ask Velvet to move off again too quickly. It's important that they don't look hurried; in dressage, horse and rider need to project an aura of calm, harmony and elegance.

After counting one hundred, two hundred, three hundred, four hundred, five hundred in her head, Megan gives Velvet the aid to trot and they continue on down the centre line towards the C marker, and turn right. Velvet's trot is as athletic and expressive as ever and, although it's a particularly bouncy trot to sit to, she hopes it will impress the judges.

Making sure they maintain balance and fluidity through the twenty-metre half circle across the arena from B to E, and the smaller ten-metre half circle from E to X in the centre, Megan half-halts Velvet, and then asks him to leg yield sideways across the arena from X to K. He does as she asks, and moves sideways without changing the rhythm or smoothness of his trot.

'Good boy,' says Megan under her breath. You're not supposed to speak to your horse during the test, but Velvet is so used to her prattling away to him, she worries he'll think something is wrong if she stays silent for too long.

As they turn across the arena, she asks Velvet to halt across the centre line. After a moment of immobility, she gives him the aid for rein back and he reverses five steps, perfectly straight. Relieved that they've done the movement well, especially as it's Velvet's least favourite, they continue on in working trot.

After the half circles in the opposite direction to the first ones, and the medium trot across the other diagonal, Megan asks Velvet to walk. This next section is the one she's most concerned about. Velvet gets bored rather easily and if she can't keep him focused on what he's doing, he'll start looking around the indoor arena, spooking at the large flower arrangements at each arena marker and the pair of bay trees at the entrance to the arena, and getting distracted by the spectators watching them from the viewing gallery.

But she doesn't need to worry. Velvet stretches out his neck and relaxes on a long stride in the first part of the walk section, and then comes back to a collected walk when asked for the second part, allowing Megan to shorten her reins without tension creeping in.

As they get closer to the A marker, Megan presses her leg against Velvet's side and asks him to canter. He gives a little squeal, and for a moment she thinks he's going to buck. But he stays relaxed, and pops into smooth, forward-going working canter.

Forcing herself not to hold her breath in case her anxiety about making a mistake passes to Velvet, Megan pilots the horse through the canter section. It passes without a problem and as they make their final halt and salute to the judges, she can't help but grin.

With the burglary, and losing her tack to the thieves, she'd almost given up hope of being able to ride in the regional finals today. But Velvet has gone like a dream, and she didn't forget the movements of the test, so whatever score they're given by the judges, she feels as if it's been the best day.

As she asks Velvet to walk forward and loops him around towards the exit of the arena, she tells him over and over what a clever pony he is. He blows out, as if to tell her he already knows that. And she laughs, crying happy tears as she rubs his gleaming black neck.

A couple of hours later, the final scores are being written onto the large scoreboard outside the indoor arena by a smartly dressed, and rather stern-looking, older lady in a burgundy quilted jacket, Hermes headscarf and smart navy trousers. The riders are gathering round, all eager to see who has the top scores, and which horse and rider combinations will go forward to the national winter championships.

Megan stays towards the back of the crowd. She hasn't yet looked at the score she and Velvet have been given, wanting to stay happy at how the test felt for a while longer in case the judges didn't like it and gave her a low score.

Up ahead, she sees Jem pushing her way through the group to the front. Her young horse, Star Child, was competing in the Elementary too, and she's already told Megan that he'll be top of the class. Megan, though, isn't so sure. She watched Jem's test from the viewing gallery and although Star Child's quality and talent is clear, today he looked tense and as if he wasn't much enjoying his work. But she didn't say anything to Jem. After all, Jem's the professional and Megan is just an amateur, so maybe she's wrong.

The scorer finishes writing the scores, and the placings, onto the board. Tucking her clipboard under her arm, she steps back. Turning towards the gathered crowd, she gestures to the board and says, 'The results are ready.'

The black-jacketed riders at the front of the group surge forward, searching to see where they ranked. Behind them, another twenty or so riders shuffle forwards, craning their necks to try and get a glimpse of the results. Megan hangs back, deciding to wait until the crowd has dispersed before approaching the scoreboard.

A loudspeaker on the wall beside them crackles into life and a plummy male voice says, 'I have pleasure in announcing the winners of our morning classes. Firstly, the Elementary Silver regional final sponsored by the BestFit Clothing Co. Along with their rosettes and prize money, winners in this class will receive a free outfit of their choice. And so onto the winners...'

'What the actual hell?' Jem's voice is so loud, it distracts Megan from the commentator.

Glancing towards the scoreboard, she sees Jem shaking her head as she stands, hands on her hips, glaring at the scores. The other competitors standing near her step away, not wanting to get caught up in any drama.

'...and in fifth place,' says the commentator over the loudspeaker, 'with a score of 67.94% we have Jenny Jackson riding Dinky. Next, in fourth place, on a score of 68.43% we have Emile Penn and Glamderry. And then...'

Megan watches as Jem marches up to the scorer with the clipboard. Although she can't hear what Jem is saying, from her furious expression and the way she's pointing her finger at the well-turned-out woman, it's clearly not a happy conversation. The scorer shakes her head and seems to be telling Jem, 'No.' Next moment, Jem starts pushing her way back through the crowd towards Megan. She looks like she's about to explode in rage.

'Are you okay?' says Megan as Jem gets closer.

'No I'm not! How can I be? 62.51% is ridiculous,' snaps Jem, glaring at Megan as she storms past. 'I'm going to put in a complaint. Obviously the scorer added the marks up wrong. Either that or the judges are entirely incompetent and have absolutely no idea what they're doing.'

Megan doesn't know what to say, so she says nothing. As the crowd has thinned out a bit, she moves forward towards the board. It's time to find out what the judges thought of Velvet and her performance.

Her heart pounds in her chest. She tells herself it doesn't matter what the score is, they've still done well to make it to the regionals. However well or badly they've fared in comparison to the other competitors, Velvet is always a star to her.

Overhead, the loudspeaker crackles again, and the plummy commentator says, 'And so on to our winner. In first place on an outstanding score of 72.85% is Velvet Mimosa ridden and owned by Megan Taylor.'

Wait? What?

Rushing forwards, Megan finds Velvet's name on the board and reads the score.

It's true. Velvet scored 72.85%.

Megan hugs her arms around herself as her heart hammers double-speed against her ribs. Happy tears prick at her eyes for the second time that day.

Oh my God. We did it.

We're going to the national finals.

CHAPTER TWENTY

WAYNE

*P*utting down the grey gelding's near hind foot that's now sporting a new iron shoe, Wayne straightens up and rubs the small of his back to ease the tension. Turning to the horse's pretty blonde owner, Nancy Neale, he smiles and says, 'Okay, he's all done.'

'Great. Let me just pop him back into his stable, and then why don't you come through to the house so I can pay you?' says Nancy, giving him a mischievous wink.

'Alright,' says Wayne. He's only recently started shoeing Nancy's horses – three Dutch warmblood dressage horses belonging to her, and a couple of Welsh mountain ponies for her twin boys. This is the first time he's found Nancy home alone. She's already told him that her husband is in the city at work and the boys are off with their grandparents for the week. He thought nothing of it at the time, but now he recognises the look she's giving him; it's the same come-hither look that he's been seeing a lot recently.

As Nancy leads the grey gelding across the yard to his stable, Wayne begins to pack up his equipment. He turns off the portable furnace and puts his rasps, hoof trimmers and hammer into his leather tool bag, then removes his chaps and folds them neatly on the rack to the right of the van doors. He's finished for the day, so he doesn't have to go rushing off anywhere. The only thing on his agenda for tonight is a few beers down the pub, and the lads won't mind if he's later than usual as long as he gets a round in when he arrives.

Once his gear is sorted, Wayne locks the van and heads across the yard towards the large barn conversion where Nancy lives. He finds the back door open. 'Hello?'

'Come in,' she says from inside.

He finds her in the kitchen, taking a bottle from the wine fridge. She's changed out of her horse clothes and is now wearing a long, stretchy dress with white-and-navy stripes and UGG boots.

Closing the fridge, she holds up a bottle of Moet and two glasses. 'Bubbles?'

'Sounds good,' says Wayne. Personally, he's not really into fizzy wine but he's learnt that the ladies like it and so he usually says yes.

Nancy walks across the kitchen towards the French doors. 'Come through to the back.'

He does as she says, although it's almost dark now and really it's too cold to sit outside. 'Where are—'

'I thought you might like a dip in my hot tub after working over that hot anvil all day,' says Nancy, suggestively.

Wayne sees the hot tub nestled in the corner of the patio, up against the side of a double garage that's been screened with some kind of climbing plant. The jacuzzi bubbles are already going, illuminated by underwater neon lighting, and the steam rising off the top makes it look as if the water is on fire.

'I don't have my board shorts with me,' says Wayne, acting coy, although from the expression on Nancy's face – half lust, half mischief – he knows that he won't be needing his swimmers.

'You'll just have to wear your birthday suit then,' says Nancy, eying him up and down. 'From your calendar picture, it looks like that's in pretty good shape.'

'I do my best,' says Wayne modestly.

'Me too,' says Nancy, pulling her dress off over her head.

Wayne inhales as he takes in the sight of her. Nancy's body is athletic and toned with the best legs he thinks he's ever seen and boobs that seem to defy gravity. Her skin has been burnished to a honey golden tan and she's wearing the tiniest white string bikini he's ever seen.

She smiles at him and climbs up the steps into the hot tub. 'You coming?'

He doesn't need to be asked twice. Pulling off his t-shirt and sweatshirt, he undoes his jeans and steps out of them. He always goes commando, and his dick is already leaping to attention at the sight of Nancy. Her expression tells him that she isn't disappointed.

Climbing into the tub beside her, he takes the glass of champagne and clinks it against hers. 'What are we drinking to?'

'Whatever you like,' says Nancy, draining her glass and setting it on the side.

'Alright then,' says Wayne, taking a sip.

He hasn't even had a chance to put down the glass before Nancy moves around to kneel in front of him and takes his dick in her hands. As the bubbles from the jacuzzi jets foam around her shoulders, she starts to stroke him. Slowly first. Then faster. He reaches out for her, wants to get an up-close look at those fantastic tits, but she wriggles away and pushes him back against the seat.

She gives him that mischievous smile again, then ducks her head down into the water. Moments later, he feels her mouth around his dick. She's sucking him, flicking the most sensitive part of him with her tongue. Jesus. It takes every bit of willpower he has not to cum immediately.

The bubbling water, the warmth of the hot tub, and the

underwater blowjob; it's surreal but hot as hell. He forces himself to think about things that aren't sexy – ironing, cleaning out the forge, the latest run of bad luck his footy team are having. He can't cum too soon. He can't let Nancy down.

But it's damn hard, as is he. And even thinking about the boring stuff isn't working. Surely she can't hold her breath much longer, he thinks. Wayne grips the edge of the hot tub and hopes that he can outlast her.

He manages to, just about.

Releasing him from her mouth, she emerges from the water and immediately turns around, pressing her bum against his dick. Not wanting to disappoint, Wayne pushes her bikini thong aside and pulls her back onto him. Nancy gasps as he enters her, then rides him reverse cowgirl style as if her life depends on it.

Grabbing her hips, he thrusts into her, matching her rhythm. In seconds, he's ready to explode. He can't hold it any longer.

'Hold on... wait.' Nancy stops moving, still impaled on his dick.

'Are you okay? Did I—'

'Shut up,' snaps Nancy.

Wayne stays quiet.

Nancy is listening to something. She turns towards him, frowning and anxious. 'Jesus, what the hell's he doing back?'

'Who?' asks Wayne, hearing the sound of car tyres on gravel on the other side of the fence, followed by the grind of an automatic garage door opening.

'Thomas,' says Nancy, springing up from the water like a dripping wet goddess and hurriedly climbing out of the hot tub. 'My husband. He's not meant to be back until later tonight but his plans must have changed.'

'Oh shit,' says Wayne. Lurching across to the steps, he clambers out.

'You need to go,' says Nancy, thrusting his clothes into his hands. 'Thomas can't see you; he'll do his nut.'

Wayne hears a car door slam shut, and the click of the side door from the garage being unlocked. 'How do I...?'

'Go across the lawn and around the house that way,' says Nancy, gesturing away from the patio and garage. 'You can climb over the post and rail and get across the front paddock to the yard.'

'Okay, but won't someone see me if I—'

'The only person I care about seeing you is my husband, and I'll make sure I keep him entertained until you're away.' Nancy lowers her voice, and shoves Wayne towards the lawn. 'Now run.'

Bare-arse naked, with his clothes clutched to his wet chest, Wayne runs across the lawn and around the side of the house. Before he's gone far, he hears a man's voice saying, 'Well, this is a surprise.'

Then Nancy replying, 'Darling, join me. I thought you might like some bubbles.'

As he yanks his clothes back on over his damp skin, and heads back to the yard and his van, Wayne wonders if Nancy knew her husband might return early. Maybe she likes to live dangerously and she gets her kicks by almost getting caught out. Maybe she's bored and looking for something, or someone, to spice things up as a preamble to sex with her husband. Whatever the truth, Wayne knows one thing for sure.

The woman gives amazing head.

CHAPTER TWENTY-ONE

HATTIE

'And you're sure you've been given the all-clear?' Daniel sounds worried as he carries Mermaid's Gold's tack across the yard to where Hattie has the chestnut mare tied up outside her stable.

'Yes, for the thousandth time,' says Hattie, trying to keep the frustration from her voice. 'I'm allowed to ride.'

Daniel looks at her. He doesn't seem entirely convinced.

Hattie doesn't blame him. She's being a bit economical with the truth, to be honest, but she's been so frustrated by not being able to ride for all these weeks, now that the doc has swapped the plaster cast on her wrist for a strong splint, she sees no reason why she shouldn't ride. She just didn't actually ask the doc if it was okay.

She gives Daniel a reassuring smile as she takes the saddle cloth from off the top of the saddle he's holding, and places it on Mermaid's back. 'It'll be okay.'

He looks sceptical. 'Well, if you're sure.'

'I am,' she says. 'But I can't lift anything too heavy at the moment, so would you mind putting the saddle on for me?'

Daniel looks at the little mare warily. 'If you think Mermaid will be okay with that?'

Hattie understands why he's concerned. Last year, after Lexi Marchfield-Wright bought Mermaid's Gold due to an ownership mix-up and sent her to Daniel's yard, Eddie tried to tack up the highly sensitive mare. She freaked out, and destroyed a saddle in the process. 'I think if I'm here it'll be okay.'

'Okay.' Daniel approaches the mare, talking calmly. 'Hey there, Mermaid. Don't worry, I'm not going to ride you. I'm just getting you ready so you and Hattie can have some fun.'

Hattie smiles. She loves that Daniel's so kind with the horses. Standing beside Mermaid, she strokes the mare's shoulder as Daniel lifts the saddle and places it gently onto the horse's back.

'There, wasn't so bad was it,' says Daniel, looking relieved that there's no dramatic reaction from Mermaid. He rubs her neck, then walks around to the other side to check the saddle cloth is smooth, then takes down the girth and passes it under Mermaid's belly to Hattie, who takes hold of it with her good hand and waits for Daniel to come back around the mare to join her on the near side.

'Good girl,' says Hattie, handing the girth to Daniel.

He fastens the girth as Hattie strokes the mare's neck. Mermaid looks relaxed and happy. She nuzzles at Hattie's pocket for a Polo. Hattie laughingly obliges. Then, with the saddle done, she takes the bridle from over Daniel's shoulder and holds it out to Mermaid, who opens her mouth for the snaffle bit.

'That's impressive,' says Daniel. 'She practically bridles herself.'

'She does,' says Hattie, as she puts the headpiece over Mermaid's ears and buckles the throatlash. It's tricky. She's still got limited movement with her injured hand and, although she's not going to admit it to Daniel, it's hurting a bit.

Once Mermaid's Gold is fully tacked up and her brushing

boots are on, Hattie puts on her jockey cap and leads the mare across the yard to the mounting block.

'Are you going in the school or hacking?' asks Daniel, joining her.

'I thought we'd go out on the little loop,' says Hattie, referring to the hacking path that circles around the Templeton Manor fields.

'If you give me a minute, I'll join you,' says Daniel. 'It'll be a good loosener before me and Rogue go in the arena.'

'Great,' says Hattie.

As Daniel hurries off to tack up Rogue, Hattie turns back to Mermaid. The little mare has already lined her body up with the mounting block, so all Hattie has to do is walk up the two steps, put her foot into the nearside stirrup and swing her leg over Mermaid's back. She takes care to land lightly in the saddle. 'Good girl.'

The mare blows out, and turns her head towards Hattie's left foot, asking for a Polo.

'Haven't you had enough?' says Hattie, laughing. Still, she takes a mint from her pocket and leans down, feeding it to the mare.

Mermaid's Gold is happily crunching the Polo when Daniel leads The Rogue out of his stable and across the yard to join them. Putting both hands on the reins, Hattie asks Mermaid to move away so Rogue can take her place at the mounting block.

After a few steps, Hattie squeezes the reins, asking the mare to halt. Pain shoots up through her injured wrist and she grimaces, clenching her jaw to stop herself gasping. It's not a good sign, definitely not good at all. Hattie's glad her back is to Daniel; at least he didn't see the pain on her face.

'You all set?' asks Daniel.

Putting both her reins into her good hand, Hattie turns Mermaid's Gold around and says brightly, 'Yes, I'm ready.'

They ride out of the yard and along the track that will take them around the outside edges of all the Templeton Manor fields. It's a beautiful morning. The frosty grass is sparkling in the sun and there's not a cloud in the sky. The landscape is looking greener than a few weeks ago, and in the hedgerows the birds are singing. Beneath her, Mermaid's Gold strides out happily but it's hard for Hattie to enjoy it. Every vibration is making the nerve-endings in her wrist jangle. Every jerky movement sends a jolt of pain through her arm.

'It's so good to see you in the saddle again,' says Daniel, smiling as they ride side-by-side along the track. 'It must feel great.'

Hattie smiles back, and forces extra brightness into her tone as she says, 'It does.'

Anything to stop Daniel realising just how much pain she's in.

CHAPTER TWENTY-TWO

MEGAN

Megan's finger hovers over the delete button. She'd signed up to OnlyFans to try and make enough money to buy Velvet a new saddle, and she's done that. But now it's two weeks since they won at the regionals, and she's still on the platform. She's receiving so many direct messages asking for exclusive content that she's lost track of the exact amount. Meanwhile, her subscribers are going up every day. She's made more money in the last three weeks than she'd usually make in a year. It's amazing, but she can't help fearing someone she knows seeing the photos or, even worse, one of her family.

Sitting on her bed, she looks around her grotty studio flat. It's basically a small bedroom with a couple of kitchen units, a sink and a two-burner hob in the far corner, and a tiny shower room that smells of mildew. The electric heater is ridiculously expensive to run, very uneconomical, and produces barely any heat and so the place always feels slightly damp. If she keeps doing OnlyFans, she'd be able to afford somewhere nicer. She could pay for more regular dressage lessons too, and maybe even manage to buy Velvet a small horsebox for travelling to competitions.

It's tempting. Very tempting.

Megan takes a breath. She's not squeamish about the photos and, although she hates the thought of people she knows in real life seeing them, there are already pictures out there now. What does it matter if she produces more? It's her body. Her life.

She makes her decision. She'll keep her account, for now at least.

Megan checks the time on her watch before opening up her messages and scanning through them. She's got half an hour before Rosalie is due to arrive for wine and pizza. She should be able to get a few requests done in that time.

Heading to the tiny cupboard where she stores her clothes, Megan pulls out her long leather riding boots, a black lacy thong and a schooling whip. She sets her phone onto the tripod she bought a few days ago, and sets it up to face the section of white wall between the kitchen cabinets and the bed. It's a neutral-looking space, with nothing to identify where it is.

Holding the tiny remote control that came with the tripod, she fluffs out her hair and gets into position. She's facing away from the camera towards the wall, so the pictures she takes will be shot from behind. Firstly she raises her arms above her head and holds the whip at both ends – the handle in her right hand, and the short lash cord in the left – forcing it into a slight bend. She takes a few shots: her looking at the wall, face not visible; hands against the wall, bum out and back arched, head back; looking over her shoulder, pouting. Then she changes pose. She takes pictures on the half-turn, and then full frontal with the whip pointing up over her shoulder, across her body, and finally brandishing it as if ready to give the viewer a spank.

She's just finishing up when the buzzer goes, making her flinch. Megan glances at her watch and realises how much time has passed. It's already five minutes later than Rosalie was due. Yanking her phone off the tripod, she chucks it onto her bed and shoves the tripod, boots and whip into the cupboard.

The buzzer sounds again. Two long blasts.

Megan pulls a baggy sweatshirt and her old jeans from the cupboard and hastily pulls them on before hurrying across to the intercom. 'Hi, sorry, I was just getting changed.'

'No worries,' says Rosalie over the crackling intercom.

Megan presses the release button for the front door. 'Come on up.'

Scooting across to the tiny kitchenette, she takes a chilled bottle of white wine from the compact fridge and opens it. She only has a narrow shelf for crockery, and ended up breaking so many glasses by knocking them off that she now only has plastic wine glasses. Taking them down, she fills them both three quarters full.

Rosalie opens the flat door and comes inside. 'Now that's a good welcome,' she says, taking one of the glasses of wine.

Megan grins and clinks her glass against Rosalie's. 'Happy evening.'

'Yay to that,' says Rosalie. 'Thank God I'm out for the night. I really can't stand another moment of being around Jem. She's totally doing my head in.'

'What's happened now?' asks Megan.

'Oh just the usual bullshit,' says Rosalie, between sips of wine. 'She's so important… what a hard life she has… does no one realise how hard she works, blah blah blah.'

'Nightmare.'

'Yeah. And if I have to sit through another one of her crap motivational speeches where she bangs on about how we're all a team and need to pull together because the competition season is revving up and at her level she is so very busy, when really what she means is she wants us to do more work and more hours for less pay, then I'm going to tell her where to stick her bloody job.'

'Amen to that,' says Megan, clinking her glass against Rosalie's again. 'You should find a new job anyway. You're too good for her.'

'I am,' says Rosalie, solemnly. 'But I'd hate to leave Peter in the lurch, especially mid-season.'

'Promise me you'll look for another job in the autumn then?'

Rosalie thinks for a moment. 'Okay. But only if I find somewhere you and Peter can come too.'

Megan smiles. 'Deal.'

'Now, more importantly, meat feast, Hawaiian or veggie supreme?' asks Rosalie. 'I'm starving.'

'Hawaiian and veggie?' says Megan. 'You know I can't resist pineapple on pizza.'

'Good choice,' says Rosalie. 'Do you want to give them a call?'

'Will do,' says Megan, walking over to the bed and picking up her phone. Tapping the screen to wake it, she quickly minimises the photo that appears and goes to her contacts – the pizza place is on speed dial.

She makes the order and pays with her credit card – now balance-free thanks to her OnlyFans money – then ends the call and looks over at Rosalie. 'Twenty to thirty minutes.'

'Cool.' Rosalie fetches the wine bottle and tops up both their glasses. 'This is good stuff, but I think we're going to need more.'

'Already thought of that,' says Megan. 'There's another bottle chilling in the fridge.'

'Excellent,' says Rosalie, grinning. Her expression turns serious. 'Did you hear about Alexander Bovey's yard getting robbed during the regionals?'

'No,' says Megan, frowning. 'Did they catch them?'

'Sadly not, and they took everything in the tack room, same as at Jem's. All the tack, equipment, and even loads of rugs. It must have been the same people.'

'Bastards.' Megan shakes her head. 'Are there any leads?'

'Not yet. The police seem totally stumped. Apparently the thieves managed to get in through the locked security gates by entering the correct code. The Boveys have no idea how they could have got hold of it, but Alexander's husband, Dillon, is freaking out about security and they're having a massive new system installed with three times as many cameras, laser and motion sensors outside, and a taller perimeter fence.'

'Wow,' says Megan. 'I guess he *really* doesn't want his fans thinking it's easy to get into his home.'

'I guess not,' says Rosalie. 'It's understandable, though. Didn't he have some kind of home invasion happen at the place they had out in LA?'

'I don't know,' says Megan.

'I'm sure they did.' Rosalie takes her phone from the pocket of her fleece and taps something into it. 'Yes, here we are, two years ago when Dillon was out in LA working on a film and Alexander was here in the UK competing, armed and masked intruders broke into their LA pad and held Dillon at gunpoint for an hour while they robbed the home. Apparently the guy in charge of keeping Dillon quiet talked to him the whole time, telling him what a huge fan of his films he was and discussing his thoughts on each one in detail. Then, just before they left, he got Dillon to sign him an autographed photo. It didn't stop the guy bashing Dillon over the head with the butt of his gun and knocking him out cold, though. Alexander and Dillon sold that home shortly afterwards.'

'That's understandable. Poor Dillon,' says Megan, taking a gulp of wine and hoping her subscribers on OnlyFans never get to that level of creepiness. She changes the subject back to the tack thefts. 'How many places have been burgled now?'

'I'm not sure. Three or four, I reckon.'

Megan frowns. 'The police *really* need to catch those arseholes.'

'Well apparently Alexander has put up a reward – £25,000 to whoever comes forward with evidence that is enough to secure a conviction – so maybe that'll help.'

'Let's hope so,' says Megan.

Although as she says it, she realises that if Jem's yard hadn't been burgled, and she hadn't lost Velvet's tack as a result, she'd never have signed up for OnlyFans. And if that hadn't happened, she would still be worrying about scraping enough money together to pay her rent, livery for Velvet and basic bills. They certainly wouldn't be drinking this eight quid bottle of wine and she wouldn't be able to afford to treat Rosalie to a pizza.

At the time, the burglary seemed like it was the worst thing that could have happened. Now, given her vastly improved financial situation, Megan almost wonders if she should be thanking the thieves.

CHAPTER TWENTY-THREE

HATTIE

'How did it go at the hospital?' asks Daniel, as he stirs a divine-smelling casserole in a big saucepan on the Aga. 'Did you get the okay to compete?'

Hattie stands in the doorway between the kitchen and the boot room, with Poppet dancing around her, excited that she's home. She leans down and strokes the puppy with her good hand, and keeps stroking him longer than usual as a delaying tactic. She didn't anticipate having to talk about what happened so soon; she hasn't even got her coat off yet. Over at the kitchen table, Eddie, Jennie and Rosalie have turned to look at her, waiting for the verdict. The hope on their faces is the opposite of the dead-woman-walking feeling she has.

'Oh, by the way, Lady Pat dropped in earlier,' says Eddie, feeding a pork scratching from the open bag on the table to McQueen. 'She's had a word with the organiser of Maxfield Horse Trials and they can get you in as a late entry for the Intermediate.'

'Which is amazing,' says Jenny, ruffling the fur on Popsy's head, the puppy being curled up inside her fleece as usual. 'That's usually a tough event to get into.'

Maxfield is in four weeks, and it would be a perfect galloping course for Mermaid's Gold. Hattie blinks. She doesn't want to get emotional, not in the kitchen with everyone here.

'Shall we have a glass to celebrate?' says Daniel, walking over to the fridge. 'Prosecco?'

'No,' says Hattie, the word coming out like a strangled yelp.

Concerned, Daniel closes the fridge door. 'What happened?' he asks gently.

Hattie feels her lower lip twitch. She swallows hard, trying to hold back tears. 'It hasn't healed properly.' She lifts her bad arm up, showing them that instead of the strong strapping, she's now back in plaster. 'It's going to be at least another four to six weeks.'

'I'm so sorry,' says Daniel, putting his arms around her and pulling her close.

She lets him hold her for a moment, but his kindness makes her feel even worse, so she moves away before the tears start to fall.

'That's really crap,' says Jenny.

'It is,' agrees Eddie.

'Although, on the bright side, at least our tack room hasn't just been cleared out like poor Ashbourne Eventing,' says Rosalie.

Daniel shakes his head. 'That's shit too.'

'True,' says Hattie. 'Although I don't have any need for tack right now.'

'We do!' says Jenny. 'And new saddles are really expensive these days.'

'Yeah, sorry,' says Hattie, feeling like a bitch. It's not her friends' fault that she can't ride for weeks. 'I wouldn't wish being burgled on anyone. Were they insured?'

'Luckily yes, but it's still awful,' says Jenny.

'There's been a whole spate of thefts over the past couple of months and the police don't seem any closer to catching the burglars,' says Eddie, shaking his head. 'It's really frustrating.'

As the others start to debate who might be behind the tack

thefts, Hattie makes herself a cup of tea. She's sympathetic to the people who've lost their stuff, but she's still reeling too much from the disappointment of having her wrist back in plaster to really engage in the conversation. Her plan of building up qualifying runs and progressing up the levels is in tatters. At this rate, she'll be lucky to have herself and Mermaid's Gold fit and ready to compete before well into the second half of the season.

Right now, her dream of winning Badminton seems even further away than ever.

CHAPTER TWENTY-FOUR

JEM

*J*em scowls as she watches Megan and Velvet do a lovely turn onto the centre line, keep their trot rhythm perfectly and come to a square halt and salute, completing their test. If Megan wins again, it'll be *really* bloody annoying. It's her, Jem, who should be the winner of this class. *She's* the full-time dressage rider – the one putting in all the hard work day in, day out. It's only fair that she does better than Megan. But, of course, that useless Rosalie didn't walk Star Child around enough before she got on him, and Peter probably gave him the wrong feed, because the horse was far too fresh and she almost got bucked off in the warmup. It took all her skill to get him to relax, but apparently the judges didn't think it was enough and his score is barely scraping into the top half of the class so far.

It isn't fair. It *really* isn't fair.

Clenching her fists, Jem turns and stomps back to the lorry park where Rosalie, assuming she's actually on time and not skiving, should have got her next horse, Zayanne, tacked up and ready to warm up for the Medium championship. The parking area is full of activity with competitors getting ready for their tests. There are grooms busying about getting horses ready, and riders talking to owners and friends with pride about a good test or disappointment at not performing well. The horses who've finished their work for the day are standing on lorries and in trailers, or tied up outside them, rugged to keep warm and munching on nets of hay.

As she gets closer to the lorry, Jem sees that Zayanne is tied up outside. She has four white warmup bandages on her legs and her saddle is on beneath the woollen show rug with 'Jem Baulman-Carter, Professional Dressage Rider' embroidered on the flanks.

Rosalie has her back to Jem and is running a cloth over the bay horse's gleaming coat. Jem has to admit Rosalie has done a good job and the animal looks well turned out, but she's hardly going to say that to Rosalie. If she does, it'll only go to her head and she'll probably want a pay rise.

Instead, Jem says, 'I'll need to be on in the next two minutes.'

Rosalie looks over her shoulder. 'No problem, I just need to put her bridle on.'

'Okay,' says Jem as she goes past Zayanne, ignoring the mare as she skedaddles sideways away from her, and stomps up the lorry steps into the living area.

Rosalie talks to the horse as she unties her and puts on her bridle, and Jem has to concentrate to shut out the annoying wittering as she puts on her dressage jacket and zips up her long boots. It's cold outside and Jem wishes she could compete with her Puffa on over the top of her dressage jacket; she does feel the chill so very acutely.

Checking her reflection in the mirror in the small shower room, Jem applies another layer of mascara and touches up her lipstick. Then, after pulling on her gloves, she fastens her spurs into place and walks over to the steps.

Rosalie is walking Zayanne in large circles. The mare is snorting at the rugs and grooming kit that have been dumped on the neighbouring lorry's ramp, and flinching as she's led past them. She looks really on her toes, and Jem makes another mental note to give Peter a talking to when they get home. If Zayanne is like this as well as Star Child, then he must be overfeeding all the horses. It's really not good enough. Sometimes she thinks she should just do everything herself; she really can't trust these grooms to get things right.

As Rosalie turns the horse back towards the lorry, Jem beckons her over. 'I'm ready.'

'Okay,' says Rosalie.

Standing on the top step, Jem waits for Rosalie to line the horse up so that the saddle is level with her. Zayanne halts initially, but as soon as Jem takes hold of the reins and goes to put her foot into the stirrup, she lurches forward and Jem is almost pulled off the steps. Cursing, she grabs for the side of the lorry to steady herself.

'Can you keep her steady, for God's sake,' Jem snaps at Rosalie.

Rosalie talks to the mare in a calm voice, then looks up at Jem. 'She's just a bit excited.'

'Well, you should have walked her around for longer to settle her down,' says Jem, taking hold of the mare's reins again, and trying to pull the animal over towards the steps more. 'How am I supposed to concentrate when I've got this nonsense to deal with?'

Rosalie doesn't reply. Instead, she asks Zayanne to move closer to Jem.

Huffing, Jem puts her foot back into the stirrup. The mare stands still this time, and so she presses her weight down and swings her leg over the horse's back. That's when the horse snorts loudly and plunges forward, yanking the reins out of Jem's hands and pitching her forward onto the horse's neck.

'Stop, steady,' shouts Jem, grabbing for Zayanne's reins and yanking the horse in the mouth. 'Stop it, you bitch.'

The mare snorts again and throw up her head, fighting against the reins. Jem see-saws at the reins, pulling the horse's head down and side-to-side. The bloody thing needs to learn its place, instead of giving her these histrionics.

That's when she sees Rosalie shaking her head. Jem feels anger rising inside her. Is Rosalie *judging* her? She's the boss, for God's sake. She has a quick look around, making sure there's no one watching them. Then, exhaling hard, she gives the mare a kick to walk forward and purposefully steers her towards Rosalie. The mare sidesteps at the last moment, but Jem's boot still connects with groom's ribs.

Rosalie gasps from the impact, winded. 'What the...?'

'Oh sorry,' says Jem, not sounding at all sorry. 'She's being really difficult to control; I couldn't stop her.'

Rosalie frowns, rubbing her side. 'That really hurt.'

Serves her right, thinks Jem, not stopping to check if Rosalie is all right. After all, why should she? After the stunt Rosalie's just pulled, she's even more pissed off at her than the bloody horse. It's Rosalie's fault that Zayanne didn't stay still. She let go of the animal too soon, and if Jem wasn't the good rider that she is, she'd have ended up dumped in a heap on the concrete. She could have broken something. Or, worse still, the incident could have been caught on camera or camera phone and put on TikTok or Instagram.

Bloody grooms, they're always letting you down. In five years of running her own yard, Jem hasn't come across a decent one yet. She always has to do everything herself. It's so exhausting. If only she could clone herself.

∽

Despite all the hardships, things actually turn out better for Jem in her second and third championship tests. After the dodgy start getting onto Zayanne, she was able to make the opinionated mare settle and produce a test worthy of her potential that put them into second in the Medium championships. Then later in the day, her top horse, Downton X, produced the winning test in the Advanced Medium championships.

It doesn't completely eclipse the irritation of Star Child's failure in the Elementary, or the frustration of Rosalie not holding Zayanne still for mounting properly, and Peter's obvious overfeeding of all the horses, but it's something. The equestrian TV channel have been filming all day, and she's just relieved that they didn't see her mishap in the lorry park. If that had been caught on camera, she'd definitely have had to sack Rosalie.

Having left the groom sulking back at the lorry, Jem rides Downton X out of the parking area towards the main arena where the championship prize-giving is going to take place. Her timing is perfect, and as she approaches the main arena, the stewards beckon her forward to lead the procession. Sitting up tall, she manoeuvres Downton X into the arena and follows the steward's directions to line up in front of the spectator stands.

The other riders line up alongside her. The classical music playing over the loudspeaker is faded down and the commentator says, 'I'm delighted to announce the winners of the Advanced Medium championship. First, and this year's champion, is Jem Baulman-Carter riding her own and Mrs Baulman-Carter's Downton X on a score of 76.98%.'

The people watching from the stands applaud.

Jem smiles as the steward calls her forward to meet the great and the good from British Dressage and the championship's sponsor. They congratulate her, and are very complementary about her test, just as they should be, as they present her with her prizes: the winner's rosette, a champion's sash for her and a rug for Downton X, plus a dressage saddle from a very high-end saddlery, and the prize money. Jem smiles graciously, even though she wishes the saddle was a new designer bag, as she's already got so many saddles to sell, and makes sure the camera guy gets her best angles.

'Congratulations,' says a male voice to her right, in second place, as the prizes are awarded along the line. 'You did a great test.'

Jem turns without smiling; this is her moment and she doesn't need some guy trying to latch onto her. But as she sees the rider on the big bay horse for the first time, she almost does a double take. Damn, he's hot: classically handsome with gorgeous eyes, high cheekbones and a chiselled jaw to die for. She's not seen him around on the circuit before. 'Who are you?'

'Daniel Templeton-Smith,' he says with an easy-going smile.

The name seems familiar. Some article she read recently about the Badminton contenders. Jem raises her eyebrows. 'The eventer?'

He laughs amicably. 'Guilty as charged.'

Guilty of being ridiculously hot, thinks Jem. 'So you've come over to the dark side, then?'

'I like dressage,' says Daniel, patting his large bay gelding's neck. 'But The Rogue here has always found it his least favourite thing. As a result, I try to get him out and about in the winter to pure dressage competitions as practice. This year is the first time he qualified for the finals.'

'Well, good for you,' says Jem, not really caring about the horse. She's been so fed up with Tyler's lack of attention recently, she rather thinks she deserves a little treat. And this guy is definitely a treat. 'You know, I was thinking I should have a go at some jumping with one of my youngsters, but I'm not really sure where to start. Do you give lessons?'

Daniel frowns a moment. 'Well, yes.'

'Excellent. I think you're based pretty close to me? I'm in Leightonshire too.' Jem holds his gaze, waiting for him to offer her some help.

It only takes a few seconds. Daniel clears his throat. 'Oh, right. Well, if you wanted to bring your horse over for a lesson, I could help start you off.'

'Sounds fun,' says Jem, licking her lips as she thinks about him getting *her* off. 'Maybe I'll do that.'

Back at the yard later that evening, Jem is relieved that Peter has finished the stables and all the horses have been exercised. As Rosalie sorts out Star Child, Zayanne and Downton X for the night, Jem takes her rosettes over to the tack room. Since the break-in, she's had the security upgraded with reinforced steel-plated walls and laser sensors, so she can feel a little more confident her belongings are safe. Removing a couple of pins from the noticeboard above the new kettle and coffee machine, she adds today's rosettes to the others on display.

As she pins up the winner's rosette from the Advanced Medium, she remembers Daniel Templeton-Smith and makes a mental note to call him in the morning and book that jumping lesson. She hasn't jumped a fence since she was seventeen and stopped going to Pony Club rallies, and she never liked jumping much in the first place. But she'll make an exception if it gives her the chance to meet up with Daniel.

'Congratulations, Jem,' says Megan, beaming as she finishes cleaning her tack. 'It's so great that we've both done so well today.'

'Both?' says Jem, narrowing her eyes. Irritated at being pulled from her thoughts of Daniel. 'What do you mean?'

'Your win and second place, and my fourth place in the Elementary,' says Megan, still smiling as she puts her saddle and bridle onto their racks. 'You must be thrilled. It's been a super successful day for the yard, hasn't it?'

Jem shrugs. 'Well, it's very sweet that you're so happy about it. Obviously you coming fourth in the Elementary is... well, Elementary is basic stuff for hobbyists rather than professional, competitive dressage riders really, isn't it? But if playing around at that level makes you happy then, really, that's lovely.'

'I'm not playing around,' says Megan, her smile faltering. 'I'm very serious about my riding, you know that.'

'Oh, well, yes, I suppose you are. For an amateur,' says Jem, tilting her head to the side as Megan's expression falls. Jem's pleased her words have hit home. Megan needs taking down a peg or two. There's only room for one star rider at my yard, thinks Jem. Megan needs to stay in her lane.

CHAPTER TWENTY-FIVE

HATTIE

*D*ress shopping has never been Hattie's favourite pastime, but she's trying to get into it today. Really, the only reason she's here in Arabella, the fanciest shop she's ever been in, is because she knows how much Liberty wants to cheer her up. That, and also because they're shopping for Liberty's outfit for her birthday party, and Hattie wants to help her friend enjoy the experience.

Arabella is an appointment-only shop, with exclusive use guaranteed for each client. After being greeted by the manager and given a glass of champagne, they've been let loose to peruse the clothes and try things on. When they're done, or if they have a question or need more fizz, there's a bell over by the counter to press and the manager will return. It's the poshest shop Hattie's ever been in. She doesn't feel entirely comfortable, although the alcohol is definitely helping.

Champagne in hand, they walk along the racks of dresses. Hattie looks over at Liberty. 'So what sort of thing are you looking for?'

'I don't know,' says Liberty, pulling a face. 'JaXX is organising everything for the party and he won't tell me anything. All he's said is "dress up" but I don't know if he means black tie or fancy dress.'

'I think you need a long gown, or a cocktail dress at the minimum,' says Hattie. The thick card invitation that had arrived in the mail for her and Daniel said black tie, although she's pretty sure whatever Liberty wore would be okay with JaXX; the guy is clearly smitten.

'Okay,' says Liberty, pulling out a couple of long black dresses, a short silver dress and a floor-length nude dress with delicate glass beading. 'Have you seen anything you like?'

Hattie shrugs. 'You know I'm no good with this sort of thing. I prefer my jeans.'

'Well, if the party is fancy, you definitely can't wear jeans,' says Liberty, laughing. She pulls another two long dresses off the rack, along with a short emerald-green cocktail dress, and thrusts them towards Hattie. 'Here you go. These would suit you.'

Hattie takes them in her good hand. 'Thanks.'

Liberty rolls her eyes. 'Sound a bit more grateful, will you? And don't tell me you can't afford one, because we both know you can.'

'Fine,' says Hattie, laughing. Liberty is the only person, aside from her newly discovered relatives, who know who her father was and how much money he left her. Hattie knows her friend is right, but she's still adjusting to the sudden change in fortune herself. After scrimping and saving her whole life, it doesn't feel real to have so much money in her account.

They walk across to the changing area. Alone in a tastefully styled private cubicle with pale grey wood-panelled walls, a bench seat with velvet grey upholstery along one side and a floor-to-ceiling silver-framed mirror at the back, Hattie hangs up the dresses on the hooks provided and tries to decide which one to try on first. She looks at the price tags – old habits die hard – and nearly chokes on her champagne at the cost of the green cocktail dress.

She checks the others. The two long dresses are almost as expensive, but one is cheaper than the other so she tries that one on first. It's black, and fits well, but the cut-outs at the waist make her a little nervous, so she takes it off and puts on the other long dress. Better. This one is a long, flowing empire-line dress with thin straps. It's pretty, but for over four hundred pounds it seems rather plain.

'How are you doing in there?' calls Liberty.

'Fine,' says Hattie.

Moments later, Liberty pulls the heavy grey velvet curtain back. 'Let me see.'

'Excuse me,' says Hattie, pretending to be annoyed.

Liberty waves her protests away. She puts her head to one side and looks at Hattie appraisingly. 'Well, it's nice, but I think you need something more dramatic. How does the green one look?'

'I haven't tried it yet,' says Hattie.

'So put it on,' replies Liberty, pulling the curtain back across the rail. 'And come show me.'

Hattie sighs. So much for not trying it on. Knocking back the rest of her champagne, she puts the glass on the bench seat and changes out of the long dress. Taking down the emerald green cocktail dress, she has to admit the material feels a higher quality than the other two dresses, but at almost eight hundred pounds, Hattie has no intention of buying it. She'll try it on though, just to keep Liberty happy.

After unzipping the back, Hattie steps into the dress and pulls it on. It's hard to zip it up on her own with one wrist in plaster, but after a bit of wriggling and contortion she finally manages it. Smoothing down the material, she turns to look at herself in the mirror and gasps.

The dress has transformed her. Figure hugging but not tight, it accentuates her curves without making her feel self-conscious. The V-neckline shows just the right amount of cleavage, and the length is perfect for making her legs look longer than they really are. The colour, not one she usually wears, is remarkably flattering.

'How does it look?' asks Liberty.

'It's okay,' says Hattie, trying to sound non-committal. She can't buy this dress; it's far too much.

'Come and show me.'

'Did I ever tell you how bossy you are to me?' says Hattie, pulling the curtain aside.

Liberty laughs. 'All the time. Now come *on*.'

The curtain to Liberty's changing cubicle is already open. When Liberty sees Hattie, her eyes widen. 'Wow. You look stunning.'

'You think?' says Hattie. She thought she looked good, but she doesn't usually wear dresses. Liberty is a far better judge of that kind of thing.

'I *know*,' says Liberty, walking around Hattie, taking in the full effect of the dress. 'You have to get it.'

Hattie shakes her head. 'It's so expensive. I can't—'

'You can,' says Liberty firmly. 'You look amazing and the dress is a classic style, so you'll be able to use it again. It's an investment piece.'

Hattie looks at herself in the mirror. She has to confess she's tempted.

Liberty gives her a nudge. 'You want to, don't you? Admit it.'

'It does look good,' says Hattie, her resolve starting to falter.

'That's settled then,' says Liberty. She smiles and takes Hattie's good hand in hers. 'You know it's really nice to see you looking happy. I know you've had a miserable time over the past couple of months with your wrist. You deserve something nice.'

Hattie looks at her reflection in the mirror. She's never liked how she looks in dresses but this one feels different. She supposes that she could splurge on it, just this once. She smiles back at her friend. 'Okay.'

'Yay,' says Liberty, clapping her hands together. 'Now let me put this beaded dress on and see what you think. If JaXX is going to all the effort of putting on a fancy party for me, the least I can do is to look the part.'

Hattie waits outside the cubicle as Liberty changes. 'How are things going with JaXX anyway?'

'Amazing,' says Liberty. 'He's the sweetest guy, and he's fun and smart and… well, great.'

Hattie smiles. She knows Liberty hasn't had the best luck with guys so it's doubly brilliant that she and JaXX have found each other. 'So is he the one?'

'I think so,' says Liberty, a smile clear in her voice. 'And Daniel?'

Hattie thinks about Daniel. They haven't known each other very long, just a few months really, but things have moved pretty fast and it's felt natural. Daniel's smart and funny. He's warm with people and kind with his horses, and it doesn't hurt that he's gorgeous too, but more than that, from the moment they met, the two of them just seemed to click. Hattie's never had that before. She nods, even though Liberty can't see her from inside her cubicle. 'I think he could be.'

'How exciting,' says Liberty. 'I'm so happy for you.'

Hattie's happy too. She just doesn't want to blow it. She's about to say something when Liberty steps out of the cubicle.

She gestures towards the dress and raises an eyebrow at Hattie. 'So what do you think?'

Hattie gives a long wolf whistle. The dress Liberty's wearing is such a close match to her skin tone that she looks almost nude, making it appear as if the strategically placed intricate beading is the only thing covering her modesty. 'You look stunning.'

Liberty grins and does a twirl, the skirt of the dress flaring out elegantly as she turns. 'It's cool, isn't it? I feel like Beyonce in that embellished sheer dress she wore to the Met Ball a few years back.'

'You look like her too,' says Hattie. 'You have to get it.'

Liberty looks at herself in the mirror again, and nods. 'I think you're right.'

'I am,' says Hattie. She's bursting to tell Liberty what she knows about the party, and the extra secret that only she and one other person know about, but she can't. So she just smiles and says, 'It's perfect.'

CHAPTER TWENTY-SIX

JEM

She hates this.

Star Child is getting stronger, pulling at the reins as they turn towards the trotting poles set up in a line of six along the quarter line of the outdoor arena. Jem tries to slow her rising to his trot, but it doesn't help and the powerful horse speeds faster. Clenching her jaw, she tugs on the reins. 'Steady, will you, steady.'

'Just go with him,' says Daniel from where he's standing in the middle of the arena. 'Let him sort his feet out. Your job is to keep him balanced on the turn and then ride straight.'

'That's easier said than done,' says Jem through gritted teeth. She yanks on the reins again. Hissing at the horse, 'Will you bloody listen?'

'Relax your hands,' says Daniel. 'Let him find his way.'

'I'm trying,' says Jem. Can't Daniel see it's not easy? She gives the rein a fraction and the horse accelerates forward, breaking into a canter.

Shit. She pulls on the inside rein, circling the gelding away from the poles. Star Child shakes his head, fighting at the reins.

Why did she book a jumping lesson? This is a big mistake.

'You didn't need to turn him away; you have to let him work it out for himself,' Daniel tells her.

'He's an idiot, and being really strong,' snaps Jem. 'If I'd let him keep going, he'd have injured himself.'

Daniel laughs. 'He'd have been fine. Horses are smart, you don't need to worry.'

Pulling the horse back to a walk, she glares at Daniel. Is he laughing at her? Can't he see what a nightmare this bloody horse is? 'It's not funny.'

'I didn't say it was,' says Daniel. 'Now, let's try that again.'

Jem forces Star Child to halt. She's had enough of this already. The arena is huge, with too much space for the horse to muck about, and as it's outdoors anyone from Daniel's yard can look over and watch her making a fool of herself. She's a dressage star, and she can't let people see her having these problems; she's got a reputation to uphold. 'Why don't you see if you can do better?'

Daniel frowns. 'I don't think it's—'

'I insist,' says Jem, already dismounting. She thrusts Star Child's reins towards Daniel.

He doesn't take them. 'I usually say a rider should work through any problems with their horse together.'

'But I'm asking nicely,' says Jem, deciding to try a different approach. She bats her eyelashes, and gives him a sweet smile. 'And I'm not one of your usual eventing-type clients. I'm a dressage rider, and this lesson has convinced me to never try and jump ever again. I'll stick to dressage. But I'd still like to see if Star Child is good at jumping.'

Daniel looks at her for a moment, and then laughs. 'Well, if you're sure?'

'I definitely am.'

'Okay then,' says Daniel. 'I'll just grab my hat.'

Jem watches him walk across the synthetic sand to the fence. He really does have a great arse.

Lifting his riding hat off one of the fence posts, Daniel puts it on and fastens the chin strap as he walks back towards her. 'Can you give me a leg up?'

Jem has never given someone a leg up in her life. She wants to get close to him, but not by acting like some groom or groupie, so she shakes her head. 'I'm afraid not.'

'No problem,' he says, although the frown on his face implies that it is a bit of a problem. Taking the reins from her, Daniel leads Star Child across the arena to the fence. He climbs up so he's sitting on the top rail, then asks the horse to come alongside.

At first the large bay refuses, curving his body away from the fence like a banana, and prancing on the spot when Daniel asks him to move over. The horse snatches at the reins, but Daniel keeps a light and even contact and after a few seconds the gelding has a change of mind and steps neatly sideways so that his saddle is lined up with Daniel. In a calm, fluid movement, Daniel puts his foot in the nearside stirrup and mounts. Star Child stands statue still.

Jem grimaces, but she doesn't say anything. The bloody horse has never been that helpful to her when she's trying to get on it.

'I'll just get to know him a bit, and then I'll bring him down over the poles,' says Daniel, starting to walk the gelding around the outside track of the arena.

'Okay,' says Jem, watching how her horse's neck is stretched long and how relaxed he looks. She purses her lips. She's always found it hard to get the creature to relax, and here he is looking like a little lamb with Daniel, who he's known all of two minutes. It's infuriating. Why doesn't the horse appreciate her more? She bloody well paid enough for him.

Jem watches as Daniel asks the big gelding to go into trot. There's no bouncing around or snatching at the reins like she's usually subjected to; instead, the bay horse transitions smoothly to the next pace. After a few trot circles, Daniel repeats the same in canter, again with no drama, and then brings the horse back to trot.

He looks over at Jem. 'He's a great horse, very responsive off the leg.'

'Yeah,' says Jem. Too responsive, she thinks.

'I'll bring him over the poles now,' says Daniel, making a smooth turn off the short side onto the quarter line, and riding straight towards the poles.

As the horse sees the line of six trotting poles ahead of him, he throws his head up and snatches at the bit. But Daniel is riding on a loose rein, and the horse finds no resistance from him, so he speeds up, moving into canter on the last couple of strides before the poles. Daniel sits quietly, and doesn't try to stop him.

On the last stride, the horse seems to realise he's in trouble. He spooks at the poles, lurching left to try and avoid them, but he's travelling too fast and there's no time to stop or divert.

Jem winces. She can hardly look. Surely they're going to end up on the floor?

Hooves clip the wooden poles as the bay gelding scrambles over the first few poles. Daniel stays in perfect balance and keeps his reins loose. He doesn't try to correct the animal.

Star Child manages not to fall. Jem's glad; the horse is insured but filling out the long claim forms of these money-grabbing insurance companies can be such a bore; even now, she's still negotiating over the amount she'll get reimbursed for the tack theft. She really can't cope with any more hassle.

Still, she's surprised that Daniel doesn't stop the horse once they're clear of the poles, and instead trots around the arena before bringing the gelding back for another attempt.

Jem holds her breath as they turn towards the line of poles. Star Child's ears prick up, and she's convinced he's about to spin round or accelerate, but he doesn't. This time, the horse maintains his gait and floats over the poles, his hooves giving each one at least a foot of clearance.

'He's smart,' says Daniel, giving the horse a pat on the neck. 'Only took him one attempt to work it out.'

'Rather you than me,' says Jem, watching Daniel repeat the poles exercise again and then change direction and come at them from the other side. 'That first time didn't look a lot of fun.'

'It's all part of the learning process,' says Daniel. He trots a large circle around Jem. 'So do you want to add a cross pole at the end? We can see if he jumps.'

'Me?' says Jem, surprised. Does he really think someone at her level should be putting up jumps? She looks past Daniel, across to the edge of the arena, and then towards the yard, but there's no one around.

Daniel nods, not seeming to notice her concern. 'Please.'

Stifling a sigh, Jem walks across to the end of the line of poles and fixes a couple of pole cups to the jump stands. She rests the end of a pole on each one, so that they cross in the middle and form a small jump. 'Okay?'

'Yes, great,' Daniel says, turning Star Child down towards the far end of the arena.

As she watches Daniel ride, Jem really hopes shagging him is going to be worth all this. She's just not used to having to do all this *menial* stuff. At her level, she really is above such things.

Still, as the horse trots rhythmically over the line of poles and pops neatly over the jump at the end, she does feel a small burst of pride. And when they add in a couple more fences, and Star Child flies them like a pro, she even breaks into a smile.

Bringing the gelding back to a walk, Daniel heads towards her and halts. 'He's a great horse. Lots of natural talent.'

'I always thought so,' says Jem.

Daniel dismounts, and runs the stirrups up on the saddle before loosening off the horse's girth. 'If you ever think he's reached his limit at dressage, he could make a good event horse.'

'I'll bear that in mind,' says Jem, smiling. Reaching out, she puts her hand on Daniel's chest and moves closer until their bodies are almost touching. She looks up at him and bats her eyelashes. 'Is it just my horse you're interested in riding?'

Daniel springs away as if she's scolded him. He shakes his head, blushing. 'I'm not looking for... I'm in a committed relationship and I—'

'I'm in a relationship too, but that doesn't mean we can't have a little fun, does it?' She smiles and gives him her best come-hither look. 'I won't tell anyone.'

'No, I... just no,' says Daniel, forcefully, backing away from her. 'I'm not interested in anything like that.'

'Okay, whatever, I get the picture,' says Jem, grabbing hold of Star Child's reins. 'Thanks for the lesson, but I don't think jumping is for me.'

'Jem, I...'

Not waiting to hear whatever it is that Daniel's wittering on about, Jem gives Star Child's reins a tug and stomps away across the arena. She has no time for timewasters like Daniel Templeton-Smith. Leading her on and then turning her down like that? It's disgusting. She's far too good for him. He clearly has no manners and zero class.

CHAPTER TWENTY-SEVEN

HATTIE

'That was quick,' says Hattie, looking up from fastening Mermaid's Gold's girth as Daniel comes into the yard from the arena. She glances at her watch to check the time but she's still got twenty minutes until Willa arrives. 'Did you finish teaching early?'

Daniel frowns. 'Jem left early. Decided she didn't want to jump after all, and then got all weird with me after I'd ridden the horse and he'd jumped well.'

'Word is, she's a bit of a diva,' says Bunty, poking her head out of the nearest stable where she's mucking out. 'A friend of mine knows this girl called Rosalie who works at her yard and apparently Jem is a real bitch.'

'I can believe that,' says Daniel, shaking his head. 'She wasn't very nice to her horse, and kept blaming him for being difficult when it was obvious she was winding the poor guy up by hanging onto his mouth.'

'Sounds like you dodged a bullet then,' says Hattie. Daniel doesn't reply. He seems really preoccupied. Hattie knows how sensitive Daniel is, how he hates not being able to get through to riders who aren't doing a good job by their horses. She reaches out and touches his arm. 'Hey, are you okay?'

'Yeah... yeah, I'm fine.' Daniel exhales, and runs his hand through his hair. 'You just don't expect professional riders to behave like that. And that poor horse, he's got quite a jump, and he's smart too – quick to learn – but Jem just seemed to want to squash all the personality out of him.'

'I guess what they say about dressage riders is true,' says Bunty from the stable.

'What's that?' says Daniel turning to face her, his tone sharper than normal.

Bunty widens her eyes, clearly surprised at his reaction. 'That they're divas.'

'Willa isn't,' says Hattie. She looks at Daniel. 'Maybe Jem will reflect on what happened in the lesson when she gets home and change her approach with the horse.'

'She might, I suppose,' says Daniel, still looking distracted. 'But I doubt it. She just didn't want to listen anything I said. It's like she had no interest in jumping or the horse.'

Hattie hasn't seen Daniel looking so rattled for a while, not since the whole Lexi Marchfield-Wright nightmare. She's learnt how to read him, and when he's worried he goes into himself. He's doing that now, and it worries her. He's clearly upset about the horse, but it seems like there's more going on. What could Jem have said to bother him so much? After all, it's hardly Daniel's fault that she's decided jumping isn't for her. Hattie's about to ask again if he really is okay when the yard gate clanks. She turns and sees Lady Pat.

'Hello, everyone,' says Lady Pat, striding onto the yard. She's wearing jodhpur boots, jeans and a Barbour gilet over a blue-and-pink check shirt. 'Lovely day, isn't it?'

'Beautiful,' says Daniel, affecting a more light-hearted tone and expression than moments earlier. 'Would you like a cuppa? I'm just about to make one.'

'That would be lovely, dear,' says Lady Pat. 'What a good boy you are.'

Bunty smirks from the stable, unseen by Lady Pat.

Even Daniel cracks a smile. 'I do my best.'

'Jolly good, that's all any of us can do,' says Lady Pat, turning towards Hattie. 'How's Mermaid's Gold this morning?'

'Ready for some work, I think,' says Hattie. 'She's been as bored as I have these past few months.'

Lady Pat nods. 'No doubt. But that's all changed now, of course. You'll be out on the circuit again in no time.'

'I hope so.' Hattie puts Mermaid's Gold's bridle on, and then picks up her own jockey skull cap and fastens it in place. 'Although I'm feeling a little rusty.'

'Nonsense, a good solid run will blow the cobwebs away,' says Lady Pat, firmly. 'But before that, you both need to build up your fitness again.' She stands back, appraising the mare. 'It looks like that might take a little while.'

Hattie knows Lady Pat's right. Mermaid's Gold is rather more rounded than usual. 'She really made the most of her time turned out in the field and the new spring grass.'

'Indeed,' says Lady Pat. 'But I'm sure you'll both get back to competition fitness soon enough, and until then there's plenty to work on, like sharpening up your dressage.' She turns towards the gate. 'Ah, good, here she is.'

Hattie follows the older lady's gaze and sees Willa Alton approaching the gate. Dressed in head-to-toe Pikeur, she looks very much the dressage professional. As Willa lets herself into the yard and Lady Pat heads over to greet her, Hattie unties Mermaid's Gold and leads her across to the mounting block. Once Hattie's onboard, they all go over to the outdoor school.

'I'll just get warmed up,' says Hattie, leaving Willa and Lady Pat to chat.

Mermaid's Gold is keen to get going, so Hattie asks her to trot and they move around the arena on a loose rein. The mare's chestnut ears are pointed and there's a spring in her stride. Hattie's thankful that her wrist and shoulder aren't hurting anymore and she can finally enjoy riding. Dressage is neither of their favourite phases of eventing, but it's an important one, so she knows they need to focus hard on getting their lateral work as established as possible before heading to their first event.

As Hattie trots and canters large circles on Mermaid's Gold, Daniel appears with a mug of coffee for Willa and a mug of Earl Grey for Lady Pat. Daniel and Lady Pat stay chatting at the side of the arena as Willa comes inside, carrying her mug as she walks across the synthetic sand to the centre.

'Okay, so now you're warmed up, start to bring her into an outline. Keep that swinging forward trot; don't collect too much yet,' says Willa.

Hattie does as she asks, shortening her reins and taking a little more contact. Mermaid's Gold responds by changing from a long and stretching stride into a slightly shortened, more powerful trot.

'Good job,' says Willa. 'Okay, start to ride a four-loop serpentine from A. Concentrate on the rhythm and balance through the turns, and on maintaining fluidity.'

Starting the serpentine, Hattie and Mermaid's Gold are halfway through the second loop when a strange, strangled noise and a sudden movement over by the fence catches Hattie's attention. Turning to look, she sees Lady Pat collapsing. Daniel tries to grab her but he's too slow and the older woman falls to the ground.

Hattie's stomach lurches. Her heart rate accelerates. She turns Mermaid's Gold and they canter across to the fence. Lady Pat is lying on the ground, her eyes closed. Her coffee mug is smashed on the ground nearby, the coffee soaking into the gravel path.

Daniel crouches over Lady Pat. He puts his hand on her shoulder. 'Can you hear me?'

Her eyes flutter. 'I… what happened… I…'

'We need an ambulance,' says Hattie, jumping off Mermaid's Gold and pulling her phone out of her pocket.

'Do it,' says Daniel, taking off his coat and making it into a cushion for Lady Pat's head. 'How are you feeling?'

'I… feel weird.' Lady Pat's skin looks ashen. Her eyes are barely open.

'Oh my God,' says Willa, joining them. 'What happened?'

'She was mid-sentence,' says Daniel, worry etched across his face. 'Then the next minute she was falling.'

Hattie dials 999. It's answered after two rings and she tells the operator they need an ambulance and gives them all the details they ask for. Hanging up, she looks back at Daniel. 'They're on their way. ETA eleven minutes.'

'Help is coming,' says Daniel, giving Lady Pat's shoulder a squeeze. 'You're going to be okay.'

'I… don't need any… bother,' says Lady Pat, her eyelids flickering. 'Just… little sleep and… right as rain.'

'Don't go to sleep,' says Hattie, sharply. 'You need to stay awake.'

'Sleepy.' Lady Pat's eyelids close. 'Need to…'

'Wake her up,' says Hattie to Daniel. Her tone is bossy but laced with fear. Daniel looks at her, but doesn't take offence. He knows that she's close to Lady Pat, but what he doesn't know is that they're as good as family. She hasn't shared that with him yet. Right now, she wishes that she had.

Daniel squeezes Lady Pat's shoulder again. 'Stay with us, Lady P. No sleeping in the middle of the day, you're not a slacker.'

A smile flicks across Lady Pat's lips. Suddenly she looks much older than she usually appears. Hattie feels her stomach lurch again. Daniel keeps talking to Lady Pat and squeezing her shoulder, trying to keep her awake.

'I'll go up to the road and wait for the paramedics,' says Willa. 'I'll tell them how they can get as close as possible to the arena with the ambulance.'

'Thanks,' says Hattie. She crouches down beside Lady Pat, opposite Daniel. Mermaid's Gold lowers her head and blows warm breath over the older woman's face.

Lady Pat gives a lopsided smile. 'Hello… Mermaid.'

One side of Lady Pat's face is hardly moving as she speaks. Hattie looks at Daniel, and she can tell from his expression that he's seen it too. Lady Pat might have had a stroke. Fear grips Hattie. She can't lose Lady Pat, not so soon after her mum, not when she's only just discovered that side of her family. Reaching out, she takes Lady Pat's hand in hers and gives it a squeeze. 'Stay with us, Lady Pat. Help is coming.'

CHAPTER TWENTY-EIGHT

MEGAN

*I*t's almost six thirty, but as she turns into the driveway Megan is relieved to see she's made it to the yard before Wayne has finishing shoeing the horses. The sun is starting to fade and the stable lighting and outside floodlights are already on.

As she gets out of the car and hurries towards the yard gate, she can see Rosalie and Peter carrying two stacks of feed buckets out of the feed room, ready to give each horse their dinner. Momento, Peter's young grey horse, is whinnying, and Jem's Star Child is banging his front leg against the stable door, demanding to get his food first, as usual. The horse has an ego that's almost as big as his rider's, thinks Megan.

Letting herself in through the metal five-bar gate, she hurries across the yard to where Wayne's van is parked. She can see Velvet tied up on the other side of it. Wayne is bending over one of the horse's back feet, fitting a shoe. Velvet's ears prick up as he spots her and he wickers.

Megan smiles. 'Hello, sweet boy.'

'Hello,' replies Wayne, a smile in his voice.

Megan blushes. 'I meant Velvet.'

'I know,' says Wayne, grinning. 'I was just having a laugh.'

'Here's the money for today and what I owe you for last time,' says Megan, waiting for Wayne to straighten up and dunk the hot iron shoe into a bucket of water, hissing loudly, before handing him the envelope of cash. 'Thanks for helping me out, I really appreciate it.'

'It's cool,' he says, taking the envelope. 'But only give it to me now if you can afford it. It's no problem if you need a bit more time.'

Megan smiles. 'I'm good, thanks. I've found a side hustle that's bringing in a bit of money.'

'That's good.' Wayne stuffs the envelope into the pocket of his jeans. He picks up a coffee mug from just inside the van, takes a sip, and then sets it back down. Nodding towards Velvet, he says, 'Okay, lad. Let's get this last shoe done and you can go back to your stable for some dinner.'

He's nice, thinks Megan, as she watches Wayne run his hand down Velvet's hind leg and wait for the gelding to pick up his foot. Velvet isn't always comfortable with men, but he seems to like Wayne. She's not surprised. Wayne's so patient and calm with all the horses that he seems to quickly gain their confidence.

'So tell me about your side hustle,' says Wayne, as he picks up the iron horseshoe that he's already shaped to fit Velvet's foot, and starts nailing it on.

Megan blushes again, and she's glad that Wayne can't see it. He's the first person she's told she even has a side hustle, and she hasn't decided how much she wants to say about it. But she can't say nothing, not when he's been so kind. 'It's... I guess you could call it a type of photography.'

'Nice,' says Wayne, hammering in another nail. 'Have you always enjoyed taking pictures?'

'I'm pretty new to it, to be honest,' says Megan, relieved she can be truthful about that part at least.

'You must be a natural at it if you're already making money.'

Wayne straightens up, still holding Velvet's hindleg, and positions the gelding's foot on the tripod stand so he can clench the nails on the outside of the hoof. 'It takes some people years to be good at that sort of thing, and some never are.'

Megan cocks her head to one side and leans against the wall beside Velvet. 'Sounds like there's a story there?'

Wayne laughs as he clenches each of the nails against Velvet's hoof, and then puts the clencher down and picks up the rasp. 'A boring one.'

'You didn't like photography?' says Megan, stroking Velvet's nose.

'It was painting rather than photography,' says Wayne, as he rasps the outside of Velvet's hoof and then clenches to make them smooth. 'And it was more that it didn't like me.'

'Do you still paint?' asks Megan.

'No,' says Wayne, continuing to rasp Velvet's hoof. 'I enjoy seeing other people's art, but as it turns out, I don't have an artistic bone in my body. I stick to footy now.'

'Football can be fun.'

'I think so,' says Wayne. He runs his palm across Velvet's hoof, checking that all the nails are clenched and smooth, then puts the gelding's foot down. Straightening up, he smiles at her. 'And you're all set.'

'Great, thank you,' says Megan, smiling back.

Wayne holds her gaze. His eyes are kind but with a twinkle to them that hints at mischief. There's an unexpected intensity to his gaze which draws her in. Suddenly, Megan doesn't want to look away.

He clears his throat. 'Would you like to—'

'Are you finished yet?' Jem's voice, laced with irritation, cuts over Wayne's as she strides towards them. 'Or just standing around wasting time?'

'I'm done,' says Wayne, turning to face Jem. 'I was just about to pack up.'

'Well, don't let me stop you,' says Jem, gesturing at him dismissively. 'I'm trying to run a yard here, not some cheap pick-up joint.'

Megan can't believe how rude Jem's being to Wayne. Or, rather, she can believe it; because it seems Jem is rude to everyone these days. 'He wasn't trying to pick me up.'

'Really? Well, that's not how it looked.' Jem looks at Megan, the disapproval clear on her face. 'But if he is going to chat you up, and if you're foolish enough to actually think about going there...' She gestures towards Wayne again. 'Then let me warn you, it's really not worth it. Rumour is, the poor love can't get it up.'

Wayne's cheeks flush. 'That's not bloody true, and you know it.'

Jem holds his gaze for a long moment, then shrugs. 'I guess I do.'

As she walks away towards the tack room, Wayne stands and watches her go, open mouthed. 'Who the hell does she think she is,' he mutters under his breath. Then he turns back to Megan. 'I'm sorry about that.'

'It's okay,' says Megan, untying Velvet from the tie-ring on the wall and turning away quickly. 'Thanks again.'

'Shall I book Velvet in for six weeks' time?'

'Okay,' says Megan, but she doesn't look round. She doesn't want Wayne to see the hurt on her face. It's clear from their exchange that he's slept with Jem, and that's okay – he's single even if Jem isn't and, anyway, what they do in their own time is up to them. It's none of her business, she knows that. And she hardly even knows Wayne.

But still, she can't help feeling disappointed.

CHAPTER TWENTY-NINE

WAYNE

He wakes with a start. Heart pounding. At the end of the bed, Albert, his Jack Russell, has his hackles raised and is growling menacingly. Question is, at what?

Then Wayne hears it again: banging on the front door. Loud and firm, like a fist against the old oak. Four times. Albert starts to bark.

'Wayne Jeffries?' shouts a male voice that he doesn't recognise. 'Open up, it's the police.'

Wayne's heart rate accelerates even more. What the hell do the police want with him?

Climbing out of bed, he hurries to the window. Pulling the curtain aside, he looks down towards the front door and, sure enough, there are two people, one male and one female, in black suits standing outside.

Shit.

He pushes up the sash window, and they look up at him. 'I'm here,' he says, hating the slight tremble he can hear in his voice.

'I'm Detective Lanson and this is my colleague, Detective James,' says the woman, raising her eyebrows. 'We need to talk to you.'

Wayne swallows hard. 'I'll come down.'

'Put some clothes on, for God's sake, man,' says the male detective, James. 'And hurry it up.'

Wayne looks down and sees that his morning glory is standing to attention as always. Yanking the curtains across the window, he curses himself for not covering himself before talking to the police. Full frontal nudity probably isn't going to endear him to them.

Pulling on a pair of joggers and an old t-shirt, he runs his hand through his unruly curls and hurries down the stairs. Picking Albert up, he holds the little dog close while opening the front door with the other hand.

The detectives stand side-by-side on the front path. Albert starts growling under his breath when he sees them, but Wayne can feel the dog's stumpy tail wagging too.

'Mr Jeffries?' asks the male officer, an athletic-looking man with ginger hair and a flinty gaze.

'That's me,' says Wayne, fighting to keep the wobble from his voice. 'How can I help you, officers?'

'It'd be best if we come inside to talk,' says Detective Lanson. She's petite, barely five feet tall, with mid-brown hair tied back in a low ponytail and minimal make-up, but her expression is even more steely than her colleague's.

'Yeah, sure, no problem,' says Wayne, pulling the door open wider and stepping to the side. 'Please come in.'

He waits for the detectives to enter, then closes the door and puts Albert down. The little dog is delighted and trots about, sniffing at the officers' trousers.

'He's totally friendly,' says Wayne. 'But he'd have kept on growling if I didn't let him check you out.'

Detective Lanson smiles and gives Albert's head a stroke, but her colleague looks unimpressed.

The cottage isn't big, just a one-bedroom, one-bathroom Victorian end-of-terrace, with a tiny patio at the back that fits two bistro chairs and a fold-out table and just enough dirt in the solitary raised bed to keep Albert happy. With the three of them standing in the front room, and Albert dancing around their feet, it feels a bit cramped.

Wayne's heart is still thumping. He gestures towards the two-person sofa. 'Do you want to take a seat?'

'Thanks,' says Detective Lanson.

As the detectives take the sofa, Wayne pulls the chunky coffee table towards him and sits down on it. There's not enough room in the lounge for an armchair as well as the sofa, and the kitchen doesn't have enough space for a table and chairs, so he's limited on seating. 'How can I help?'

'It's about the saddlery thefts that have been taking place in the area,' says Detective Lanson, her expression serious. 'We've had some information come to light.'

'Well, that's great news,' says Wayne, feeling relief spreading through him. 'I know a few people who've been hit by those burglars and it'd be great if—'

'We know you do,' says Detective James, holding Wayne's gaze. 'And that's something we need to talk about.'

Wayne frowns. 'I don't understand.'

'Can you tell me if you've visited equestrian properties belonging to the following people in the last two months?' asks Detective Lanson. 'Freddie Chalfont, Jem Baulman-Carter, Deana Malone, Alexander Bovey and Delia Ashbourne.'

'Yes, I've been to all those places at least once in the last two months,' he says, his frown deepening. 'They're all clients of mine.'

'And you're a farrier, right?' says Detective James.

'Yes,' says Wayne, nodding. His tone is starting to sound rather defensive, but he can't help it.

Detective Lanson looks serious. She glances at her colleague. 'Wayne Jefferies, can you tell us where you were on the following occasions?'

Detective James takes a small notebook from his jacket pocket and flips the pages until he finds what he's looking for. Then he reads out five dates and times.

Both detectives look at Wayne expectantly.

'You can't seriously think I'm involved in the tack thefts?' says Wayne.

'Answer the question please, sir,' says Detective James.

Wayne shakes his head. 'I'm not sure, I... can I get my diary?'

'Okay,' says Detective Lanson. 'But stay where we can see you.'

'It's just over here,' says Wayne, standing up and moving over to the kitchen counter.

Detective James stands as well, watching Wayne with the intensity of a hawk eyeing up a sparrow.

Picking up his diary, Wayne walks back to the lounge and sits down on the coffee table again. Detective James returns to the sofa.

As he goes through his diary, reading the entries for each of the five dates, his pulse continues to accelerate. It's the same situation for nearly all the dates and times. He looks back at the detectives. 'I was here, with Albert, on most of those occasions, but the third date you mentioned, I was... erm... staying at a friend's place.'

'And you were with this friend all night?' asks Detective James.

'Most of the night,' says Wayne.

Detective Lanson holds his gaze for a long moment. The cop doesn't blink once. 'And they'll give a statement to that effect?'

'They might,' says Wayne, running his hand through his hair. 'Truth is, I only met them at the pub that night. It was late, probably after ten. I don't actually know her last name.'

Detective James frowns. 'So you have a first name for this woman? Do you have her number?'

'Her first name is Polly, but I never got her number.'

Wayne detects disapproval on the male detective's face as he asks, 'Can you tell us where she lives?'

'She used to rent the second cottage on the left in Chairmaker's Close, down in the village, but I heard that she moved to London for a new job about a month ago,' says Wayne. He wishes he'd asked for Polly's number now, but how was he to know he'd need an alibi?

'And on the other nights, can anyone aside from the dog confirm you were here?' asks Detective James, his expression grim.

Wayne looks from Detective James to Detective Lanson. It's Sod's Law, but he's got to tell them the truth. 'I'm sorry, but no.'

The detectives stand up, and Wayne does the same.

Detective James moves closer, blocking his exit from the lounge. The detective's voice is no-nonsense as he says, 'We're going to need you to come with us to the station.'

'Am I under arrest?' says Wayne, the fear clear in his voice now.

'Not at this time,' says Detective Lanson. She holds his eye contact for a beat longer than usual. 'But we need to take your fingerprints and DNA so that we can compare them to those found at the scenes of the crimes.'

Wayne exhales hard. He can't believe this is happening. 'Are you going to cuff me?'

'I don't think that will be necessary if you agree to come willingly,' says Detective Lanson. 'Are you going to come willingly?'

'Yes, of course. Anything to help,' says Wayne, noting that Detective James looks almost disappointed.

Having grabbed his parka from the hook by the door and pushed his feet into a pair of old trainers, Wayne points to Albert's tartan bed beside the radiator and says to the little dog, 'Go in your bed.'

Albert looks unimpressed, and for a moment Wayne thinks he's going to have to pick the Jack Russell up and put him into his bed, but then the brown-and-white dog walks slowly across the kitchen and gets into the bed.

'Good boy,' says Wayne, stroking the dog's head.

Giving Albert a biscuit, Wayne ushers the two detectives out of the front door, pulling it tight behind the three of them and deadlocking it.

As they walk down the path towards the road, Wayne looks at the female detective. 'You said earlier that my name came up in some new information you received.'

'Yes,' says Detective Lanson, her tone neutral and impossible to read.

They reach the detectives' car, and halt beside it. Wayne hopes his neighbours are still asleep so they don't see this happening.

'Where did that information come from?' asks Wayne, as he waits outside the unmarked car while Detective James opens the rear passenger door for him.

'I'm afraid I can't tell you that, sir,' says Detective Lanson. She sounds almost sorry.

Wayne sighs, and climbs into the back of the police car. He's not surprised, really. And he's already got a good idea of who it was that gave his name to the police anyway.

What he doesn't understand is why.

CHAPTER THIRTY

HATTIE

'It's alright, you don't need to speak in hushed tones,' says Lady Pat. Her speech has greatly improved, but it's still a little slower than usual. 'I'm not dead just yet.'

Hattie smiles. It's a relief that Lady Pat is back to her usual forthright self. For the first couple of days in the hospital following her mini stroke, it was awful to see this usually vibrant and no-nonsense woman reduced to barely speaking. Hattie had felt the fear of losing her like a physical pain to the chest, and it's only now that the pain is starting to subside. This last week, thankfully, Lady Pat has been improving every day, and when they discharged her home three days ago, she was well on the way to being back to her old self. 'How are you doing?'

'Still stuck in this old thing,' says Lady Pat, slapping the palm of her hand against the bed's mattress. 'And having to rely on poor Michelle for everything, but feeling perky enough otherwise, and at least I have the view.'

Hattie looks in the direction of Lady Pat's hand gesture, and has to admit the view from her bedroom is magnificent. The huge multi-pane window looks out over the parkland that would once have belonged to Lady Pat's home, Missenden Croft, and is now a National Trust-run garden. There's a clear view all the way to a large lake and the swans and water birds that have made it their home.

'That's good,' says Liberty, stepping into the room beside Hattie. Along with her canvas tote bag slung over her shoulder, she's carrying a tray with a pot of tea, cups and a plate of biscuits that Michelle, the home help Robert Babbington has hired to help Lady Pat while she's recovering, prepared for them.

'What did you bring me?' says Lady Pat, eyeing the carrier bag that Hattie is carrying. 'Not more grapes, I hope? Bloody things. Only good use for them is making wine.'

'It's not grapes,' says Hattie, laughing.

'Or wine,' says Liberty, setting the tea tray down on one of the large oak dressers. 'I don't think the doctors would be pleased if we brought you alcohol.'

'Nonsense,' says Lady Pat. 'A bit of medicinal wine never hurt anyone.'

Hattie and Liberty don't comment. Instead, Hattie puts her bag on the floor and removes the contents. 'It's hot chocolate and macaroons, from me.'

Lady Pat smiles. 'Lovely. I do enjoy a macaroon.'

'And I brought you something nice to look at as you convalesce,' says Liberty, taking the calendar she's brought out of her bag and handing it to Lady Pat.

'Why do I need a calendar?' says Lady Pat, looking at it, confused. 'It's nearly May. I already have one.'

'You don't have one like this,' says Liberty with a wink. 'This one is more for the pictures than for practical use.'

Lady Pat takes her glasses from the bedside table and puts them on. Peering at the calendar, she reads the title out loud. '"Rural Pleasures"? What is this?'

'Open it and see,' says Hattie, smiling as she glances at Liberty.

'Hmmmm,' says Lady Pat, opening the calendar and flicking through the pages. She stops on Mr March. 'Well, I say!'

'I know, right?' says Liberty, laughing. 'We thought you might enjoy it.'

Lady Pat taps the picture with her index finger. 'Indeed, a very thoughtful gift. This farrier chap looks quite impressive, I must say.'

'Word is that he's recently been interviewed by the police about all these tack thefts,' says Hattie, setting out the cups and pouring the tea into them. 'So many local yards have been burgled in the last few months, it's really worrying.'

'And they think this rather splendid young man is responsible?' says Lady Pat, taking a cup of tea from Hattie without taking her eyes off the picture.

'I don't know,' says Hattie, passing Liberty a cup, and then taking a biscuit from the plate. 'They didn't arrest him, so maybe he's a witness or something. It's weird, though, as the police have had numerous thefts to investigate but seem no closer to finding the thieves.'

'How interesting,' says Lady Pat, looking up from the calendar. There's a twinkle in her eyes, something that's been missing since the mini stroke. 'Maybe we can help.'

'Us?' asks Liberty. 'How?'

'Well, we're well connected in the local horse world and I for one have a lot of time on my hands at the moment. I'm feeling thoroughly useless shut up here in my bedroom the whole time. A little criminal conundrum might be just the ticket to help keep the old grey cells occupied.'

'You want to play Poirot or Miss Marple?' says Hattie, putting her tea down on the dresser. She'd been expecting to talk Lady Pat through her plan for the second half of the event season – how if she and Mermaid's Gold were fit enough in time, she thought they could start with Great Witchingham in early July and, after a few runs, aim for the CCI3*S at Cornbury in the autumn.

'I think it would be rather fun, and as you'll be heading off to Badminton tomorrow, I'm going to be extremely bored here all by myself,' says Lady Pat, in a firm voice that makes it clear she's deadly serious. 'So, tell me everything about these tack thefts.'

CHAPTER THIRTY-ONE

MEGAN

*E*ven though it's barely eight o'clock and the cross-country jumping doesn't start for hours, there seems to be a lot of people wandering along the main walkway between the stands at the scoreboard end of the Badminton international arena. Staying to one side of the thoroughfare, Megan takes another sip of the takeaway coffee she's just bought and makes her way to the Doxford Millar trade stand. She ducks through the gap between it and the stand next door – a rather fancy jewellers – then undoes the small entrance flap in the canvas awning and goes inside.

She's the first one here, of course. Evelyn is unlikely to show up until a few minutes to nine, and Georgie, the teenager who helps out in the shop some weekends, is being driven in by her parents so they've probably been held up in traffic – the Badminton country lanes are notorious for lengthy queues on cross-country day.

Looking round, Megan tries to decide what to do first. The Doxford Millar trade stand has been in demand over the dressage days, and they've already sold out of the popular sizes of their special Badminton limited edition boots, the Gloucestershire.

Thousands of people have been inside the stand over the past couple of days and it's beginning to look a bit tatty, not at all on brand. So Megan decides that the first thing she needs to do is get things smartened up.

Grabbing a bucket and some soapy water, she sets about wiping down the cabinets and plinths to remove the finger marks and dirt. It takes a while, and she's pretty warm after doing it, but she's pleased with the result. Putting the bucket down, she checks her watch; it's eight thirty and there's still no sign of the others. She thought Georgie would have arrived by now.

As she goes to pick up the bucket again, she glimpses her reflection in one of the mirrors. She looks rather dishevelled from all the cleaning – her hair is coming loose from her chignon and her cheeks have a rosy glow. It gives her an idea.

Unbuttoning her blouse so the neckline is a low V, exposing her black lace bra, she leans forward towards the mirror, damp sponge in hand, and takes a few photos of her wiping the mirror. She takes care that they're in close up, so the trade stand isn't really visible behind her, then has a look at the results. Not bad, thinks Megan. They're pretty tame shots, but will do as a couple of bonus pictures for her subscribers. Quickly, in a process that's well practised now, she loads them onto her OnlyFans.

'Sorry I'm so late.'

The sudden sound of Georgie's voice behind her makes Megan flinch. Shoving her phone into her pocket, she quickly refastens her blouse before turning round.

'The traffic was a nightmare,' says Georgie. 'The queues went on for miles. My dad was going bonkers.'

'Well, you're here now,' says Megan, relieved that Georgie didn't arrive a couple of minutes earlier and find her mid-photo-shoot. 'I've finished most of the smartening up, so if you can check all the cabinets in here are fully stocked, and fetch more from the van if needed, that'd be great. I need to freshen up before we let in the hordes.'

'No probs,' says Georgie, walking over to the nearest boot cabinet, and making a start on the stock check. 'Has it been busy so far?'

Megan picks up her bucket and sponge. 'Very.'

'Cool,' says Georgie, grinning. 'I hope we get some of the big event riders in.'

~

Having tidied away the cleaning products and sorted out her own hair and make-up, Megan makes her way to the front of the stand. Georgie is ready at the till but Evelyn still hasn't arrived. Still, it's two minutes after nine so they really can't leave it any longer to open.

As she unfastens the front flap of the awning, Megan sees a group of keen-looking shoppers have gathered outside. They're younger than the usual customers they get in the shop. Evelyn will be pleased – she's been desperate for the products to gain a cult following among the younger country set and the urban types, and has been sending new products out to Instagram influencers for months. Maybe it's starting to pay off.

Megan smiles as the girls hurry into the stand, cooing loudly over the boots, their phones already out as they grab a few selfies. It's going to be another busy day.

That's when she notices him for the first time: an older guy standing a few metres away from the stand. He's smartly dressed in beige chinos, a check shirt with a Barbour jacket and brown boots. He's got salt-and-pepper hair, and the sort of tan that indicates he spends a lot of time outside.

As her eyes meet his, he smiles and raises his hand to wave.

Megan frowns.

Does he think he knows her?

He waves again, more enthusiastically. Not wanting to appear rude in case he's a customer she doesn't recognise, Megan raises her hand and waves back with a smile. But, as she turns away and walks towards the queue of girls that has already formed to try on the boots, Megan can't help but shiver. There's something about the way the guy was looking at her that seemed overfamiliar, even sexual.

A few moments later, having fetched a few pairs of boots for the shoppers to try, Megan glances over her shoulder, expecting the man to have gone. But he's still there, now sitting on the bench in the middle of the walkway. And he's staring right at her.

Megan shivers again.

Why is he still there? Is he the dad of one of the young shoppers?

Whoever he is, he's giving her the creeps.

CHAPTER THIRTY-TWO

HATTIE

*H*attie feels sick. The nerves she felt when she was watching Daniel compete at Tweseldown are a million times worse today. Badminton Horse Trials is one of biggest, if not *the* biggest, challenge in the eventing world. As Daniel and The Rogue canter around the warmup area and pop over a couple of the practice fences, Hattie stands beside Eddie and tries not to let on how she's feeling.

'You okay?' asks Eddie. There's concern on his face.

Clearly her attempt at hiding her nerves has failed. Hattie grimaces. 'I feel worse than if I was riding. I just want them to get round safe and clear.'

'Me too,' says Eddie. 'But they're ready. They did a good dressage yesterday and The Rogue's jumping has never been better.'

Hattie nods. Eddie's right, of course, but she still worries. In eventing, you can do everything right and still have things not go your way. There are so many variables; things like an unexpected divot, a slippery patch of ground, or a loose dog can put you off your stride and cause disaster.

Over by the walkway through to the main arena, the tweed-jacketed and bowler-hatted steward gives Daniel a wave and holds up the index finger of their right hand, giving him the one-minute warning. Turning The Rogue, Daniel walks him across to Eddie and Hattie. He looks paler than usual, but there's no mistaking the determined set of his jaw. 'I'll be in next.'

'He's looking good,' says Hattie, handing Daniel a bottle of water.

Eddie steps forward and runs through the final checks: making sure all the gelding's tack and boots are in place and secure, and that there's enough event grease on the front of the horse's legs to help him slither over a fence if he accidentally leaves a leg too low when jumping. When he's finished the checks, he runs a damp sponge across The Rogue's lips, then steps back and looks up at Daniel. 'You're all set.'

'Thanks,' says Daniel. 'I'd better head over.'

'Good luck,' says Hattie. 'You're both going to be amazing.'

Daniel gives her a nervous smile. 'I hope so.'

And with that he's gone, walking The Rogue purposefully towards the tweed-jacketed steward.

'See you in a minute,' says Eddie, picking up the spares bucket and hurrying after Daniel. As The Rogue's groom, Eddie is allowed into the main arena until Daniel and The Rogue have gone under starter's orders. That way, if there's a problem with a bit of equipment, Eddie is on hand to sort it.

Hattie follows them up the walkway as far as the entrance to the arena, and then goes through the gap that takes her into the special section of the grandstand for riders, owners and grooms to watch. As she finds a seat, she hears the commentary over the loudspeakers.

'And our next starter will be number 83, The Rogue, ridden and owned by Daniel Templeton-Smith.'

Her stomach lurches and a wave of nausea floods through her. Over at the far side of the arena she can see Daniel and Rogue circling beside the starting box – a three-sided post-and-rail structure painted white. There are several tweed-clad stewards with clipboards, and the main starter – a tall, distinguished-looking man holding a stopwatch and wearing cords with a green tweed jacket and matching cap.

She sees the starter say something to Daniel. Daniel turns The Rogue towards the starting box. And as the countdown pips sound, The Rogue steps into the box, takes a stride of walk, and as the final elongated pip sounds, the big bay gelding launches out of the start box and into a gallop.

As Daniel and The Rogue leap over the first fence – a flower box spread with the year planted in yellow blooms – the crowd in the grandstand cheers. The pair gallop across to the end of the arena and then out across the pasture beyond, disappearing from view. Hattie swallows hard. She waits, watching on one of the huge TV screens positioned around the arena as Daniel and The Rogue make light work of the second fence – a huge hayrick – then she gets up and hurries out of the grandstand to find Eddie in the riders' tent alongside the warmup area, where they can watch Daniel's round streamed live to the television screens in the tent.

It's busy. Riders who are going later in the day are watching to see how the course is riding, and the sponsors, owners, grooms and supporters of the riders out on the course or about to set off are watching too. The atmosphere feels supercharged, the tension palpable.

Finding Eddie at the side of the tent, Hattie weaves her way through the people and joins him. Onscreen, Daniel and The Rogue are galloping between fences. Eddie leans closer. 'They're over fence five.'

Hattie nods. That means they've cleared the quarry and the narrow ditch-brush. Huntsman's Close is at six, a sequence of narrow logs off-set at different angles. It needs precise riding and a responsive horse. On the screen, The Rogue looks to be pulling. Hattie hopes the gallop to fence six will help settle him and he'll listen to Daniel.

As they start the turn to the first log, Hattie holds her breath. But she doesn't need to worry. The Rogue comes back to a punchier gallop and jumps smoothly through the logs as if they're Pony Club cavaletti. As Daniel gallops away from the fence, she sees him patting the gelding's neck. So far so good, but there's a long way to go.

The technical questions come thick and fast on this part of the course. After a large table fence, they approach the first jump at the lake. As one of the iconic sights of Badminton, the lake is a huge crowd puller and the banks are packed with spectators. The Rogue jumps confidently over the heavy hanging log into the lake, then heads out of the water and around the edge of the lake towards the more technical jumping sequence at the far end of the rectangular expanse of water.

Hattie watches as Daniel shortens his reins, asking the big bay gelding to steady before they turn to the narrow log which will drop them down into the lake on landing. The Rogue's ears are forward, and the horse is clearly focused on the jumps. He leaps over the log and lands well, cantering through the water to the skinny brush fence that lies a couple of strides before the bank. Taking it easily in his stride, The Rogue continues on a smooth arc, past the ornamental trees and model swans, and over the second skinny brush fence on an angle before leaping over the next fence built from two pick-up trucks parked back-to-back. The crowd goes wild, and a grinning Daniel gives the horse an enthusiastic pat as they gallop away across the country.

Hattie glances at Eddie and smiles. He smiles back, but neither of them speaks. They don't want to say anything or get too excited yet; they're too fearful of jinxing the round.

Back on screen, Daniel and The Rogue fly over a few large spread fences and another technical fence, before coming to the second water. This one is more of a pond than a lake, and the timber is narrow silver birch rails rather than the chunky logs and brushes of the first, but it still needs a lot of respect from horse and rider.

The Rogue is pulling hard, and Hattie feels her stomach clench as Daniel tries to steady the horse and the big gelding throws up his head in protest, missing the turn. Daniel does a good job of quickly getting the horse back to a steadier pace, and turning him towards the rail into the water. The Rogue jumps in boldly, but the late turn means they're not lined up straight for the narrow parallel spread fence coming out of the water. Hattie wonders whether Daniel will change course and take the long route, but he doesn't; instead, he keeps their forward momentum and steers The Rogue towards the parallel. Honest as ever, The Rogue leaps the fence with ease.

There's a brief let up over a large roll-top log spread, and then they arrive at the third water. They pop over the big and imposing log pile and make the four strides to the hanging log into the water look easy. Hattie exhales hard. They're three-quarters of the way round the course now.

Daniel and The Rogue take the Trakehner with ease, and head towards the legendary Vicarage Vee – a post and rail fence offset at an angle to a huge yawning ditch. It needs bold riding and a brave horse. Daniel and The Rogue make it look easy.

'Come on,' says Eddie beside her.

Hattie's stomach is churning with nerves. 'Only a few more.'

On screen, Daniel and The Rogue pop through the Shogun Hollow – a combination of narrow fences with a ditch in the middle – and gallop on, over the maximum-sized spread of the hayrick, then steadying up for a combination of three corners. The Rogue jumps well, but Hattie wonders if he's starting to feel tired. She claps her hands together, willing him on safely as he and Daniel set off on the gallop back across the open parkland.

The long gallop can tire horses at this stage of the course but Daniel's letting The Rogue cruise along in a good rhythm and he looks happy enough. Hattie hopes he's got enough petrol in the tank for the last few jumping efforts.

They jump the table fence and the huge bullfinch, and make it through the following technical fence of a large spread on the crest of a hill followed by a couple of skinny brush fences. The Rogue finds the distance a little long, and chips in an extra stride before the final brush, putting Daniel off balance. Hattie gasps as Daniel falls forward, but he manages to get back into the saddle quickly and they clear the fence okay.

'That was close,' says Eddie.

'Yeah,' says Hattie. 'Is he okay?'

Eddie nods. 'He looks alright, and it's not far now.'

Hattie hopes Eddie's right. They stand side-by-side, both tense and both focused on the image of Daniel and The Rogue on the screen as the pair make the turn towards the main arena and the last few fences. The Rogue leaps over the ditch-hedge and flies the penultimate fence, a huge tree trunk.

Hattie and Eddie turn and rush out of the tent, sprinting towards the main arena as soon as they're past the crowd. As they reach the arena, Daniel and The Rogue gallop through the archway beneath the grandstand, towards the final fence. Daniel takes time to steady the horse, making sure that he's got plenty of power in his stride, as they turn towards the final flowerbed fence. The Rogue gives an impatient toss of his head, leaps over the jump as if it's nothing and storms through the finish.

'They're clear,' says Hattie, breathlessly. 'Oh my God, they've done it.'

'So much for thinking he was getting tired,' says Eddie, grinning.

Daniel gradually slows The Rogue to a steady canter, then a trot and finally back to walk. As Hattie runs to meet him, she sees he's patting the horse's neck and telling him how brilliant he is. The Rogue is striding out purposefully with his ears pricked, looking thoroughly pleased with himself.

As Daniel jumps off the big gelding, Hattie hugs him and gives him a bottle of water, then sets about loosening Rogue's tack as Eddie sponges water over the gelding to help cool him. 'You were both amazing.'

'He was amazing,' says Daniel, taking a swig of water. 'He was so brave and brilliant, the whole way round.'

They hug again, and the commentator announces that Daniel and The Rogue were clear within the time, and have gone into fourth place after the dressage and cross-country. Hattie feels herself welling up. After all the heartache Daniel went through last year, she's so happy that he and The Rogue achieved their dream this year. They so deserve it. And it gives her hope. Dreams really can come true.

CHAPTER THIRTY-THREE

MEGAN

Finally, the crowds are starting to clear. The stand has been busy non-stop since they opened this morning, so much so that Megan wonders if some people come to Badminton purely for the shopping and never even watch the horses. Evelyn hasn't allowed her or Georgie to take more than a half-hour break the whole day, so Megan didn't get a chance to see any of the cross-country, but she's heard that Daniel Templeton-Smith – who lives in Leightonshire like her – is in fourth place on the leaderboard as the competitors go forward to the show jumping tomorrow.

'Okay, girls, I need this place smart and ready for the morning,' says Evelyn, clapping her hands together and then gesturing around the stand. 'Georgie, you can sort out the boots, and Megan you're on hats. I'll go into the van and check our stock levels.'

'Okay,' says Megan, glancing at Georgie, who rolls her eyes. They've both been rushing about serving customers all day, but Evelyn, as ever, seems to have managed to get away with regular trips to the van for 'stocktaking'.

At least I don't have to go far after this, thinks Megan. Her tent is pitched in the area designated for those working on the trade stands. It's a relatively short walk away, and she's heard there's going to be a big party this evening, with a barbeque and drinks. It sounds like fun. She just hopes that she doesn't fall asleep before then.

Megan gets to work straightening out one of the hat displays. It's looking rather sparse with just three hats left of the original eight. Leaning down, she opens the cabinet beneath the plinth and pulls out a few more hats to add to the display.

A sudden chill makes her shiver, despite the warmth of the afternoon, and Megan has the distinct feeling that she's being watched.

Then, behind her, over by the boots, she hears Georgie say, 'Hello, can I help you?'

A plummy, male voice replies, 'I'd like to speak with this young lady, actually.'

Turning round, Megan sees that the older guy in the Barbour from this morning is walking towards her. He's smiling, laughter lines crinkling around his eyes, and looks friendly, expectant, as if he recognises her and is waiting for her to recognise him. But she doesn't know him, she's sure of it.

As he reaches her, he puts his hand out. 'It's so lovely to finally meet you in person.'

Confused, but not wanting to seem rude, Megan shakes his hand. 'I'm really sorry, but I don't think I know you?'

'No, no, of course you don't. We haven't met, not in real life anyway, but I do know you, you little minx,' he says, with a wink. He steps a little closer. 'I'm a big fan of yours, Megs Moore.'

Megan's breath catches in her throat. As soon as she hears him say the name she goes by on OnlyFans, she realises what's happened: he must be a subscriber. She looks round, panicked. Georgie is arranging the long boots, her back turned towards Megan and the man, and Evelyn is nowhere to be seen. This is bad, really bad. Megan has to get him out of the stand, right now. She can't have Evelyn finding out about her side hustle.

Taking hold of the man's elbow, Megan tries to steer him towards the exit. 'I'd love to chat but I'm so sorry, we're actually closed now. I'm going to have to ask you to—'

'My daughter is a big fan of this brand,' says the man, stopping alongside a display of ankle boots and looking at them admiringly. 'It was when she dragged me here this morning to get a hat that I spotted you. I wasn't sure at first but—'

'I'm sorry, sir, but I really do need to ask you to leave.' Megan steps forward, trying to encourage him to keep walking. 'We're closing up and—'

'Yes, yes, of course,' says the man, patting her on the arm but not moving towards the exit. 'As I was saying, I had another look at those exclusive pictures you sent me, and I knew it was you. And then I realised that those new pictures you posted this morning, they were taken here in the trade stand, weren't they? Very foxy.' He beams. 'Of course it makes absolute sense, you—'

'Is this man bothering you?' says Evelyn, hurrying over.

Megan flinches. She hadn't realised her boss had come back into the stand. She tries to keep her voice calm and casual. 'No, not at all.'

Evelyn frowns. 'Are you sure?'

'Yes, it's fine.' Megan wishes Evelyn would go back to stock-taking. 'He was just about to—'

'I was just saying that Megs working here makes complete sense,' says the man, smiling. 'It gives her easy access to all your wonderful boots.'

'Well, yes,' says Evelyn. 'All our staff get a discount on Doxford Millar products.'

The man nods enthusiastically. 'That must be so useful.' He looks at Megan. 'I imagine you must need a good selection of them to keep up with all the demands.'

Evelyn looks confused. Megan wishes the ground would open up and swallow her.

The man looks from Megan to Evelyn, then back to Megan. 'I don't suppose I could get a picture with you, could I? Not a saucy one, just a regular selfie? I'm happy to pay the usual fee.'

'Why would you want to pay for a photo with her?' says Evelyn, snootily.

The man raises an eyebrow. 'I would've thought that was obvious. Megs here is an OnlyFans superstar.'

CHAPTER THIRTY-FOUR

HATTIE

*D*aniel and The Rogue are going into the show jumping in third place. They'd been lying in fourth after dressage and cross-country, but this morning at the trot up the ground jury sent the horse who'd been in third place overnight to the holding box as they felt it wasn't quite sound, and the rider chose to withdraw rather than re-present for inspection.

As the horses and riders show jump in reverse order of their ranking, it means that they have a long time to wait before they're due in the ring. The course has been causing quite a few problems. The most influential part of the track is a related distance from a double of oxers to a maximum height upright – three yellow planks with a white pole top and bottom. It's riding as a short four strides or a long three strides, and at least a third of the horses who have jumped so far have had the top pole of the upright down.

As Hattie watches Daniel warming up The Rogue, she wonders how he'll ride the distance between the double and the upright. When they walked the course earlier, he said the three strides would usually suit The Rogue, but if the horse felt tired he'd go for the four. Looking at the horse now, Hattie thinks he looks on great form but she knows that his efforts yesterday could cause him to tire more quickly today. She hopes whichever route they take, they do a clear round.

The Rogue pops happily over the practice fences, and after a quick spruce up by Eddie, they all walk up to the collecting area just outside the entrance to the main arena. The horse currently in fourth place is jumping. Daniel will be in next.

'Good luck,' says Hattie. 'You're going to be great.'

'Thanks,' says Daniel. Outwardly he looks calm, but she can see from the tightness in his jaw that he's nervous.

The Rogue has no such worries, and pushes his muzzle against the pocket of Hattie's jeans, hoping for a ginger biscuit. Hattie laughs and strokes his nose. 'They're for after you've done your jumping.'

'Okay, you're all set,' says Eddie, giving The Rogue's shoulder a final wipe down and then stepping back.

The tweed-jacketed steward gives Daniel the nod. Daniel looks at Hattie and Eddie and gives them a nervous smile. 'See you on the other side.'

As Daniel rides into the main arena, Hattie and Eddie hurry to the riders' and supporters' section of the grandstand. All the seats are full, so they stand at the bottom, leaning on the white railings, and watch Greta Wolfe and Washford Bay complete their show jumping round clear. It means that Greta's guaranteed at least fourth place and, if Daniel or the two riders currently in second and first places make any mistakes, that she and Washford Bay could rise higher in the placings.

'That puts the pressure on,' says Eddie.

'Yeah,' says Hattie, nodding.

The atmosphere in the stands is electric. Every seat is taken, and over in the VIP and members' enclosures at the opposite end of the arena it's standing room only. Everyone is on tenterhooks. The winner of this year's Badminton Horse Trials will be decided by how well the next three horses jump.

Over the loudspeaker, the commentator says, 'And next to jump we have Daniel Templeton-Smith riding his own, The Rogue. They come forward on their dressage score of 29.6.'

Daniel salutes to the judges, then puts The Rogue into canter and circles around towards the start of the course. Hattie feels as if her heart is beating in double time. Reaching out, she grips the top of the white railings, hanging on as if her life depends on it as she wills them to go clear.

The Rogue makes light work of the first fence, an upright of green poles, and puts in a cheeky buck afterwards. There's laughter from the crowd, who clearly enjoy the big gelding's antics, but the buck makes the distance between the first and second fence, another upright with white-and-blue poles this time, a little tight and the horse has to put in extra effort to spring up and clear the fence. Then it's on to a huge square oxer with red, white and blue striped poles and a filler painted like the Union Jack, then a maximum height upright. After a sweeping turn around the bottom corner of the arena, The Rogue pings over a double of oxers followed by a related distance to an upright white gate, and a dogleg turn to another maximum-height upright. The Rogue is jumping well, but he slips a little on the dogleg and doesn't quite get enough height at the upright. His front hooves rap against the top pole and Hattie clutches the railing tighter as the crowd gasp. But although the pole jiggles in the cup, it doesn't fall, and they continue on to the next fence, clear.

Daniel expertly guides The Rogue through a tightish turn to a large oxer of white poles with a blue water tray beneath. The fence has caught out more than a few riders today, but the big gelding flies over without a second glance and pops over the next fence easily too.

They're nearly finished. There's just the tricky combination to go.

As Daniel makes the turn towards the double of oxers, he asks

The Rogue to steady, but the horse has other ideas and puts in another cheeky buck.

The crowd gasp again. Hattie holds her breath.

Eddie mutters, 'Keep it together.'

The Rogue jumps in confidently over the first oxer and makes the one stride between that and the second oxer look easy. As they land, Hattie sees Daniel push the gelding on, and she realises he's going for the three strides. It's a risky move. The show jumping course is long, and after the galloping cross-country yesterday, the horses can tend towards flatter jumping, especially if they're getting tired.

The Rogue doesn't look at all tired, though. He leaps over the tall yellow-and-white upright with a foot to spare, then puts in two big bucks on landing. Daniel, taken unawares by the second buck, only just manages to keep himself in the saddle.

The crowd jump to their feet, cheering and applauding. Daniel grins as he pats Rogue's neck over and over.

'And Daniel Templeton-Smith and a rather frisky-looking The Rogue jump clear within the time,' says the commentator over the loudspeaker. 'They finish the competition on their dressage score of 29.6.'

Daniel and The Rogue are guaranteed third place.

Hattie hugs Eddie, and as they hurry out towards the collecting ring to congratulate Daniel, she realises that she's crying.

∼

Daniel and The Rogue ride back into the collecting ring. The Rogue is looking very pleased with himself and as soon as he sees Hattie he opens his mouth, demanding his ginger biscuit. Hattie laughs. She looks up at Daniel. 'Well done. That was such a great round.'

'He was amazing,' says Daniel, rubbing the horse's neck. 'I still can't believe it.'

'You were a very clever boy,' says Hattie to The Rogue, breaking one of the biscuits in her pocket into two and feeding the big bay gelding one of the halves.

'Almost too clever,' says Eddie, waiting for Daniel to dismount and then throwing a rug over the gelding's hindquarters. He looks at Daniel. 'Well sat.'

'Thanks,' says Daniel, shaking his head with a smile as he runs up his stirrups and loosens the horse's girth. 'He just loves showing off to a big crowd.'

'You rode it perfectly,' says Hattie, hugging Daniel and then handing him a bottle of water. 'And you looked so calm.'

'I was shaking inside,' says Daniel. 'But I wanted to give him the best round so I tried to stay focused on the fences rather than the terror.'

Hattie smiles. 'Well, it definitely worked.'

The three of them walk big circles with The Rogue around the nearly empty warmup area, knowing that once the jumping is finished there'll be a mounted prizegiving that Daniel and The Rogue will need to attend. As the horse in second comes out of the main arena, and the last horse to jump, Dodger, ridden by Fergus Bingley, goes in, the warmup area is deserted. While they walk around the bottom end of the area, far from the main arena, Daniel gives them a blow-by-blow account of how it felt to jump the course, and Hattie feeds The Rogue more ginger biscuits.

It's a few minutes later when they realise a bunch of people up in the collecting ring are waving frantically at them.

'The jumping must have finished,' says Daniel, breaking off from his description of the water tray fence. 'We'd better head back up.'

As they walk back towards the collecting ring, Greta Wolfe trots over on her bright bay mare, Washford Bay. She's shaking her head and Hattie wonders what's wrong; are they late?

'You are so very strange, Danny,' says Greta, bringing Washford Bay to a halt beside The Rogue. 'The stewards have been calling and calling for you, and here you are going on a hike with your horse.'

Daniel looks confused. 'I thought we had a while until the prizegiving.'

'Yes, yes, we do, but still. You do not know which prize it is that you are getting,' says Greta as Washford Bay falls in step with The Rogue. 'There has been much drama.'

Hattie feels her heartbeat quicken. 'What sort of drama?'

'Well, Jonathan had a fence down, and as you know he had less than a fence in hand,' says Greta. 'So I went up to third, you went up to second and poor Jonathan went down to fourth.'

'Second?' says Daniel.

Hattie feels sorry for Jonathan Scott. She worked with some of his trickier horses at the end of last year and he's become a friend, but she's thrilled for Daniel. She grins at him. 'Oh my God, that's amazing, congratulations.'

'That is not the end of the story,' says Greta. She pauses theatrically.

Daniel stops walking. The Rogue halts beside him, and nuzzles Hattie's pocket for more ginger biscuits.

'What *is* the end of the story?' asks Eddie.

'You won,' says Greta, pointing at Daniel with a flourish. 'Fergus had two fences down. You are the winner now, Danny. And I am second.'

Daniel stands there, rooted to the spot, unable to speak. Hattie and Eddie cheer and pull him and The Rogue into a group hug.

'You won. Oh my God, you won!' says Hattie.

The Rogue tosses his head, as if to say, 'Enough hugs and more biscuits.'

Daniel laughs and kisses the horse's neck, then pulls Hattie to him and kisses her.

Eddie takes a step back. 'No kissing needed, mate.'

Daniel laughs again, and claps Eddie on the back. 'We won,' he says, looking from Hattie to Eddie, still clearly in shock. 'We actually bloody well won.'

∼

Later, as she watches Daniel and The Rogue being presented with the Badminton Horse Trials trophy, Hattie feels as if she might burst with pride. The tears fall down her face and she cheers and claps along with the rest of the crowd as Daniel and his big, brave bay gelding canter around the main arena in their victory lap.

Today has been an amazing day.

CHAPTER THIRTY-FIVE

MEGAN

*E*velyn hasn't said anything yet. Yesterday evening, after the guy happily left the Doxford Millar trade stand after taking a selfie with Megan, her boss asked her what he meant by OnlyFans. Megan fobbed her off, saying it was like Instagram, and Evelyn nodded and then barked more orders about tidying up. It was clear Evelyn had no idea what OnlyFans actually is, but Megan wonders how long it will be until she discovers the truth.

Now that the competition is over, all that's left to do is to pack everything up and go home. Today has been super busy again and they've run out of stock in most of the boots and have very few hats left. Megan's glad, because it means it'll be quicker to get the van loaded. She's looking forward to getting home and seeing Velvet. She's also got a lot of requests to fulfil for her OnlyFans, having not been able to do many pictures over the last few days. She hopes it won't take her too long. She's longing for a hot shower and a takeaway.

Beside her, Georgie leans a little closer, her voice low. 'OnlyFans, huh?'

'Shush,' says Megan, glancing towards Evelyn. 'Don't.'

Georgie gives her a knowing smile. 'Fair play.'

Megan feels her face flush. Georgie is a teenager and even she knows about OnlyFans. She trusts her not to talk about it to their boss, but there's no way Evelyn isn't going to find out. Megan grimaces. Evelyn is such a prude, Megan can't imagine she'll react well.

She tries to concentrate on the work, but the fear of Evelyn finding out feels like a belt being tightened ever tighter around her chest. Having boxed up the remaining stock and cleared out the cabinets in the trade stand, Megan and Georgie get to work loading the van. Evelyn watches over them, ticking off the boxes on her list as they're loaded.

Megan's relieved when it's done. She turns to Georgie, smiling. 'Good work.'

'And you,' says Georgie. Her cheeks are flushed from the effort, but she raises her hand and high fives Megan. 'We've really earned our money today.'

'Definitely,' says Megan. 'I'm looking forward to my day off tomorrow.'

'I bet,' says Georgie. She frowns. 'I'll be back at school.'

Evelyn catches Megan's eye. 'Can I have a word?'

Something about her boss's tone makes Megan's heart rate accelerate. 'Sure.'

'In private,' says Evelyn, looking at Georgie, who's loitering beside the van.

'Okay, fine. I'm going home then; my dad's already messaged to say he's here,' says Georgie. She looks at Megan. 'See you next weekend.'

'Have a good week,' says Megan, smiling.

Evelyn waits for Georgie to pick up her rucksack and walk away towards the car park. She watches the girl for a long moment, then turns back to Megan. Her expression hardens. 'You're fired.'

'I... what?' Of all the things Megan was anticipating, it wasn't this. She thought Evelyn would lecture her or belittle her, but not fire her. 'Why?'

'For bringing the company into disrepute with your... unsavoury sideline.' Evelyn gestures towards Megan like she's a piece of dog poo. 'It's gross misconduct, I'm afraid. So there'll be no pay in lieu of notice. You'll be paid up to today, but that's it.'

'Can't we talk about this?'

Evelyn narrows her gaze. 'You've been taking pictures of yourself naked beside from Doxford Millar products, and selling those pornographic images for money, so no, it's not up for discussion.'

'But I'm a good employee,' says Megan, her voice getting louder. 'I work hard and I've always covered for you when you go off on your extended lunch breaks.'

Evelyn shakes her head. 'Like I said, it's not up for discussion. Your employment with us is terminated as of now. We'll email you your P45 next week.'

'You can't do this. I... what does Thomas say?' Megan asks. Thomas Doxford is one of the co-founders of the company, Evelyn's business partner. He has an equal say on what happens in the company, and has always seemed a fair and reasonable man.

'Don't think you can get around Thomas with your charms,' says Evelyn, shaking her head. 'I spoke to him at length yesterday evening and he agrees one hundred percent with me. Doxford Millar can't be associated with someone like you.'

'Like me?' says Megan, her fists clenching. 'What do you mean?'

'A... sex worker,' says Evelyn, spitting out the words as if they're poison. 'It's disgusting, what you do. You're disgusting.'

'It isn't disgusting,' says Megan, heat flushing across her neck and face. 'And I'm *not* a sex worker.'

Evelyn gives a cold, barking laugh. Her expression is haughty and her tone laced with condescension. She looks Megan up and down, then shakes her head. 'You're deluded, dear. You'll get naked for any man who'll pay you. So yes, you absolutely are a sex worker.'

Megan bites her lip, and anger and humiliation burn through her. Blinking hard, she fights back tears. She's taken so much crap from Evelyn the whole time she's been employed by Doxford Millar, never feeling good enough, smart enough or polished enough for this humourless, snooty woman. Well, she's had enough. This is enough. She's going to stop taking crap from mean, self-centred people, starting right now.

She meets Evelyn's gaze. 'I'm an entrepreneur and a model, not a sex worker. But, if I was one, I'd rather be that than a bitter, hated-by-everyone, arsehole like you.'

Leaving Evelyn standing there open mouthed, Megan turns and walks away.

CHAPTER THIRTY-SIX

JEM

*J*em downs her glass of champagne as if it's a shot of tequila and then holds it up for the waiter to refill. From her seat at the head of the table, she looks at all the people chatting and laughing as they drink the alcohol and eat the food that she's paid for, and wishes she could relax and enjoy it more. It's her birthday, after all, but no matter how much fizz she has, she can't shake the tension headache that's tightening across her brow. If she's honest, the music – a birthday playlist she's carefully curated – and the heat in the room is making things worse. She barely tasted the quail egg and caviar starter.

This is not how she'd hoped her birthday would be.

It's Tyler's fault, of course. All she wanted was for him to be the perfect boyfriend, not too much to ask, surely? But no, he got her a rubbish present – a last season Gucci bag that she guesses is probably from some outlet and she knows for a fact would have been on sale – and he's spent most of her party chatting to girls from a couple of rival dressage yards.

Jem takes a big mouthful of her refreshed glass of fizz, and then sighs. Why is her life always so hard? She's beginning to wish she hadn't invited all these people. She hardly knows some of them, and actively dislikes others. She only invited most people so that she'd be guaranteed a good crowd. After all, she needs to do an Instagram live from their private dining room here at the Lounge, so she needed to be sure of enough guests; she can't not look popular to her followers.

In fact now, as the waiting staff finish bringing in the main course, is the perfect time to go live. Tyler is still talking to the blonde sitting opposite him, and Jem deserves more attention on her birthday. She knows her followers won't disappoint.

After smoothing down her hair, and making sure her new Cartier necklace is visible in shot, she goes live. 'Hi, everyone. I'm here at the Lounge, the coolest place in town, for my birthday party. The food is sublime and the fizz even better. I feel so lucky to be sharing my special day with you all. Wish you were here.'

As the hearts appear onscreen, and the comments wishing her a happy birthday start to pop up on the feed, Jem blows a kiss to the camera. For the first time today she feels closer to happy. 'Thank you all so much. I'd better eat my food before it gets cold. Catch you all later.'

As she stops the live recording, and puts her phone back into her bag, Jem feels the happy feeling start to recede. Tyler is leaning far too close to that tarty little cow, Kallie, from Alexander Bovey's yard.

Jem reaches out and jabs Tyler in the ribs.

He turns towards her. 'What the hell?'

'Why are you paying her more attention than me?' hisses Jem under her breath.

Tyler frowns. 'I'm just being sociable. You were doing your social media thing so...' He shakes his head. 'I should've known you expect me to sit quietly next to you like a good little lapdog.'

'Don't say that, I don't—'

'Yeah, you do,' says Tyler. 'You expect me to be your bitch. But

I'm a person in my own right, yeah? The world doesn't just revolve around you. I have my own shit going on.'

'Oh that's nice, tell your girlfriend she's not important.' Jem shakes her head. 'You have zero class. You're—'

'Look, I can't deal with this, I'm going,' says Tyler, dropping his knife and fork onto the plate with a clatter. 'That way you won't have to be disappointed in me any longer.'

'But it's my birthday, you can't just leave.'

'Why not?' says Tyler. 'You've been going on at me all day about how the present I gave you wasn't good enough, and I'm not making an effort. I've tried to give you what you want, but it's *never* enough. I doubt anyone could be good enough for you. So done. I'm going.'

Jem's hand flies to her chest. This can't be happening. Is Tyler dumping her at her own birthday party? He can't dump her. If anyone is going to getting dumped, it's her who should be dumping him. But she doesn't want to cause a scene, not with all these people around. So she shrugs. 'Go home then. I'll see you later.'

'Fine,' says Tyler.

'Good,' says Jem. As Tyler stomps away from the table, Jem fixes a smile on her face and turns to the waiter. 'Get me some more fizz, yes?'

As he hurries off to fetch some, Jem looks around at the partying that's carrying on, everyone else seemingly oblivious to the fact that Tyler's gone. Jem frowns. Most of these freeloaders either envy her or hate her. They're only here for the free meal and the kudos of saying they were at her party. In fact, now she thinks of it, she doesn't really have any proper friends, only acquaintances and staff. It's never bothered her before – after all, if you have a goal like she does, that's what matters most. But right now, in this moment, she can't shake the feeling that she'd like to have a friend. Someone to tell her that she's too good for

Tyler. That she should go home and throw him, his gaming chair and the rest of his crappy stuff out.

She feels her eyes start to water. No, this can't happen, not here, in front of these people. Getting up, Jem battles to hold back the tears as she walks to the ladies' loos. She refuses to let anyone see her cry. Absolutely refuses.

She's doing okay, holding it together. That is until she sees Daniel Templeton-Smith. He's sitting at a table in the corner, laughing at something the ginger-haired guy on his left is saying. There's a woman sitting on his right and, as she gets closer, Jem sees that Daniel's holding her hand.

Jem feels her cheeks redden at the memory of him giving her the brush-off. This woman must be the person he's dating, although she looks frightfully plain. Could Daniel really have rejected her for this scruffy-looking woman? She's hardly even wearing any make-up. Jem can't believe it. It's only when Daniel glances in her direction and his eyes widen that Jem realises she's been staring.

Looking away, she hurries past the table and into the ladies' toilets. Pushing past the women preening themselves in the mirrors over the sinks, Jem hurries into the nearest stall. Slamming the door behind her, she sits down on the loo. Outside the stall, she can hear the other women chattering away like they haven't got a care in the world. The door opens and closes as they leave, then more women enter. Jem wishes they'd all just go.

Can this evening get any worse?

It's hard to think how.

Jem bites her lip to stop it from quivering. Tyler's gone. And it's bloody typical that Daniel Templeton-Smith is here to remind her of how he rejected her. It's not fair. It's her *birthday* and everything is a disaster. She lets out a sob.

A few seconds later, there's a knock on the stall door.

Jem frowns. 'Yes?'

'Erm, are you okay?' says a female voice that she doesn't recognise.

Jem rolls her eyes. Can't she ever get any peace? This is all she needs; some do-gooding busybody poking their nose into her business. 'I'm fine.'

'Well, okay, if you say so.' The woman's tone implies she's not convinced.

Jem clenches her fists. Feels the anger building inside her. So now this do-gooder is judging her. How dare she? Standing up, Jem flushes the loo and yanks open the stall door. The woman is still standing on the other side.

'You?' says Jem, her tone filled with contempt.

The woman takes a step backwards. She looks confused, but Jem doesn't care. She wants to hurt Daniel the way he hurt her, and mess up his happy little relationship with his nothing woman. She jabs her finger towards the plain woman's face. 'You should be less concerned by other people's business, and more concerned about who your precious boyfriend is carrying on with behind your back.'

'I don't understand... have we met?' says the woman, frowning.

'No, we haven't. But I know your boyfriend *very* well, if you know what I mean,' says Jem, giving her a wink. 'It's sad, really, but I just don't think Daniel knows the meaning of the word loyalty.'

The plain woman's mouth opens and shuts like a landed fish. 'Daniel? What has he got to do with—?'

'Ask him, darling,' says Jem, waving away the woman's question and heading towards the exit. 'Just ask him about all the devilish things he's been up to.'

For the first time that evening, as she pushes the door open and strides back across the restaurant towards her party, Jem feels like she's beginning to enjoy herself.

CHAPTER THIRTY-SEVEN

HATTIE

*I*t's been a fun night. Hattie has never been to a restaurant as expensive as the Lounge before, but they needed to do something unique to mark Daniel and The Rogue's big Badminton win, and the food has been amazing. The only thing that's put a bit of a damper on the evening is the weird encounter in the ladies' loos.

Hattie didn't know it was Jem Baulman-Carter in the toilet stall when she first knocked, but she'd heard a distressed woman crying and didn't want to ignore her in case she needed help. When Jem opened the stall door, Hattie recognised her right away from the time she visited Templeton Manor for the lesson with Daniel, and it was clear from what Jem said that she knew Hattie was with Daniel. But aside from that, her words didn't make much sense. Jem seemed to imply Daniel had been playing around – suggesting that she herself knew him intimately and that he wasn't loyal.

Had something happened when Jem came for the lesson a few weeks back? Or had it been happening before and it ended then? Was that why Daniel seemed so shell shocked and weird after Jem left?

No, thinks Hattie. That's ridiculous. Daniel wouldn't do that.

It's just the champagne making me paranoid, surely.

'Home sweet home,' says Eddie, the designated driver for tonight, as he steers the Land Rover into the driveway of Templeton Manor and they bump along the gravel track.

Pulling up outside the house, the five of them get out of the vehicle and head towards the house. That's when they hear the dogs barking: McQueen's distinctive throaty bark taking the lead, with the two higher-pitched spaniel puppies joining in as the chorus.

'That's odd,' says Eddie. 'McQueen never usually barks when we get home.'

'Maybe the puppies are winding him up,' says Bunty.

'Yes,' says Jenny, laughing. 'Poor McQueen's probably desperate for us to rescue him.'

'They probably just want to be let out,' says Daniel, putting his arm around Hattie as they walk round to the back door.

Hattie's not sure though. Aside from the dogs everything is quiet, yet she has an uneasy feeling. 'Shall we go and check the horses?'

'Sure,' says Daniel, unlocking the back door. 'The dogs can come with us.'

As if reading his mind, the three dogs hurtle out of the back door and sprint off across the gravel towards the yard.

'Charming,' says Eddie, with a rueful smile. 'All that barking and I don't even get a hello.'

Hattie gazes into the gloom after the dogs. She knows they're safe – the whole place is fenced so they can't get off the property. But it's strange that they've just run off. They're always so keen to say hello. 'They're certainly on a mission.'

'They must have heard a fox out here, or a deer,' says Daniel, frowning. 'Let's go and check the horses.'

'I'll put the kettle on,' says Bunty, heading into the house. 'Teas all round?'

'Sounds good,' says Hattie.

'Camomile for me, thanks,' says Jenny, looping her arm through Eddie's as they set off towards the yard.

It's dark, but the full moon is bright, illuminating their way. Even so, Hattie's feeling of unease intensifies as they approach the yard.

'What the...?' Daniel rushes forwards to the gate.

Following him, Hattie gasps. 'Oh shit.'

Lying on the gravel beside the gate is the reinforced padlock and chain that usually keep the parking area near the yard secure. Daniel picks them up. 'They've been cut through with bolt cutters.'

'Shit,' says Eddie.

Hattie feels her heart start to race. 'The horses?'

Jenny inhales fast. 'Maybe we—'

Not waiting to hear the rest of what Jenny's going to say, Hattie yanks open the gate and runs towards the yard. The second gate that borders the yard has had its padlock and chain cut off too, and the gate is standing half-open.

Sprinting into the yard, Hattie flicks on the lights. She hears a whinny and is thankful to see Mermaid's Gold's chestnut face looking out over her stable door. In the stable beside her, The Rogue puts his head over the door, blinking sleepily. Hattie feels a wave of relief flood through her. One-by-one, the rest of the horses wake from their sleep and put their heads out over their stable doors.

Daniel catches up with her. 'Are they...?'

'No, they're all here. The horses are okay,' says Hattie, the relief clear in her voice. That's when she notices the door to the tack room is ajar. 'What the...?'

Heart hammering against her ribs, she hurries across the yard to the tack room. Daniel is at her side. As they get closer, Hattie sees the deep grooves in the side of the door where it's been crowbarred away, the barrels of the bolts still embedded in the frame. The combination lock lies in pieces on the concrete nearby.

Daniel pulls open the door. 'Oh my...'

Hattie gasps.

Everything has gone. The saddle racks and bridle hooks are empty. The doors of the equipment cupboards hang open, the rugs, boots and saddle cloths gone. The freestanding wooden saddle stand in the centre of the room has been tipped onto its side, and a jar of coffee has fallen from the worktop over by the sink and shattered on the concrete floor.

The three dogs are rushing about, following the unusual scents. Hattie slaps her palms against her thighs to get the dogs' attention. 'Hey, Poppet, Popsy, McQueen, come here, guys.'

The dogs ignore her, too fixated on the unknown smells. Worried they'll cut themselves on the broken glass, Hattie sets off in pursuit. She grabs Popsy, and is leading her back towards the door before trying to catch the others when Eddie appears at the door.

'We've checked the horses in the paddocks, they're all fine,' says Eddie as Bunty and Jenny join him in the doorway. He takes a sharp intake of breath. 'What the...?'

'Everything's gone,' says Daniel, turning back towards them. 'The bastards have even taken the Badminton winner's rug, the one Rogue took a bite out of – it was lying over the saddle stand waiting for me to fix it.'

Hattie hands Popsy to Jenny, and tries again to catch Poppet and McQueen, who seem to think it's a great game and start racing around even faster. As Eddie comes into the tack room to try and help Hattie catch the dogs, Bunty stands there, shaking her head. She looks as if she might cry.

'Have you got insurance?' asks Jenny, her usually strong and confident voice laced with concern.

'Yeah, it'll all be covered,' says Daniel. 'But it's very inconvenient and the cheek of the arseholes that did this. I mean, they're so bold; we've got cameras…'

'They spray-painted the lens black; I noticed it on our way back from the fields,' says Eddie, taking hold of McQueen's collar firmly to stop the collie going back into the tack room. 'We should call the police.'

'I'll do it now,' says Daniel, taking out his phone and dialling the non-emergency police number.

As Daniel gives the details of the break-in, Hattie and Eddie finally manage to grab Poppet. When the call is finished, with the police due to come out to see the crime scene the next day, they all head back to the house with the dogs.

No one feels like celebrating anymore.

CHAPTER THIRTY-EIGHT

WAYNE

It happens so fast. One moment he's settling the youngster's front foot between his knees and picking up the iron shoe to fit, the next he's being tossed into the air like a ragdoll. He lands with a crash on the concrete yard. It's his own fault. His mind wandered and he was thinking about the police investigation into the tack thefts rather than the youngster he's shoeing for the first time. He's been tense and distracted ever since the police questioned him, and although they haven't arrested him he's still a person of interest. Now that's landed him on his arse, literally.

The leggy youngster is prancing around on the end of its lead rope, wild eyed and snorting, but the owner doesn't seem to have noticed. In fact, Wayne has no idea where Netta Sharpe is. She said she was going to make him a cuppa but that was over half an hour ago. The gelding rolls his eyes and pulls back on the rope, trying to get further away from Wayne, clearly spooked by a human lying on the yard rather than standing.

'It's alright, boy,' says Wayne, trying to keep his tone calm even though he feels really groggy. 'Steady there. You're okay.'

The youngster snorts loudly but stops leaping around. He stands, trembling, with his ears pricked and the whites of his eyes showing.

'Good boy,' says Wayne, trying to ease himself up to sitting.

What the...

Wayne gasps. The pain shooting up his right leg and exploding in his lower back is like nothing he's ever felt before. It's so intense, he thinks he might vomit. There's no way he's going to be able to get to his feet anytime soon.

The horse is still looking at him as if he's a terrifying monster. Any loud noise or unfamiliar movement could set the gelding leaping again. Wayne knows as long as he's sprawled on the concrete, he's vulnerable.

'Netta?' calls Wayne. His voice sounds small, weaker than usual. 'Netta, I've got a problem. Can you come back onto the yard?'

He waits a few minutes, but there's no sign or sound of Netta. She must still be in the house making tea, and there's no way she'll be able to hear him from there. The yard is in the centre of a horseshoe-shaped wooden stable block. There's an all-weather arena along the bottom end of the concrete and fields beyond. The house is nearby, but across the quarter-acre gardens. There's no clear view from the house to the yard because of all the trees between them. Wayne suddenly feels very alone.

He tries to sit again. This time, he manages to make it a couple of inches before the pain intensifies so much he cries out. Something is badly wrong. Getting up unaided is impossible. He needs to get help.

Grimacing from the pain, he slowly eases his phone out of the pocket of his jeans. Scrolling through his contacts, he finds Netta's number and presses call.

The phone rings a few times before she answers. 'Hello?'

'Netta, it's Wayne the farrier,' he says.

'Wayne?' Netta sounds confused. 'But aren't you here on the yard?'

'I've had an accident. Can you come and help me?'

'Is Bubbly okay?' says Netta, the panic clear in her voice. 'My husband paid a fortune for that horse, if he's—'

'Bubbly's fine,' says Wayne, his voice getting weaker as another wave of nausea engulfs him. 'It's me who's not.'

'Oh, Wayne. I didn't mean... I'm on my way.' Netta ends the call.

He can't face the pain that will come from the movement of putting his phone back into his pocket, so he holds onto it and hopes Netta hurries. Above him, the youngster is still looking at him suspiciously but he's stopped shaking and doesn't look quite so freaked out. It's the opposite to Wayne, who has started shivering and, as the initial shock of the fall fades, the fear of what he's done to himself increases.

He looks up at the grey horse. Tries to keep his tone light. 'Help is on its way, Bubbly. It'll be okay soon.'

Wayne really hopes things will be okay.

Moments later, he hears the gate between the garden and the yard being unfastened, then hurried footsteps approaching from behind him. He tries to turn towards them, and immediately regrets it. The movement causes pain to sear through his back. Every nerve ending feels as if it's on fire. Black spots dance in front of his eyes. The nausea intensifies.

'Wayne?' says Netta. He hears the footsteps change from walking to a run. 'Oh my God.'

Netta crouches beside him. Her black kohl-lined eyes widen. 'What happened?'

Wayne tries to speak, to tell her about his back, but he can't get the words out.

Netta leans closer, her expression increasingly fearful. 'What's that, Wayne? I didn't catch what you said?'

He shivers harder. He feels cold, so cold.
'Wayne?' says Netta. 'Stay with me, stay with me.'
He wants to, but he can't. His vision is fading. The light too. After that, there's nothing.

CHAPTER THIRTY-NINE

HATTIE

She couldn't have hoped for a better round. As Mermaid's Gold gallops towards the final fence on the Great Witchingham cross-country course, a maximum-height square log pile, and leaps over with ease, Hattie has to fight the urge to punch the air in triumph. It feels so good to be back competing with the little mare, and from the way she's flown around the course today, Hattie can tell Mermaid's Gold feels the same.

They gallop through the finish and Hattie leans forward, patting the mare's neck and telling her how clever and brave she is. Mermaid's Gold's chestnut ears are forward and she still feels full of running. As Hattie gradually slows her to a canter and then back to walk, she's thankful that she was able to replace her tack and equipment quickly after the burglary, so they didn't lose much time in their preparations for the event.

The theft was several weeks ago, but the police still don't seem to have any leads. The good news is that the insurance company has paid out and Daniel has been able to replace most of the items taken. The bad news is some of the equipment stolen was irreplaceable – the Badminton Horse Trials winner's rug, and a couple of saddles won as prizes at events – but Daniel seems to be taking the knock-back in his stride.

'Brilliant round,' shouts Lady Pat from over behind the ropes where she's sitting on a folding camping chair beside her nephew, Robert – Hattie's half-cousin. 'Inside the time too, by my reckoning.'

Hattie smiles and gives Mermaid's Gold a rub on her neck. The mare twists her head round, opening her mouth for a Polo, and Hattie laughs.

'Alright then,' she says, as she jumps off, loosens the girth and then takes a mint from the pocket of her breeches and feeds it to the happy mare. 'Here you go.'

'Heading back to the lorry?' asks Robert. He's more used to playing polo and it shows in his attire; his shirt, smart blazer and cream chinos make him look rather out of place at a regular, non-championship horse trials.

'I'm going to walk her around here for a few minutes until Daniel's finished,' says Hattie. Daniel was setting off on Pink Fizz two horses behind her. He'll be on the early part of the course now and she'd like to be at the finish when he completes. Pink Fizz is super talented but can be tricky. She hopes the roan gelding is on form today.

Hattie wants to listen to the commentary as she walks, hearing Daniel and Pink Fizz's progress around the course, but Lady Pat has other ideas. Instructing Robert to help her, she links arms with him and walks with Hattie and Mermaid's Gold around the perimeter of the cross-country area. Lady Pat is still supposed to be in bed, but Hattie knows there's no way of changing the older woman's mind, so she slows her pace to enable Lady Pat to keep up with her and the little mare more easily.

'So what have the police said about the burglars?' asks Lady Pat. 'What leads are they following?'

Hattie shakes her head. Since being laid up in bed for a while,

Lady Pat has developed a very strong interest in the local tack thefts. 'Nothing really. They haven't told us about any leads, and they've not managed to locate the stolen tack.'

Lady Pat frowns. 'That's unusual, surely? Not recovering any of it? Assumingly, these criminals would want to sell the stuff to get money.'

'You'd think so, or why would they bother,' says Hattie.

'It's bloody ridiculous,' says Robert, shaking his head. 'If they come on my land, I'll take them out with the shotgun.'

'I'm not sure that would be wise, dear,' says Lady Pat, wheezing a little as she walks. 'Probably better just to call the police.'

Robert rolls his eyes.

Hattie slows her pace even more; she can see Lady Pat is struggling. As Robert bangs on about bringing back corporal punishment, Hattie tries to tune him out and listen to the cross-country commentary coming over the loudspeaker. Daniel is clear and over fence nineteen.

When they've finished one lap of the cross-country area and reach Lady Pat's canvas chair, Hattie halts Mermaid's Gold and grabs the sweat rug folded over the back of the chair. Putting it across Mermaid's hindquarters, Hattie says, 'Why don't we wait here. Daniel should be finished any moment.'

'Very good,' says Lady Pat, taking a seat back on the canvas chair. 'Now, back to these thefts. I've been thinking. It seems to me, given that the yards have all been targeted when the people who live there are out, these aren't random, spur-of-the-moment burglaries. These places are rarely left without at least one person home – they have yard staff and live-in help, so finding a time when no one is there would be hard.'

Hattie nods. It's something she's thought about the burglary at Daniel's yard. It's probably only once or twice a month that everyone is out at the same time.

Encouraged, Lady Pat continues. 'So it has to be someone with insider knowledge.'

'A horsey person?' asks Hattie. 'You think someone we know stole the stuff?'

'Not necessarily someone you know well, but someone who is connected with the world, yes, I think so,' says Lady Pat.

'But if you can't trust horse people, who can you trust?' says Robert, frowning. 'It's a bad state of affairs when country people start robbing each other.'

'Like I said,' says Lady Pat, firmly, 'I'm not saying these are friends, just that they have enough connection to the horse world to be able to pinpoint the precise times people are away and their yards are unattended.'

'We know the police talked to a farrier about the break-ins,' says Hattie, nodding slowly.

'Ah yes, Mr March.' Lady Pat pauses for a moment. 'Well, it's true that a farrier would have inside information on the yards themselves, but they wouldn't know the movements of their clients outside of the times they're actually on the yard.'

'The chap could've asked though, yes?' says Robert, sharply. 'He could have found out that sort of information by sweet-talking the staff, and then snuck back to the properties later on to steal the tack.'

'It's possible,' says Lady Pat. 'But I think the police are wrong about that particular farrier. You see, he doesn't shoe horses at all of the targeted yards, so even if he was involved as a mole or spy or suchlike, he wouldn't be working alone.'

'So we're looking for more than one person?' says Robert.

'There'd have to be more than one,' says Hattie, nodding. 'There's no way a lone operator could have removed the amount of equipment taken so quickly. They'd have wanted more hands to get in and out of the properties fast.'

'Indeed, it has to be a criminal group,' says Lady Pat. 'So that is what we must focus our efforts on.'

Hattie's about to ask her what efforts, but as she opens her mouth, she sees Daniel come into view, galloping towards the last fence. Mermaid's Gold, who was dozing beside Hattie, lifts her head and wickers at the sight of her stablemate.

'Ah, jolly good, here he is,' says Lady Pat. 'Come on, Daniel.'

Daniel and Pink Fizz fly the last fence and thunder through the finish.

As Hattie rushes to congratulate him, the commentator announces that the final riders have now finished in the Intermediate and Open Intermediate sections D, F and H. As they list the provisional scores and placing of the top ten in each section, Hattie and Daniel are thrilled to hear that they've come second and fourth respectively.

As Daniel kisses her, and Mermaid's Gold nuzzles her pocket for another Polo, Hattie puts all thoughts of criminals and burglaries from her mind. The sun is shining. Her first event of the year has been a success. Today has been a good day.

CHAPTER FORTY

MEGAN

She hadn't expected to feel this nervous. Holding onto the dish of lasagne with one hand, Megan uses the iron knocker to rap on the door. The sound seems to echo around her.

As she waits, she looks at the white roses blooming from the archway above the door. This place is very picturesque. On the plaque inset into the middle of the row of cottages giving the name, Lavender Cottages, there's a year – 1902 – etched into the stone. She hadn't expected Wayne to live somewhere like this; she thought he'd have gone for something sleek and modern. It's nice that his tastes are more traditional.

She hears barking inside and then Wayne's voice. Moments later, the door opens and a tan-and-white Jack Russell rushes out to greet her.

'Sorry,' says Wayne. 'Albert's a bit overfriendly.'

'It's fine, honestly,' says Megan, trying to stroke the little dog with her free hand while holding the lasagne out of his reach with the other. 'He's great.'

'He's an attention-seeker,' says Wayne, smiling. 'But anyway, come in.'

Megan follows Wayne into the cottage. Albert dances around

them in excitement, sniffing at the lasagne. It takes Wayne, who is decidedly lame, a lot longer to cover the short distance to the kitchen.

'It's so nice of you to do this,' says Wayne, turning to face her.

'It's nothing,' says Megan. When she heard from Rosalie that Wayne had been in an accident, she found his number on the board in the tack room and gave him a call to see how he was doing. He sounded so low and in pain that she offered to bring him dinner. It was only as she was standing on his doorstep, lasagne in hand, that she realised she didn't really know much more about him than that he's a great farrier and that he slept with Jem at some point. She shrugs. 'You were so kind when I was struggling with money, it's the least I can do.'

'It seems like a lot to me, and I'm grateful.' He gives her a genuine smile.

'I didn't make it,' says Megan, nodding towards the lasagne. 'I bought it from the farm shop on the way over.'

'Well, I'm still grateful,' says Wayne, his smile widening. 'How about I put it in the Aga to cook, and then get us some drinks?'

'Sounds good,' says Megan. She leans against the wooden kitchen counter, watching Wayne wince as he slowly bends down, opens one of the Aga doors and slides the lasagne inside. The cottage is tiny; the ground floor is one open space, with the kitchen to the right of the front door and the sitting area to the left. It's bigger than her flat, but not by much. It's a lot prettier though, with an oak floor, original beams across the ceiling, and a large fireplace with a log burner in the little lounge area. It's the type of place that immediately makes you feel relaxed. 'How long have you lived here?'

'About a year now,' says Wayne, setting a timer and putting it down on the counter next to the Aga. 'It was in a right state when I first moved in, but I've managed to fix it up.'

'It's lovely.'

'Thanks,' says Wayne, smiling. 'What can I get you to drink – beer, wine, or something else?'

'Beer is good,' says Megan.

Wayne takes a couple of beers out of the fridge and opens them, handing one to Megan. 'The doc says I'm okay to drink now, as long as I take it easy. I gave my head a bit of a whack on the concrete when I fell.'

'Seriously?' says Megan. She knew he'd torn the muscles in his back, but she hadn't realised he'd fallen that hard.

'Yeah, the doc said I'd given my brain a proper shake-up,' Wayne says, with a rueful smile. 'I felt really sick, and it took a while to get Netta back to the yard to help. Then just as she'd arrived and I was telling her what happened, I passed out. It was right there on the concrete. Not my proudest moment.'

'How did she react?' asks Megan.

'I don't remember really. But when I woke up, her horse, Bubbly, was back in his stable and there was a pillow under my head and a blanket over me. I stayed like that until the ambulance arrived.' Wayne gestures towards the lounge area. 'Shall we sit down?'

'Sure,' says Megan, following Wayne across to the sofa where a small tortoiseshell cat is curled up. As she approaches, the cat opens one eye and looks at her.

'Hello,' says Megan, leaning down to stroke the cat's silky head and smiling when the cat starts to purr.

'That's Dora. I'm afraid she thinks she owns the sofa,' says Wayne. 'But she'll probably share if you don't mind her sitting next to you as you eat?'

'That's fine. I like cats,' says Megan. She looks around the rest of the cottage but the only place to sit is the sofa. 'What about you though?'

Wayne grimaces as he sits down onto a chunky wooden coffee table. 'This is better for me, to be honest. I find it hard getting up from the sofa at the moment. It's too squashy.'

Megan nods. 'Okay, if you're sure.'

'I am,' says Wayne. 'Cheers.'

Megan takes a sip of beer. 'You said it took a while before Netta came to help you after the accident – what happened?'

'She wasn't on the yard as she'd gone back to the house to make tea,' says Wayne. 'But then she got a call from the Pony Team selectors telling her Tilly would be on the main team at the next international. After that, she was calling Tilly at school to tell her, and then messaging her husband the good news.'

'Ah, okay,' says Megan, nodding. 'Have the doctors said how long you'll need to be off work?'

Wayne grimaces. 'At least six weeks.'

'That's tough,' says Megan. 'Will you be okay?'

'Financially, yes,' says Wayne. 'My farrier mates, John Mackie and Steve Burrows, said they'll take on as many of my clients as they can for the next few weeks, so the business side should be okay. But it's going to be hard sitting here all day every day for weeks.'

'I totally get that,' says Megan. 'I like to be active.'

Wayne frowns. 'It's my fault, though. I let my mind wander when I was shoeing Bubbly.' He exhales hard. 'It's just since the police questioned me about all the tack thefts, I've not been able to stop thinking about it.'

Megan can't hide the surprise in her voice. 'The police questioned you?'

'Yeah. They came here and then took me to the police station to quiz me. Apparently they'd had an anonymous tip-off saying I was involved in the thefts.' Wayne frowns, then adds quickly, 'Which I'm not, by the way.'

'I never thought you would be. But an anonymous tip – who would do that?'

'That's what I've been wracking my brains to try and work out.' Wayne runs a hand through his black curls. 'There's only one person I can think of who'd be so petty and mean.'

'Who?' says Megan, stroking Dora the cat's head.

'Jem Baulman-Carter. It was just after she saw us chatting at the yard.'

Megan nods slowly. Jem had been extra bitchy when she saw the two of them chatting. But why would that prompt her to call the police? 'It seems a pretty extreme reaction to finding us chatting.'

Wayne shakes his head. 'I think she was jealous.'

'But nothing was going on,' says Megan. 'Why would she react like that?'

Wayne takes a swig of beer.

'Is there something going on between the two of you?' says Megan, frowning.

'No, I…' Wayne's cheeks flush red.

'Are you sure?' Megan raises her eyebrows. 'I mean, Jem certainly implied she'd seen you naked.'

Wayne exhales hard. Shakes his head. 'Yeah, well, something did happen a few months back, but we certainly don't have anything going on. It was only the one time, and she made it extremely clear immediately afterwards that she was just using me.'

'Right,' says Megan. The thought of Jem and Wayne together makes her feel rather sad, but she tries not to let it show. After all, they're all adults, and it's not like her and Wayne are anything more than acquaintances really.

'I know it sounds far-fetched, but since the "Rural Pleasures" calendar came out, things have been a bit crazy.'

Megan doesn't really want to know, but she can tell Wayne's keen to talk about it. '"Rural Pleasures"?'

'It's a charity thing, you know, rural hunks posing naked. I'm Mr March,' says Wayne. 'There's a copy hanging up in the tack room at Jem's.'

'I don't think I've noticed it, sorry,' says Megan, giving Dora the cat another stroke.

'It's okay. I know some people don't like that sort of thing.'

'No, it's not that,' says Megan, worried he now thinks she's a prude. 'I just tend to be focused on Velvet when I'm at the yard.'

'I get that,' says Wayne, smiling.

Megan smiles back. Wayne really does have the nicest smile. He's sexy, but in a friendly, easy-going way. Their eye contact seems to intensify. Megan feels her stomach flip.

Then the timer beside the Aga starts beeping, and the moment is gone.

CHAPTER FORTY-ONE

HATTIE

Tonight, it's a full house at Templeton Manor. Daniel has been showing off his cooking skills with a delicious meal, and they've spent several hours chatting and laughing around the kitchen table as they eat. Eddie and Jenny seem as loved-up as ever, and tonight is the first time that Bunty has invited her new boyfriend, the young farmer Tom, to come over for dinner.

As Hattie tops up the wine glasses, Daniel takes the huge pasta bake out of the oven and carries the steaming cast iron dish over to the table.

'That smells amazing,' says Jenny.

'McQueen thinks so too,' says Eddie, laughing as McQueen and the two young spaniels, Poppet and Popsy, start sniffing the air around the table.

'It's not for them,' says Daniel, going back to the Aga and collecting the garlic bread from the second oven compartment, and the bowl of salad from beside the sink. He carries them across to the table and sets them down. 'There, this should keep us going for a while. Dig in.'

They all serve themselves and start eating. It's delicious.

'This is amazing,' says Hattie. 'How did you learn how to cook like this?'

'I've always enjoyed cooking,' says Daniel, dipping a chunk of garlic bread into the pasta sauce. 'I find it really relaxing. I've just learnt stuff from TV programmes and YouTube really.'

'It's top notch,' says Tom, shoving pasta into his mouth. 'Better than my mum.'

'Yeah, better than the Lounge too,' says Bunty, nodding.

Daniel smiles. 'Well, luckily it's pretty cheap and cheerful to make, unlike that place. With all the stuff that needs fixing and maintaining here, I can only afford a meal like that once a year.'

Eddie looks serious. 'Have you had any more thoughts about getting more liveries?'

'Yeah, I'd like a few more,' says Daniel, thoughtfully. 'But I don't want just anyone coming in; they'd have to be the right fit. The yard works well as we are, but the more people who come, the more we risk losing this small team feeling.'

Hattie nods. She loves the friendly atmosphere on the yard; there's no competitiveness between any of them, just a lot of mutual support and laughter.

'You could advertise and see who replies,' says Eddie, feeding a piece of meat to McQueen.

'Yeah, I could,' says Daniel. 'I do need to find another way to bring in regular income.'

'Well, as this is so amazing,' says Bunty, gesturing towards the food on her plate with her fork, 'maybe you should moonlight as a chef in the evenings. That'd be a way to bring in more cash.'

'Not sure I could combine eventing and being a chef,' says Daniel, smiling. 'They're both pretty full-on careers.'

'Definitely not when you're riding multiple horses,' says Jenny, gently pushing Popsy's front paws off the edge of the table to stop the spaniel puppy staring and licking at the food. 'I struggle sometimes to find the time and energy to train and compete on just one horse alongside work. More than one would be really hard.'

'Very true,' says Eddie, nodding. 'And with The Rogue and the others going so well, you need to keep your focus on them.'

Daniel nods. 'Yeah, you're both right. But this place really needs a new roof and the damp situation is getting worse.'

Hattie reaches out and gives Daniel's hand a squeeze. It's been a fun evening until this moment, but now, suddenly, Hattie feels uncomfortable. The conversation about money is putting her on edge. It's because of what she herself *hasn't* said about her own finances – the secret she's still keeping from Daniel.

He turns to look at her and smiles. 'Don't worry, I'll find a way to keep this place going. Even if I do have to get a second job as a chef.'

Hattie forces a smile, but she feels even worse now. With the money sitting in the bank account her late father set up for her, she could easily help fix up Templeton Manor, but she's holding back from telling Daniel about the money and her father's identity. She needs to know that he's serious about this relationship first, that she can trust him. And although her heart tells her Daniel is the one, there's a nagging worry in the back of her mind – the memory of Jem Baulman-Carter sneering about Daniel's loyalty, and the image of Daniel returning from teaching the lesson with Jem and looking visibly shaken. It's planted a tiny seed of doubt. So, even though she feels guilty, Hattie stays quiet, keeping her secret to herself a while longer.

CHAPTER FORTY-TWO

JEM

'Do you want to spank me, baby?' says Jem, in a breathy voice that's very unlike her usual tone. Walking over to where Tyler is standing in the doorway to their bedroom, she looks up at him through her fake lashes and bats her eyelids. 'I've been a very bad girl.'

'Erm.' Tyler looks confused. He looks at her silk negligée and knee-high suede boots, and then across to the speakers where soft music is playing. 'I thought you went to bed ages ago?'

'I was waiting up for you,' says Jem, biting her lip and trying to stay in character. She holds out a black dressage whip with a diamanté handle and smiles seductively. 'I thought you might like to play.'

'Okay.' Tyler takes the whip from Jem. 'If you're sure?'

'Yes,' says Jem, pressing herself against his chest and playfully biting his neck as she undoes his jeans and yanks them and his boxers down. She runs her hand up and down his dick. 'Spank me.'

'This looks like it might be a bit painful,' says Tyler, looking doubtfully at the dressage whip.

'That's kind of the point, isn't it?' snaps Jem. 'Do you want to do it or not?'

'I said yes, didn't I?' says Tyler, glaring at her.

'Well, good,' says Jem, scowling back. 'Then get on with it.'

It's not exactly the sexy encounter Jem had planned. Tyler seems reluctant to use the whip, and she isn't especially enjoying having to be subservient to him. But since he left her at the Lounge, he's been even more distant and she's been worrying that he might dump her. That just can't happen. They need to stay together for at least another six months before she can break things off with him and tell her parents they'd grown apart. Any earlier than that and she'll look stupid for letting him move in here, and she can't allow herself to look stupid. She read in a magazine that men like this type of thing and, as they haven't had sex in forever, Jem needs something to spice things up and get them back on track. So she forces the irritation from her voice and coos, 'Spank me, baby, I've been so naughty.'

She's surprised when Tyler suddenly seems to get into it.

Grabbing her waist and shoulder, he pushes her against the bedroom wall, growling, 'You *have* been naughty.'

'Yes, baby. So naughty.'

Tyler yanks her negligee up so her bum is exposed, and Tyler spanks it with his hand. 'You like that?'

'Oh yes,' says Jem. Really, she can take it or leave it, but she's pleased that he's actually giving her some attention now. 'Harder. Use the whip.'

She hears the thwack of the whip. Next moment, she's gasping from the pain. 'What the hell?'

'You said to spank you,' says Tyler, his voice unsure. 'I just did what you—'

Turning around, Jem takes one look at Tyler's limp dick and shoves him out of the way. She can't believe she's in this much pain and Tyler hasn't even managed to get it up. Pathetic. 'I didn't mean that hard, you idiot.'

'But, you said—'

'It was roleplay,' shouts Jem, shaking her head. 'You don't whack anything with a dressage whip; it's for light refined movements. Everyone knows that.'

'Well, I'm sorry but *I* don't,' says Tyler, pulling his boxers and jeans up. 'I'm not one of your chinless wonder horsey-types.'

'Yeah, that's very obvious,' yells Jem. 'You have no bloody class.'

'No class?' says Tyler, his tone dangerously low. 'You parade around on camera half the day, telling strangers your business, and you say *I've* got no class?'

'That's right, I'm an Instagram influencer,' shouts Jem. 'At least people like me.'

'Do they?' says Tyler, raising an eyebrow. 'Or do they just think you're something to watch, like a freak show? Who really is your friend, Jem? The people who work for you hate you, and I've never once seen you meet up with a proper friend. The only people around you are either paid to be there or are hanging onto you for your money.'

'Does that include you?'

'What?'

'You heard me. These people hanging around me for my money – are you one of them?'

Tyler pales. 'That's not what I meant, and you—'

'Isn't it, Tyler? Because that's exactly what it sounded like you meant.' Jem fights back tears. She can't let him see he's hurt her. 'You said no one likes me, and the only people around me are paid or cling-ons. And as I don't pay you, and God knows your shitty band doesn't make you any money, you must be a cling-on.'

They stare at each other. Neither speaking. Neither looking away.

Jem feels the rage building inside her. After everything she's put up with from Tyler. After letting him move into her home, and arguing with her parents about his intentions, now she discovers they were right all along. She's the one to break the silence.

She moves towards him. Shoves her hands against his chest. 'You've used me, Tyler. You don't give a crap about me, and you certainly haven't supported me. All you wanted was a free place to crash.'

Tyler's expression turns to shock. He must realise that he's overstepped the mark. He takes a step towards her. 'But, Jem, that's not true, I've been here for you when—'

'No, you haven't,' says Jem, shouting again now as she shoves him away. 'You've belittled my struggles, and—'

'I've never belittled you. I've just tried to help you see that you're in a pretty good position compared to—'

'That's crap, and you know it,' shouts Jem. 'And you don't even want to shag me anymore. What's the point of us being together if you—'

'I'm surprised you'd be able to fit me in when you're shagging half the county already,' yells Tyler.

'What?' Jem stares at him. How can he know?

'I'm not an idiot, Jem, and I've heard all the rumours,' says Tyler, his voice lower now. 'You fucked the farrier, and the feed delivery guy before him, and probably that Daniel bloke you went for a lesson with. I expect there are others too. So don't try to make out you're the victim here. You've *never* been exclusive to me.'

Jem feels like she's taken a punch to the chest. She thought she'd been so discrete. How could Tyler have found out? It's not like she doesn't *want* to be exclusive, it's just that she gets horny and if he's not around she has to find another way to satisfy the itch, and if he's pissed her off, then she just needs a little something to make her feel better. 'Baby, I—'

Tyler throws up his hands. 'Don't *baby* me.'

Jem runs her hand down his chest to his trousers. 'It's you I want. I thought you didn't want me.'

'I always wanted you,' snaps Tyler. 'And you look really hot in those boots, far hotter than Megan on her OnlyFans.'

'What OnlyFans?' says Jem angrily.

'Megan does this OnlyFans thing with hats and boots. It's good, but…' Tyler pauses. He moves closer to Jem, staring into her eyes, intense and hungry. 'Like I said, you're far hotter.'

Jem pouts as she sees the bulge in his jeans. Licking her lips, she presses herself against him and whispers, 'Then fuck me.'

Tyler glares at her, and for a moment Jem thinks he's going to storm out. Then he grabs her and throws her onto the bed. Ripping the silk negligee from her body, he thrusts into her. Gasping from his vigour, she bites his shoulder and smiles to herself.

Got you.

CHAPTER FORTY-THREE

MEGAN

Her thighs are burning. All these sitting trot serpentines are a killer, but Jem shows no sign of giving her a let-up. In fact, Jem seems to be enjoying causing her discomfort even more than usual, and her tone is unrelentingly harsh.

'Stop bouncing around on that poor creature's back and sit up straight,' instructs Jem, from the centre of the arena. 'You look awful, like an uncoordinated sack of potatoes.'

Megan tries to draw herself up straighter in the saddle. She's tired; they must have been doing the four loop serpentines on repeat for nearly fifteen minutes. Her core is aching, and she knows she's not riding as well as she was at the start of the session. Usually she does whatever Jem tells her when she's having a dressage lesson, but this amount of sitting trot without a break is ridiculous. Velvet's a young horse and she has to be careful with him.

Asking Velvet to ease back to walk, Megan lengthens the reins to let him stretch. The gelding extends his neck and blows out, relaxing.

'What the hell are you doing?' Jem shouts. 'I didn't say you could stop.'

'I need a breather.' Megan looks across at her, apologetically, as she strokes her horse's neck. 'Like you said, I was bouncing on Velvet's back and that isn't fair on him.'

Jem shakes her head. 'You're never going to amount to much in dressage if you can't even master a basic sitting trot.'

'I can do a sitting trot,' says Megan, turning Velvet into the centre of the arena and halting. 'But Velvet's a young horse and it doesn't make sense to keep pushing on if I'm fatigued and not riding my best.'

'Ridiculous,' says Jem, putting her hands on her hips. 'You mollycoddle that horse. He's a sports horse, not a baby. He needs to toughen up.'

'It's up to me how I choose to treat my horse,' says Megan, thinking she'd rather build a partnership then try to drill the absolute obedience and zero personality that Jem expects of her horses. 'At least I treat my horse like a living being rather than a machine to win things on.'

Jem glares at her, her tone becoming menacing. 'What the hell do you mean?'

Megan hesitates. She's never said what she thinks of the way Jem treats her horses, and never questioned her methods direct to her face, but she's had enough of being meek and mild; all that gets you is people thinking they can walk all over you. 'I mean you treat your horses almost as badly as your staff – like they have no feelings, are stupid and are vastly inferior to you.'

Jem stares at her open mouthed.

'You don't care about anyone but yourself,' says Megan, unable to stop herself now she's started. 'You refused to lend me a saddle after the burglary even though you had far more freebies given to you than you needed and you knew I'd be unable to go to the regionals without one. You treat Rosalie and Peter like dirt, and you treat the horses as a means to an end – winning being far more important than their confidence and comfort. It's not—'

'Okay, okay, shut up, you've made your point,' says Jem. Her face is flushed, and her brow creased. 'And there I was thinking we were friends.'

Megan refuses to feel bad. Jem started this – she always criticises how other people ride and handle their horses – and it's about time she learns how it feels. 'We've never been friends. You've always made it explicitly clear that I'm a livery and a pupil, not a friend.'

'And that seems to have upset you,' says Jem, raising an eyebrow.

'No, I've got plenty of real friends, thanks,' says Megan lightly.

They stare at each other. Megan's unsure what to do next. She's still got another twenty minutes until the lesson ends, but after this she can't see how she can continue; not the lesson or keeping Velvet at the yard. She's about to say something when Jem speaks.

'At least I don't sell naked pictures of myself,' says Jem, the disgust clear in her voice. 'That's a real low, even for someone like you.'

Megan clenches her fingers tighter around the reins. Velvet throws his head up against the pressure. 'Someone like me?'

'A riding school kid.' Jem makes a dismissive flick of her wrist in Megan's direction. 'An ideas-above-her-station dressage wannabe.'

'I'm deadly serious about my riding,' says Megan through gritted teeth. 'And the fact my parents couldn't afford to buy me a pony when I was a child doesn't mean I'm inferior to you.'

'Really, darling, it's so sweet that you think that, but you'll never succeed in the dressage world,' says Jem, dismissively. She looks at Megan as if she's worse than dirt. 'Someone like you, well, you simply don't have the pedigree.'

CHAPTER FORTY-FOUR

HATTIE

*A*fter months of planning, the day of Liberty's birthday bash has arrived. They're all dressed up and ready to party. When Hattie turns off the narrow lane into the long driveway of High Drayton Manor, Daniel's mobile starts to ring. As the Land Rover chugs along the drive, Hattie watches as Daniel takes the phone from his pocket and does a double take at the name on the screen.

'What is it?' she asks.

'It's the chair of the selection committee,' says Daniel, the colour draining from his face.

'Well, answer it then,' says Jenny, leaning forward from the back seat. 'It could be important.'

'Okay, wish me luck,' says Daniel, taking a breath and then pressing answer. 'Hello?'

The noise of the Land Rover's engine is too loud for Hattie to hear what's being said by the person on the other end of the call, and Daniel's side of the conversation is mainly nodding with the occasional 'yes' or 'I see' added in. As the call continues, all three of them – Hattie, Jenny and Eddie – find themselves leaning towards Daniel, trying to make out the conversation.

They're almost at the top of the driveway, and the magnificent High Drayton manor house has just come into view, when Daniel thanks the caller and ends the call. He sits in the passenger seat, phone in hand, staring out of the windscreen, silent.

'So what did they say?' asks Hattie.

Daniel doesn't answer.

'Danny?' says Eddie, leaning forward and tapping Daniel on the shoulder. 'Mate, are you in?'

Daniel turns towards Hattie. His eyes are brimming with tears.

'Tell me,' says Hattie. 'Whatever it is, it'll be okay.'

'We've got a place,' says Daniel, his voice so quiet it's almost a whisper. 'Me and The Rogue. We've got a place on the World Class Programme. We might be going to the Europeans next year.'

Squealing, Hattie slams on the brakes and throws her arms around him. 'Oh my God, that's amazing. Congratulations.'

Eddie and Jenny cheer from the back seat.

'I can't believe it,' says Daniel. 'It feels unreal.'

'Well, it's real, mate, and you've earned it,' says Eddie. 'Congratulations.'

'It's brilliant,' says Hattie, finally letting Daniel go and driving the Land Rover forward again. 'It's what you've been working towards for so long.'

Daniel looks as if he's in shock. All he can do is nod.

Hattie holds Daniel's hand tight as she steers one-handed and follows the wooden signs to the field designated as the car park. She's so happy for him, and she knows he's thrilled too, even if he can't find the words to talk about it. Parking the Land Rover, she turns off the engine and says, 'Okay, let's celebrate.'

∽

Liberty's birthday party is as wonderful as it is over the top. The gardens of the manor have been transformed into a carnival-themed wonderland. There's a Ferris wheel, an old Victorian 'Golden Gallopers' merry-go-round, a bunch of games including a giant Jenga and a huge bouncy castle and inflatable slide. On the patio immediately outside the house, there's a buffet set up on the long tables with every kind of vegan food you can imagine, and the special cocktail, a 'Liberty Fizz' – made with champagne, lychee and tequila – is the drink of the night.

JaXX started the party with a heartfelt speech about how brilliant Liberty is. Liberty looked gorgeous in the floor-length beaded dress, if a little embarrassed at being the centre of attention. Since then, they've danced, played the carnival games and ridden the Ferris wheel twice. Liberty has had a huge grin on her face the whole time.

It's now almost nine thirty, but the warm August evening means Hattie doesn't feel at all cold in her emerald-green cocktail dress. The DJ has finished his set, and the band are setting up to play. Liberty, Hattie and Daniel are talking with Lady Pat, who looks great in a white tuxedo and is now almost back to full strength.

'Great news about you joining the squad,' says Lady Pat to Daniel, clinking her glass against his. 'About time too.'

'Thanks,' says Daniel. 'The Rogue really deserves it.'

'As do you,' says Lady Pat. She turns as Willa and Tony Alton join their group. Willa looks lovely in a long pink dress, and Tony has one of his trademark Hawaiian shirts paired with a tuxedo. 'Hullo.'

'I just came over to say thank you,' says Willa, her voice a little weaker than usual. 'I'm afraid I'm heading home.'

'Oh no, stay, please,' says Liberty, reaching out and taking Willa's hand. 'JaXX is going to play next. His first live gig in years – you can't miss it. And then there'll be fireworks at eleven.'

Willa shakes her head. 'I'd love to, but I've got this awful headache that I just can't shift and it's making me feel rubbish. Tony is staying though. I'm going to drive home and he'll get a cab back later.'

'You're sure I can't persuade you to stay?' says Liberty.

Willa nods. 'Thank you for a wonderful evening. Your party has been amazing.'

Liberty beams. 'JaXX did all of it. I'll pass on your thanks.'

'Feel better,' says Hattie, as Willa turns to go, assisted by Tony.

'Yes, I hope your head clears soon,' says Daniel.

Willa gives them a smile. 'Thanks. See you both on Tuesday.'

'Looking forward to it,' says Hattie. They've got lessons booked in on Tuesday.

Lady Pat raises her hand to wave Willa goodbye, then turns back to the group. 'So, what do you think the odds are of someone here at the party getting their tack room broken into tonight?'

Hattie frowns. 'You think that's likely?'

'I do,' says Lady Pat. 'In fact, I'd put good money on it. Because every time one of these burglaries happens, it coincides with a big event of some kind – something that means a yard that would usually have at least one person around is left unoccupied.'

'Really?' says Daniel. 'What about when they broke into the Templeton Manor tack room? We weren't out at some big event.'

'True,' says Lady Pat, nodding. 'But you had just won Badminton Horse Trials – a fact that was well publicised – so it would stand to reason that you might want to take your whole team out to celebrate.'

'I suppose,' says Hattie. 'But how would they know it would be that particular night?'

'They were probably watching you,' says Liberty. 'Winning Badminton made you a target – then it was just a question of waiting until you all went out.'

Daniel frowns. 'I'm not convinced.'

'Well, I've been giving it quite a lot of thought, and I think there's something to it. The police seem fixated on this farrier chap and, although I think they're not far wrong – I believe the people behind the crimes are linked to the horse world somehow – I don't think the farrier is our man. I've spoken to a few friends who know him and, by all accounts, although he's a bit of a ladies' man, they don't believe for one moment he's a criminal.'

'So who do you think's behind it all?' asks Liberty.

'Well that, dear, is what I'm trying to find out,' says Lady Pat. 'It's been rather tricky while I've had to be holed up at home recuperating, but now I'm able to get out and about under my own steam again, I've got a list of things to investigate.'

Hattie frowns. She's not sure it's wise for Lady Pat to be off conducting her own investigation. After all, she's still meant to be taking things easy. 'I don't—'

At that moment the band starts up, and the music drowns out the concerns Hattie was going to voice.

Liberty claps her hands together as JaXX struts onto the stage dressed in a black dinner suit with thousands of glinting rhinestones, silver cowboy boots and an over-sized, silver top hat. With the Deciders' drummer playing the beat, JaXX takes hold of the microphone. 'I hope you're all having a great night? This party is my gift to my wonderful girlfriend, Liberty, and this is the song I've written for her. I love you, baby.'

As Liberty watches, enthralled, JaXX and the Deciders launch into a beautiful ballad. The lyrics are so heartfelt and the tune so emotive that Hattie feels her own breath catch in her throat. She looks at Daniel and she knows she loves him and that she needs to tell him the secret she's held back. But as he turns to her and kisses her cheek, then takes her hand and squeezes it, the words that Jem Baulman-Carter said to her in the ladies loo a couple of months ago replay in her mind.

'Daniel doesn't know the meaning of the word loyalty.'
'Ask him about the devilish things he's been up to.'

Suddenly, Hattie feels as if she might be sick.

CHAPTER FORTY-FIVE

MEGAN

'I'm done. I can't stay there.' Megan puts the extra-large pizza onto the coffee table as Wayne fetches two beers from the fridge. 'And there's no way Jem would let me even if I wanted to.'

'And do you want to?'

'Hell no,' says Megan, as she sits down on the sofa beside Dora the cat. Albert the Jack Russell immediately jumps onto her lap looking for some attention, and she strokes his tan-and-white head as she continues. 'After what she said to me, she can stick her pretentious, better-than-everyone attitude up her arse.'

'Good,' says Wayne, laughing. 'That's the spirit.'

Megan frowns. 'It's not funny though, is it? She genuinely believes she's better than me.'

'And me,' says Wayne, putting the beers down on the coffee table and sitting down on the other end of it. 'She thinks she's above all of us people who have to actually work for a living.'

Megan shakes her head. 'It's so messed up. She thinks she works so hard when all she does is ride a couple of horses and boss poor Peter and Rosalie around. She's forever going on about how she wishes she could clone herself, and how things are much harder for her at her *much higher* level.'

'Higher level of bullshit more like,' says Wayne, clinking his beer bottle against Megan's.

'Totally,' says Megan, taking a sip of beer. 'But Jem always thinks she's completely right. It's scary really. I mean, I actually used to feel a bit sorry for her because she always seemed stressed. And that boyfriend of hers never seems to show any interest in what she does, and I've never seen her with any friends – not even on her birthday. It's sad. But given how she treats people, it's not surprising, is it? She needs to get over herself.'

'Yeah, she does,' says Wayne. 'But she's not your problem. She's a grown woman.'

'I know,' says Megan, opening the pizza box and holding it out towards Wayne so he can take a slice. 'But I feel bad. I wanted to base myself with her because she was a successful dressage rider and I thought I could learn from her.'

'And how's that going?' asks Wayne before taking a large bite of pizza.

'Well, it was okay at first,' says Megan, thoughtfully. 'But I don't agree with the way she treats her horses, and I just can't stay there now, not after what was said.'

'It won't blow over?' says Wayne.

Megan shakes her head. 'We said too many things. Anyway, I don't think she wants me on the yard after what she's found out about me. Someone "like me" would be lowering the tone far too much.'

Wayne finishes his pizza slice and frowns. 'That's such shit. Why would you lower the tone any more than the rest of us riff-raff?'

Megan looks at him. Can she trust him? She hopes so. She hasn't known him long but already he feels like a good friend. She doesn't want to risk that by telling him the truth.

'What?' says Wayne, smiling. 'Has she discovered your murderous past? Or that you're a fraudster or, worse still, you don't like her favourite clothing designer?'

Megan doesn't laugh. 'It's worse than that.'

'Is that right?' says Wayne, raising an eyebrow. 'Worse than being a fraudster or a murderer? Interesting. Well, seeing as you're sitting in my house and drinking my beer I reckon you should tell me this awful secret.'

Megan feels her stomach lurch. She should tell him; after all, now Jem knows it's only a matter of time before she spreads the gossip. 'Okay.'

'Good.' Wayne smiles. 'What is it then?'

'I'm on OnlyFans. I sell pictures… of myself.' Megan holds her breath, waiting for his reaction.

'Really?' Wayne laughs. 'You actually had me thinking you did something bad for a minute, but OnlyFans? Why's that an issue for Jem?'

Megan exhales, relieved that Wayne isn't throwing her out. 'Bringing the yard into disrepute and, as I said, I'm lowering the tone.'

'That's ridiculous. You can earn your money anyway you want,' says Wayne, taking another slice of pizza. 'I think it's kind of cool.'

'You do?' asks Megan, surprised.

'Sure,' says Wayne, nodding as he chews a mouthful of pizza. 'It's just like a modern-day page three thing, isn't it, but you get all the money? Fair play to you, I say.'

'Thanks,' says Megan. She smiles as she takes another slice of pizza. 'That means a lot.'

'No worries,' says Wayne. He holds up the remains of the pizza slice. 'This is great, by the way.'

'I know you love a Hawaiian.'

Wayne nods enthusiastically. 'Ham and pineapple, what's not to like?'

Megan laughs. 'A lot, some people would say.'

'Not me,' says Wayne, grinning. 'It's the dream team. Now what are you going to do about finding a new yard?'

'I'll ring round a few places tomorrow,' says Megan. 'But it might be hard to find the right type of place at short notice. We're in the middle of the season so I bet most competition yards will be full.'

'Well, good luck,' says Wayne. 'Let me know if I can help at all.'

'I will,' says Megan.

As she meets Wayne's gaze, his expression seems to intensify. Megan's stomach lurches again. She can't look away.

She's about to say something when Albert takes advantage of her being distracted. Leaping up from her lap, the little terrier grabs the pizza slice from her hand and sprints away across the room.

'Albert!' says Wayne. 'You naughty little dog!'

'It's okay,' says Megan, laughing.

When she looks back at Wayne, the moment is gone.

CHAPTER FORTY-SIX

HATTIE

JaXX and the Deciders played an amazing set. Everyone danced, even her and Daniel. She felt weird at first, struggling to push away the memory of what Jem Baulman-Carter had said to her, but after a while the memory and the nausea faded, and they had a good time. Daniel loves her, she's sure of it; the way he looks at her, the way they get on so well – it can't be faked. Jem Baulman-Carter has a reputation for being a bitch. Hattie shouldn't believe a woman like that over her own experience, should she?

As the band packs up, Hattie and Daniel say their goodbyes to Liberty and JaXX and make their way back to the parking area. Eddie and Jenny left about an hour ago – getting a taxi back to Templeton Manor as Jenny was due on the early shift the next day. So when Hattie spots Tony Alton, weaving a little as he walks up the driveway, she calls over to him. 'Are you okay?'

'No cabs,' says Tony, holding up his phone as if it's proof. 'All too busy.'

'We can drop you off,' says Hattie. 'There's room in the Land Rover, and I haven't been drinking tonight.'

'Really?' says Tony, grinning at her as if she's just told him he's won the lottery. 'That would be great. I wasn't looking forward to the walk. Exercise isn't really my thing.'

Hattie's not surprised. It's quite a few miles back to Tony's house. The walk would've taken him forever.

'Come with us,' says Daniel, clasping Tony on the shoulder to help hold him steady. 'You'll be home a lot faster.'

'Very kind, very kind,' says Tony, smiling drunkenly.

∼

As Hattie drives them back through the lanes, she glances at Tony in the rear-view mirror. He's conked out, fast asleep with his head lolling back against the seat, snoring. She smiles. She doesn't think she's ever seen Tony drunk before. He's usually the sensible designated driver, or busy looking after the kids – his and Willa's twin sons are rather a handful. It's nice to see him letting his hair down for once.

'Here we are,' says Hattie, turning into the gateway of Tony and Willa's house – Palisade Heights.

Tony does a loud snort, then wakes up. 'Oh, great.'

Hattie drives through the gates and up to the house.

'How did you do that?' asks Tony.

'Do what?' asks Hattie, stopping the Land Rover outside the front of the house.

'Open the gates?' says Tony, twisting round to look back down the drive. 'They're automatic. Did Willa give you the code?'

'They were already open,' says Daniel, glancing at Hattie, concerned.

'Perhaps Willa left them open?' says Hattie.

'She'd never do that,' says Tony. 'She's really hot on security, and the gates would have shut and locked behind her.'

Hattie turns off the Land Rover's engine. 'I don't like this,' she says to Daniel.

'Me neither,' replies Daniel. He looks into the back seat at

Tony. 'We'll come in with you, and just double check everything's okay.'

Tony swallows hard. 'Thanks.'

The three of them get out of the Land Rover. The house is in darkness, and when Tony opens the front door and they go inside everything looks neat and tidy. It's nearly half eleven so it's very likely Willa's been in bed a while.

'There's nothing out of place,' says Tony, frowning. 'Maybe the gates malfunctioned and Willa didn't realise.'

'Do you want to check she's okay before we go?' says Daniel, the tension audible in his voice.

'Okay,' says Tony. 'Wait here.'

They wait in the foyer as Tony hurries up the grand staircase to check on Willa. Daniel leans closer to Hattie, his voice lowered. 'I don't like this. I think we should check the yard – the tack room.'

Hattie remembers what Lady Pat said earlier about how she'd put a bet on someone at Liberty's birthday party being targeted by the tack thieves during the party. Maybe she was right. She nods. 'Agreed.'

There's an agonised scream from upstairs, and Tony rushes down the stairs towards them. 'She's gone. Willa's gone. I don't think she's even been in the bed.'

'We need to check the yard,' says Daniel. 'Show us the way.'

'The yard?' says Tony, confused. 'She won't be with the horses at this time, she—'

'The tack room,' says Hattie, trying to get Tony to understand.

'Oh no,' says Tony as the realisation of what they mean hits him. 'Do you think the thieves are here?'

'We need to check,' says Daniel.

'This way,' says Tony, stumbling along the hallway, through the kitchen and out into a large boot room. He unlocks the back door and they follow him across the garden towards a large stable block.

Hattie feels her heart beating in double time. The lights are on in the stables. The gate from the garden to the yard is hanging open.

'This is always shut,' says Tony, hurrying through.

Hattie glances at Daniel as they follow Tony through the gate. Daniel grimaces. He's probably thinking the same as her – that she wishes they'd brought a weapon of some kind to defend themselves. Up ahead, she spots a shape on the ground. Hattie's breath catches in her throat.

Tony sprints forward. 'Willa? Oh my God. Willa, can you hear me?'

Hattie and Daniel follow fast behind him. Across the yard, the door of the tack room is open and it's obvious that all the tack has been cleared out. A few feet from it, Willa lies on her side on the concrete. There's a bloody wound on the side of her head, and blood has pooled beneath her. Her bag is open on the ground beside her. The contents have been taken.

'Willa, can you hear me?' asks Hattie as she drops to her knees beside her friend.

There's no answer.

Willa's not breathing. Her lips look blue. Lifeless. Tony's crying and trying to hug his unconscious wife. Hattie gently feels along Willa's neck, trying to find a pulse. Behind her, she hears Daniel call 999 and ask for an ambulance.

'Get them to hurry,' says Hattie. 'I can't find her pulse.'

CHAPTER FORTY-SEVEN

WAYNE

The knock on the front door makes him jump. He's not expecting anyone.

Albert leaps up from the sofa where he'd been lying beside Dora, and starts barking.

'No barks,' says Wayne, easing himself up to standing and hobbling over to answer the door.

He's halfway across the room when the person knocks again. Louder this time.

'I'm coming,' says Wayne. He tells Albert to get back from the door, then opens it. 'Oh, hello.'

Detective Lanson and Detective James are standing a couple of feet back from his doorstep. Detective James glances at his partner, then takes a step closer to the cottage. 'Can we come in, Mr Jefferies?'

'I guess so,' says Wayne, looking from Detective James to his slightly friendlier partner, Detective Lanson. 'What's this about?'

'There's been another tack theft,' says Detective Lanson, her tone neutral. 'We'd like to talk to you about it.'

'Well, okay,' says Wayne, wincing as he pulls the door open wider and shuffles to the side to let the two detectives in. 'But you should know that I've been here, under doc's orders, for the last few weeks.'

'Alone?' says Detective James, his tone sharp.

'Not always,' says Wayne.

The detectives don't sit down, instead choosing to stand in the kitchen area. Wayne could do with sitting, but he doesn't want to be lower than them; the power balance would feel even more skewed. Instead, he leans against the front door. 'So what do you want to know?'

'Where were you last night between the hours of seven and eleven thirty?' asks Detective James, his expression serious.

'Like I said, I was here,' says Wayne.

'And you were alone again?' asks Detective James.

Wayne tries not to rise to the bait even though he hates the judgemental tone to the detective's voice. 'No, I wasn't.'

'Who else was here?' says Detective Lanson, opening her notebook.

'A friend of mine,' says Wayne, looking towards the female detective. 'Megan Taylor.'

'And she was here the whole night?' says Detective James, the suspicion still clear in his tone.

'No,' says Wayne, shaking his head. 'Not the whole night, but until just after midnight.'

'Right,' says Detective James, clearly disappointed. He runs his hand across his jaw and glances at his partner before making eye contact again with Wayne. 'And you didn't leave the house *at all* during that time?'

'No. I didn't,' says Wayne, firmly. He knows the detectives have a job to do, and he wants the tack thieves caught so Megan can get some justice for what she lost to them, but the detective's behaviour is starting to feel like bullying.

'Can you give us Ms Taylor's contact details?' says Detective Lanson, giving him a slight smile. 'Just so we can confirm this with her, for the record.'

'Sure,' says Wayne. Taking his phone out of the pocket of his jeans, he finds Megan's number in his contacts and reads it out to the detectives. 'There you go.'

'Thanks,' says Detective Lanson. 'We appreciate it.'

Wayne takes a breath, the female detective's manner making him feel a little calmer. 'Can I ask who they burgled last night?'

'It wasn't just a burglary,' says Detective James, grim-faced. 'Last night they attacked the home owner. She's in the hospital and it doesn't look good.'

'Oh shit,' says Wayne. 'I mean, I'm sorry to hear that.'

Detective James nods but says nothing.

'Thanks for your help, Mr Jefferies. That's all for now,' says Detective Lanson, moving towards the door.

'Does this mean you believe I'm not a criminal?' asks Wayne.

Detective James unfastens the door then turns back towards him. He shakes his head. 'Let's see if your alibi checks out. Don't go on any holidays or trips, okay?'

Wayne waits until the detectives are almost at the front gate, then closes the door and turns around, leaning his back against the solid oak. He exhales loudly. His alibi – Megan – will check out. And if he was here with her, he couldn't have been out thieving and attacking some poor person. The detectives will have to remove him as a suspect in the burglaries then, surely?

He really hopes so.

CHAPTER FORTY-EIGHT

HATTIE

Hattie feels the relief wash through her as she ends the call. She turns to Daniel, who is standing over by the tack room sink, cleaning. 'That was Tony. Willa's awake, and she's going to be okay.'

'Thank God,' says Daniel.

'They're keeping her in a few more days to be safe, but all the signs are good – no lasting damage.' Hattie shakes her head. 'When we found her on the ground like that... I thought she was dead.'

'I did too,' says Daniel, putting down his tack sponge and putting his arms around Hattie. 'I'm so glad she's going to be okay.'

They stand with their arms around each other. Hattie rests her head against Daniel's chest. His warmth and the softness of his polo shirt are comforting. It's been a hellish twenty-four hours waiting for news on Willa. Hattie has been getting the lorry ready to travel Mermaid's Gold to the Intermediate at Cotters Hall Horse Trials tomorrow, but her mind hasn't been focused. She feels almost weak from the stress.

Daniel clears his throat. 'Hattie?'

There's a strange tone to his voice. Hattie looks up. 'You okay?'

He nods, moving his body away from hers a fraction.

Hattie frowns, worried. 'What is it?'

Daniel swallows hard. 'Look, after what happened with Willa... it made me think. I know we've not been together that long, but I love you, Hattie, and I know I want to be with you.' Daniel pauses. Takes a breath. 'I wanted to ask you to move in with me.'

Hattie feels a riot of emotions rollercoaster through her. Her first instinct is excitement. She loves Daniel, and she wants to go to the next stage in their relationship. They get on so well, she thinks living together would be fun. But then she remembers that she's not yet told him about the money she was left by her father; she wanted to be sure he loves her for her, not for her money. And right now, as she looks at his kind, hopeful face, she can see the love in his eyes; she knows he's genuine.

But still she doesn't say yes.

There's something else holding her back now. Another doubt.

The memory of what Jem Baulman-Carter said to her in the ladies' loos at the Lounge comes back to her, the words repeating over and over in her mind: *doesn't know the meaning of loyalty... devilish... what he's been up to.*

She doesn't want to believe what Jem said, but Hattie still remembers how shaken Daniel was after Jem stormed off during the lesson he was teaching. Could something have happened between the pair of them? Or had Jem seen Daniel doing something he shouldn't and challenged him on it?

Indecision twists in her stomach. She should ask him, she knows she should, but if he was playing away would he actually admit it? And if he lied, would she be able to tell?

'What do you think?' asks Daniel, his voice gentle, his gaze loving.

'I…' Hattie shakes her head, pulling away from him. 'I'm sorry, but I don't think I can.'

CHAPTER FORTY-NINE

MEGAN

It's been over a week since her argument with Jem, but Megan still hasn't managed to find a yard where she can move Velvet. It's as she feared: with the competition season in full swing, every stable is full. The earliest anyone can accommodate Velvet is in six weeks, after the event season has finished, but that's too long. She needs to get out of Jem's yard now. The atmosphere is unbearable.

She's taken to brushing Velvet inside his stable rather than on the yard as a way of avoiding Jem as much as possible, and hacking out rather than schooling whenever Jem is already in the arena but, even so, Megan finds herself feeling stressed and anxious the whole time she's at the yard. She doesn't feel like she was wrong to say what she did, and she isn't going to apologise, but at the same time she hates confrontation and every moment she's here the potential for Jem to come and have a go at her is there.

Today she's waiting for the vet to come. It's just a routine visit as Velvet is due his annual flu and tetanus jabs, but it means she's had to wait around on the yard a lot longer than usual. The vet gave her the one-hour slot of midday to one o'clock for the visit, but then the time got pushed back as the vet was diverted to an emergency call. Megan runs her tail comb through Velvet's long black tail for the hundredth time and hopes, again, that the vet will arrive soon.

So far she's busied herself with taking Velvet on a hack through the lanes and an extra-long grooming session. She needs to clean her tack but Jem has come out of the house and is criticising Rosalie's work on the stable beds, making her remove some of the wood shavings from one bed and add more to another when, as far as Megan's concerned, they all look perfect already.

Feeling her phone vibrate in the pocket of her breeches, Megan takes it out and looks at the screen. It's an unknown number, but a local one. Pressing answer, she keeps her voice low as she says, 'Hello?'

'Am I speaking to Megan Taylor?' The voice is professional and no-nonsense, and definitely not someone Megan recognises.

'Yes, this is Megan.'

'I'm Detective Lanson from Leightonshire Police. I've been given your name by a Mr Wayne Jefferies.'

Megan frowns. 'Okay. How can I help?'

'Can you confirm if you were with Mr Jefferies last night?' asks Detective Lanson.

'Yes, I saw Wayne last night. I went to his house and we had dinner – pizza.'

'That's helpful, thank you,' says the detective. There's the sound of a phone ringing, and a group of voices talking in the background. 'Can you tell me exactly what time you arrived and left?'

'Yes, erm, I must have arrived around six thirty, and then it was a bit after midnight when I went home.'

'Okay, good,' says Detective Lanson. 'And did Mr Jefferies leave your sight at any time during that time?'

Megan frowns. 'For a couple of minutes to go to the loo.'

'And, just to confirm, aside from that he was with you between the hours of six thirty and midnight?'

'Yes,' says Megan, feeling relieved as she sees a black Land Rover with the veterinary centre's logo on the door pull into the parking beside the stables. 'Does this mean there's been another yard burglary?'

'I'm afraid I can't give out that information, but you've been most—'

'I keep my horse at Jem Baulman-Carter's yard and was a victim of the theft there. I lost all my tack and equipment so I think I have a right to know if there are any developments in the case, don't you?' says Megan, surprising herself with her own boldness.

'Hold on,' says Detective Lanson. There's the sound of tapping against a keyboard and some mouse clicks, then the detective clears her throat. 'Ah, yes, I can see you listed against the theft at the Baulman-Carter yard. I thought your name sounded familiar.'

'Okay.' Megan stays silent, hoping it will force the detective to tell her more.

'I can't give you any details,' says Detective Lanson. 'But, yes, there has been another incident.'

'Wayne wasn't involved, he was with me,' says Megan firmly. 'I hope you're going to make this a priority and find the bastards who are responsible.'

Detective Lanson clears her throat again. 'This is a priority case for us.'

'Good,' says Megan. 'And if that's all, I have to go.'

'That's all. Thank you for your help, Ms Taylor.'

Ending the call, Megan shoves her phone back into her pocket and opens the stable door. Slipping out onto the yard, she hurries across to the parking area and the vet's Land Rover.

A ruddy-faced woman with kind eyes and a broad smile gets out as she approaches. 'Megan Taylor?'

'Hi, yes, are you Jenny?' asks Megan.

'I am. Sorry to be running so late. There was a nasty colic over in the Claythornes. It took a while to get the horse right,' says the vet, climbing down from the driver's seat. 'Now, I'm here for a flu and tet jab, is that right?'

'No problem, and yes, that's right,' says Megan, handing Velvet's passport to the vet.

'Great,' says Jenny, flipping through the equine passport until she reaches the vaccination record, and then having a read of the dates and jabs of his previous injections. She nods. 'I'll just grab the stuff and we can get it done.'

Megan waits as Jenny takes some equipment from the back of the Land Rover – syringe, needle, and a bottle of the combined vaccine – then leads her across the yard towards Velvet's stable.

'Nice place,' says Jenny.

'Yes,' says Megan, although she knows her tone doesn't sound very enthusiastic.

Jenny doesn't say anything in response. Instead she smiles as Velvet pricks his ears and wickers at Megan. 'Lovely horse.'

'Thanks,' says Megan, smiling. 'He's a good boy.'

'Do you mind bringing him out of the stable for this? It's easier to have a bit more space, just in case he reacts to the needle.'

'No problem,' replies Megan, although she'd rather they were hidden away in the stable. She can't see Jem at the moment, but she doubts she's far away.

As Jenny prepares the injection, Megan puts a headcollar on Velvet, picks out his feet so that he doesn't scatter wood shavings from his hooves across the freshly swept concrete, and leads him out onto the yard. He stands quietly beside her as Jenny gives him a quick check over and listens to his heart and lungs.

'All good,' says Jenny, putting her stethoscope back around her neck. 'How is he with needles usually?'

'He doesn't mind,' says Megan, taking a packet of Polos out of her pocket. 'I'll keep him occupied with these.'

'Great,' says Jenny, moving along the gelding's body to his rump. With experience born of repetition, she bangs on Velvet's rump twice with the heel of her hand, and on the third time puts the needle into his skin. The horse doesn't react, letting her attach the syringe and inject the vaccine. It's over in seconds. 'There we are, all done.'

'Well done, Velvet,' says Megan, giving him a Polo. 'Such a brave boy.'

'You sound ridiculous,' says Jem, walking across the yard towards her. 'It's a horse, not a baby.'

'I can talk to my horse however I want,' says Megan, taking care to keep her tone neutral. She doesn't want another fight, especially in front of the vet.

'Is that how you talk to your subscribers?' asks Jem, cocking her head to one side. She looks at Jenny the vet. 'You know what she is, don't you? She's one of those people who sells naked pictures of themselves on OnlyFans.'

Megan feels heat flush up her neck to her face. She can't believe Jem would say that to the vet. Scratch that, she *can* believe it, but that doesn't make it any less shocking. And Megan knows why. Jem's popularity on Instagram was short-lived and her followers have been unfollowing her in droves. Megan, in contrast, has been gathering more paying fans by the day, so many now that she can barely keep up with the private requests and specials, even though she's working on it full time. She turns towards Jem. 'I don't see how that's relevant.'

'I just thought your vet should know the sort of *person* she's dealing with,' says Jem, the way she emphasises the word making it obvious the disgust she feels. She looks at Megan. 'I looked up your page, you know. You have thousands of subscribers. I don't know how you can stand it, all those dirty old men looking at you. Haven't you got more self—'

'As long as they're not breaking the law, I have no interest in how my clients make their money, actually,' says Jenny the vet.

Megan looks at Jenny gratefully.

'Really?' says Jem, raising an eyebrow. 'How very liberal of you.'

Megan's still trying to think of a pithy reply when Jem turns and stomps off across the yard to the tack room.

'Wow,' says Jenny. 'She's quite something.'

Megan nods. Although not entirely unexpected, Jem's attack has upset her more than she anticipated. She turns towards Velvet and strokes his face, trying to stop herself from crying. 'Yes.'

'It's okay to be upset,' says Jenny.

Megan looks at her. There's sympathy in her eyes.

'Does she usually speak to you like that?' asks Jenny.

'She's always been difficult, but recently, since Velvet's been having some success at Elementary and she found out about my OnlyFans, she's become vicious.'

Jenny shakes her head. 'You shouldn't have to put up with it.'

'I want to move,' says Megan, her lower lip quivering as she speaks. 'But I can't find any competition yards with space, so I'm stuck.'

Jenny looks thoughtful, then rips a bit of card from the box she brought the injection kit over in, and jots a telephone number down onto it. 'Look, give my friend Daniel a call. He's just started doing liveries, and if I let him know the situation I'm sure he'll be able to fit you in.'

'Is his yard local?' asks Megan.

'Yes, he's at Templeton Manor. It's only a few miles away.'

Megan tries to contain her surprise. 'Daniel Templeton-Smith, the eventer?'

'That's him. He's a nice guy and very good with the horses.' Jenny glances over towards the tack room. 'And a lot more respectful to his liveries, I can tell you.'

'Thank you,' says Megan. 'Thanks so much, I can't—'

'Give him a call,' says Jenny, giving Velvet a pat before turning towards the parking area and her Land Rover. 'And get out of here as soon as you can so you don't have to deal with that woman anymore. Honestly, life's too short for that kind of nonsense.'

CHAPTER FIFTY

HATTIE

She hasn't seen Daniel since yesterday afternoon. Things were so awkward after she turned down his idea of them moving in together that she slept at her rental cottage last night, and then set off extra early this morning on the drive to Cotters Hall Horse Trials. As a result, she's arrived here at the event far too early. They're doing dressage today, but not until later this afternoon. Then they have the jumping phases tomorrow.

It seems strange to be arriving entirely alone, but Cotters Hall is a four-hour drive from Leightonshire and Daniel's scheduled to compete at Blair Castle International in just over a week's time so he can't take three days out of his schedule to come here with her. Usually Lady Pat and Liberty would be here, but Liberty and JaXX are away in Miami for a week, and Lady Pat has a hospital appointment tomorrow. So it's just Hattie and Mermaid's Gold on this trip.

Maybe it's what I need, thinks Hattie, as she unloads Mermaid's Gold from the lorry and sets off towards the competitor stabling. A bit of time away on my own might do me good.

The temporary stable block – four lines of wooden stables with canvas roofs – has been put in a sheltered corner of the overnight lorry field, well away from the hustle and bustle of the competition. There are already quite a few horses here, and it isn't long before Hattie locates Mermaid's Gold's stable. There are a couple of bales of wood shavings inside, ready for Hattie to lay a bed for the mare on top of the grassy floor.

Leading Mermaid's Gold into the stable, Hattie moves the bales to the corner and removes the mare's halter. 'There you go. You can eat the grass before I put your bed down if you like.'

The mare doesn't need telling twice. She puts her head down and starts eating, not even asking Hattie for a Polo first. Hattie smiles as she watches the little horse munching happily. Things are so much simpler with horses than they are with humans.

As Mermaid's Gold enjoys the grass in her stable, Hattie makes a few trips back and forth to the lorry, bringing water buckets, rugs and mucking out equipment that she can store outside.

She says hello to Greta Wolfe and her tall groom, Helga, and waves hello to a couple of people she recognises from other competitions. Back at the stables, she stops to catch up with Jonathan Scott – the medal-winning Australian rider who she helped out with a few of his trickier horses towards the end of last year.

'How's my favourite horse whisperer?' says Jonathan, pulling her into a hug. 'Still shagging Templeton-Smith?'

Hattie laughs. Subtle, Jonathan is not. She's aways been well aware of his love of threesomes; he even invited her to one when they first met before she made it clear that wasn't her thing. 'I'm good, and yes, we're still together.'

'That's good,' says Jonathan. 'And how's the little mare going?'

'She's great. We had a slow start to the season because I broke my wrist but we're back on track now.'

Jonathan shakes his head. 'Sorry about the wrist; injuries are a real bugger in this game.'

'It wasn't a horse, actually,' says Hattie, setting him right. 'It was a deer.'

Jonathan raises his eyebrows. 'Deer whispering your new thing, is it?'

Hattie laughs. 'Thankfully no. We were rescuing an injured one and it kicked me. I'm safer around horses.'

'Well, I'm glad you're all fixed now,' says Jonathan. He looks thoughtful. 'I was going to give you a call actually. I've a few youngsters and one established horse that's developed a few issues that I'd appreciate your help with once the season's ended. Would you be up for it?'

'I'd love to,' says Hattie, smiling. Jonathan's yard isn't that far from Templeton Manor, and it would be nice to spend some time there. There's always a good atmosphere and a plentiful supply of coffee and biscuits.

'Great,' says Jonathan. 'I'll let you get on, but I'll call you in a few weeks to make the arrangements.'

'Look forward to it,' says Hattie.

～

Having got Mermaid's Gold's stable set up just right, Hattie has spent the last hour plaiting the mare's mane as she stood munching hay, and then tacking her up. She's got about forty minutes until her dressage test so it's time to get on.

As she leads Mermaid's Gold out of the stable, Hattie hears a voice behind her.

'Hello there.'

Turning, she sees Fergus Bingley is looking over a door a couple of stables along. 'Hi, Fergus.'

'You off to the dressage?' he asks. 'How's your lovely mare?'

'She's great,' says Hattie, leading Mermaid's Gold across to an upturned water bucket that will do as a mounting block. 'Are you riding today?'

Fergus nods. 'I had a couple in the Novice today, but they're all finished. Thought I'd take Matilda here for a hack; she's not competing until the Advanced tomorrow.'

'Great. Well, have a nice hack,' says Hattie. Turning away from Fergus, she springs off the mounting block, swinging her leg over Mermaid's Gold's rump and landing lightly in the saddle.

'If you ever think about selling that mare, do let me know. My offer still stands,' says Fergus. 'She's real dynamite.'

'Thanks,' says Hattie, smiling. 'But I'll never sell her.'

As they head out of the lorry park and towards the dressage warmup, Hattie knows she can't keep dwelling on the situation with Daniel. She has to focus on the competition – it's not fair to Mermaid's Gold if she isn't fully present.

But she feels bad about how she left things with Daniel yesterday. She has to talk to him about what Jem Baulman-Carter said, but yesterday the timing felt wrong; she'd been drained from worrying about Willa and the nerves of coming away to compete today.

Riding through the gateway into the dressage field, Hattie sees the warmup area is already quite busy with twelve other horses and riders all getting ready for their tests. The five arenas across on the far side are all being used, and closer to her is a parked Range Rover with two ladies in fluorescent pink tabards and holding clipboards sitting on the tailgate. One of the ladies, with long grey hair tied up in a pink scrunchie that matches her tabard, raises her hand in a wave.

Nodding to the steward and asking Mermaid's Gold to walk towards the Range Rover, Hattie decides to have the conversation with Daniel when she gets back to Templeton Manor. She won't put it off any longer; it's not fair on either of them.

With that decided, she fixes a smile on her face and forces herself to put Daniel out of her mind. From now on, she's just going to focus on Mermaid's Gold and the competition.

CHAPTER FIFTY-ONE

WAYNE

The anticipation is killing him.

He's lying on his bed, naked. The lights are off; the room lit only by moonlight. Over by the door, Megan is performing a striptease. There's music playing. A slow, sexy saxophone solo. Megan dances in time to the beat. Slowly she unbuttons her shirt, slipping it off over one shoulder, then the other. Next she peels down her little flared skirt, wriggling her bottom and revealing a black lace thong.

Oh blimey.

Wayne thinks he's going to explode.

Megan smiles and dances closer to the bed. Wayne wants to reach out and touch her but he can't. That's when he realises his hands have been shackled to the bed with a pair of red fluffy handcuffs. The delaying of gratification only makes him harder.

Reaching behind her back, Megan unhooks her black lace bra and throws it at Wayne. He flinches as it hits his chest. Inhales and smells the heady scent of her perfume. His body aches for her, but she continues to dance, prolonging the sweet agony of waiting.

All he can do is watch.

Megan kneels onto the bed. She's barely a foot away from him. 'Do you want me?'

Wayne groans.

'I need you,' he wants to say, but somehow he can't speak. He tries to nod, but he can't move his head.

Smiling, Megan moves across the bed until she's astride him.

His heart is pounding like a jack hammer in his chest. His dick feels like steel. He needs to be inside her. 'Megan… please…'

Wayne gasps as he wakes. His hand is around his dick. He feels groggy, disorientated.

He pushes himself up to sitting and looks around the room. There are no handcuffs, no music and no Megan. He's alone. It was a dream: a hot, realistic and incredible dream.

He flops back onto the pillows, deflated. He wishes Megan was here.

Shit.

He's tried to avoid admitting it, even to himself, but he can't pretend any longer. He's got feelings for Megan, and not just sexual ones. He enjoys being with her; they have a real connection. Whether it's watching TV, or cooking dinner, or taking Albert for a walk and laughing as he chases the leaves and carries sticks, everything is fun with Megan. It's been a long time since he's felt like that with a girl. Hell, he's *never* felt like this.

He's got it bad but it's hopeless. She's made it clear that she only sees him as a mate. He's been friend-zoned, completely. And it's doing his head in.

He has to come up with a way to move from the friend zone to boyfriend material.

Wayne swallows hard.

Boyfriend material?

He's never been that. Never wanted to be until now.

What is he going to do?

CHAPTER FIFTY-TWO

JEM

*H*ow dare he come here? thinks Jem, watching Daniel Templeton-Smith parking his horsebox in the area to the side of her yard. Who the hell does he think he is?

From her spot in the doorway of the tack room, Jem looks across the yard to where Megan is fussing around with her stupid horse's travel boots and swears under her breath. At her level, she really shouldn't have to deal with this. Megan should have apologised to her for being so rude. But instead, she moped about for a week and then gave notice that she would be leaving. She's supposed to have given a month's notice, but she only told her this morning – less than an hour ago, in fact. But there's nothing Jem can do, because Megan says she'll pay the full month in lieu. It's infuriating. And now that arsehole Daniel Templeton-Smith is here, in *her* yard. The audacity of the man, coming here after turning her down.

Jem scowls.

Daniel Templeton-Smith might think he can just waltz in here and steal her livery, but she's sure as dammit not going to make it easy for him. Striding out of the tack room, Jem crosses the yard and stops in front of the gate. Daniel is out of the lorry now and heading towards the gate. If he wants to come in, he's going to have to ask her to move.

Glancing round, Jem catches Megan's eye and shakes her head. She smiles inwardly as she sees the mortified expression on the girl's face. Serves her right for being a traitor and leaving. Jem might have to let her go, but there's nothing in the contract that says she has to make it easy.

'Hello, Jem,' says Daniel, reaching for the latch to undo the gate.

'Daniel,' says Jem, her tone frosty. She puts both hands on the top rail of the gate to prevent it being opened. 'What are you doing here?'

'I'm collecting Velvet.' Daniel gestures across the yard towards Megan. 'He's moving to my yard today and as Megan doesn't have transport, I said I'd lend a hand.'

'How generous of you,' says Jem, cocking her head to one side. 'What a nice guy you are.'

Daniel ignores the mocking tone in her voice. 'I try to be.'

'Really?' says Jem, opening the latch and shoving the gate hard towards him as she turns away. 'That's not my experience.'

When she turns back to him, she's pleased to see that he looks rather embarrassed. Watching as he comes through the gate and walks over to where Megan and her stupid horse are, Jem feels her anger building. The horse seems to feel it too as the creature skedaddles away, almost knocking Megan over as she bends down to adjust a strap on one of his travel boots.

'What the...?' Megan turns towards her. She doesn't even look sorry for the hassle she's causing. If anything, she looks annoyed.

I'll give her annoyed, thinks Jem. 'I'm glad you're going. Saves me the trouble of kicking you out.'

Megan fusses over the horse, talking to it in a baby voice and stroking its neck. If it were Jem, she'd give the stupid animal a few sharp tugs on the lead rope and then it would know who was boss.

Jem looks at Daniel and raises her voice a little more. 'You obviously don't care about the quality of clientele at your yard, then?'

'I don't know what you mean,' says Daniel, frowning. He looks at Megan. 'Are you ready to go?'

Megan nods. 'Yes, I'm all set. All my stuff is in the car, so it's just Velvet now.'

Daniel smiles. 'Okay, let's get him loaded.'

'She does porn,' says Jem, raising her voice louder as she gestures towards Megan dismissively. 'Naked photos and worse, on OnlyFans. It's disgusting.'

'What Megan does is her own business,' says Daniel. 'Not mine.'

'Wow,' says Jem. She shakes her head. 'I'd heard a rumour that you're strapped for cash, but if you're taking liveries of dubious morals I guess the rumour is true.'

Megan's cheeks flush, but she says nothing as she leads Velvet out through the gate and up the ramp of Daniel's horsebox. The black gelding walks straight up the ramp and waits patiently while Megan ties him to one of the quick-release rings inside. Daniel brings the back gates across and puts the ramp up.

With Velvet loaded onto the lorry, Megan exits it via the living area and walks back to close the yard gate. She looks across at Jem. 'Bye, then. Thanks for everything.'

Bitch, thinks Jem. If she actually was thankful, she wouldn't be leaving. 'I meant what I said, you know.'

Megan frowns. 'What do you—'

'You'll never make anything of yourself in the dressage world,' shouts Jem. 'You've got no class, no style and zero talent. You should give up now, because you're only ever going to fail and you're almost certainly ruining that horse.'

The redness of Megan's cheeks intensifies. Her eyes go watery. 'How can you be like this? I've never done anything to—'

'Ignore her, she's not worth it,' says Daniel, putting his arm around Megan and leading her away towards the cab of the horsebox. 'She's a bully; don't let her see you're upset.'

Megan sniffs. Nods her head. Her shoulders shaking.

'Don't cry. It's going to be okay,' says Daniel, pulling Megan into an awkward hug.

Jem clenches her fists. Furious.

I'm not worth it? Me?

Taking her mobile from her pocket, Jem snaps a few photos of Megan and Daniel. By angling the camera, she manages to make the pair of them look rather intimate. More like lovers than the new acquaintances that they are.

Jem smiles.

She knows exactly how to use these pictures to get her revenge.

CHAPTER FIFTY-THREE

HATTIE

*T*hings have been going well at Cotters Hall Horse Trials. After a good dressage, and just one down in the show jumping, Hattie and Mermaid's Gold are well in contention as they head into the cross-country phase. The course is big and requires accurate riding and a bold horse. Hattie thinks Mermaid's Gold is going to love it.

She pops over the practice fences for a third time and then brings the mare back to walk. The weather is perfect – not too hot or too cold – and the going on the old, springy turf is great. Mermaid's Gold gives a toss of her head, impatient to be out on the course, and Hattie laughs.

'Not long now, girl,' she says, giving the mare's neck a rub.

Glancing across the field, Hattie sees the horse before them is in the start box getting counted down by the starter. That means they've still got a few minutes until it's their turn.

As Hattie completes her final preparations and checks the girth is tight enough, she feels her phone vibrate against her chest. Damn. She totally forgot that she wedged it between her shirt and her body protector after Daniel messaged her good luck when she was getting ready. She'd meant to leave it back at the stables. She certainly can't ride out on the course with it.

But there's no time to ride back to the stables now, so she'll have to leave it with someone here. Hattie looks around but there's no one in the cross-country or spectating at the start or finish that she knows. Pulling the phone out, she decides to go over to the start box and ask if she can leave it there while she's out on the course. That's when she catches a glimpse of the screen. There's a photo message from an unknown number.

Frowning, Hattie taps on the image. As it opens the app and the picture becomes clearer, she feels her stomach lurch. Onscreen is a picture of Daniel. He's got one arm around a beautiful woman, while he's cupping her face with the other. It looks loving. Intimate.

She doesn't recognise the woman. She's young, barely in her twenties, Hattie would guess, with shining brown hair and freckles across her nose, and although she's wearing a loose-fitting t-shirt there's no denying her impressive curves.

There's a message beneath the picture. It's short and to the point.

YOU SHOULD KNOW THE TRUTH ABOUT DANIEL. Jem x

Hattie's breath catches in her throat.

Did Jem Baulman-Carter send her the picture? Is this what she meant about Daniel not being loyal and his devilish ways?

Hattie feels a pressure building in her chest. Then the one-minute call from the starter pulls her attention from the photo, reminding her of where she is and why she's here.

She swallows down the nausea she's feeling. She *has* to focus and do the best job she can piloting Mermaid around the course. She *cannot* allow whatever Daniel is doing to jeopardise that.

Taking a few deep breaths to compose herself, Hattie shortens her reins and rides over to the starter. Dropping her phone onto the grass beside the start box, she confirms to the starter that she's ready and walks the mare in a circle as the countdown commences.

'Ten seconds.'

Hattie bites her lip and shortens her reins again.

'Five.'

Mermaid's Gold gives a little jig, keen to get going.

'Three, two, one... go.'

As the starter says 'go', Mermaid's Gold leaps out of the start box towards the first fence. She jumps it easily and the pair of them gallop on to the second jump.

As they fly across the country, Hattie lets the tears fall.

She wishes she could gallop away from Daniel and her feelings for him just as easily.

CHAPTER FIFTY-FOUR

WAYNE

It's Wayne's third day back and he's pleased to be working again, but after six weeks out he's finding the long days and intense physical labour far more tiring than he did before. It's been a warm day, and although the temperature is starting to drop now, it must still be well into the twenties. At least he's almost finished. He's trimmed the hooves of the two Welsh mountain ponies and just needs to finish off this set of shoes for Nancy Neale's Dutch warmblood, then he can head off home.

Wayne checks the time; it's almost four o'clock. Megan is coming over tonight and he's promised to cook her his speciality, spaghetti bolognese, made the way his Italian grandmother taught him back when he was a little boy. He can't wait to see Megan. It's been three days since they last got together and he's already having withdrawal symptoms. Not that she knows that, of course. They're still just mates.

As he lifts the sturdy Dutch warmblood's hind foot and gives it a final rasp and tidy, Wayne is thankful that the horse is a steady, well-mannered sort. Even wearing the lower back support given to him by the physio, he's feeling sore and looking forward to a warm shower to ease the tension in his muscles.

Finishing off with the rasp, he puts the horse's hind foot down and winces as he straightens up. He looks around for Nancy but can't see her, so he starts to pack his equipment into the van. It takes him a few minutes, but when he's finished there's still no sign of her, so he gives the patient Dutch warmblood a pat and leads him across to the empty stable where the gelding's dinner and hay are waiting.

He's just finished closing the stable door when Nancy and a blonde friend strut onto the yard. Nancy's long white-blonde hair cascades across her shoulders and down the front of the blue maxi dress she's wearing. Her friend, with her more golden-blonde hair worn in a short pixie cut, seems barely dressed in a tiny crop top and a minuscule pair of denim hotpants.

Wayne smiles at them both. It felt a little awkward when he first arrived, given that the last time he'd seen Nancy he'd had to run across her paddocks naked to avoid her husband spotting him, but they soon laughed it off. She's already paid him by bank transfer so he can say his goodbyes quickly and go home. 'I've just finished, so I'll be off now. See you in four weeks.'

Nancy comes closer and puts her hand on his arm. She looks back at her blonde friend. 'This is Mr March, the guy I was telling you about. He's just as good in the flesh as he is in his picture.'

'Definitely,' says the blonde, running her tongue across her bottom lip. 'Even better.'

Wayne smiles uneasily. This feels like an ambush.

'My husband's away on business until the weekend. And don't worry, he's definitely there – I just spoke to him,' says Nancy, slipping one arm around the blonde woman beside her, and caressing the front of Wayne's plaid shirt with the other. She bats her lashes at him. 'We thought you might like to stay and play for a little while? The hot tub is fired up and ready.'

'Well, that's a kind offer but—'

'Don't be shy, sweetheart,' says the blonde friend, winking. 'We'll be gentle.'

Wayne takes a step towards the van. 'It's not that... I just need to get back.'

'Really?' says Nancy, seductively. 'Are you sure we can't do something to persuade you?'

'We'd love to try,' says the blonde friend. 'I think you'd enjoy it.'

Wayne takes another step towards the van. 'Sorry, but I really can't. Thanks though, for the offer.'

Turning, he jumps into the driver's seat and fires up the engine. As he speeds away down the driveway, the memory of Nancy's surprised expression is vivid in his mind. Normally, he'd have been well up for a threesome, what guy wouldn't? But today the idea doesn't appeal at all. The only thing he wants to do is get home, have a shower, and start preparing dinner. He wants to make a meal that Megan will love.

Oh my God, thinks Wayne. I've really changed.

CHAPTER FIFTY-FIVE

HATTIE

They won.

As other riders come up to her, congratulating her on first place in her Intermediate section, Hattie smiles and thanks them. But now the competition is over, and Mermaid's Gold is safely tucked up in her stable waiting to travel home, the photo of Daniel and the unknown woman is foremost in Hattie's mind.

She hasn't been able to bring herself to look at it since that first glimpse before she went cross-country. Just thinking about Daniel with another woman makes her feel nauseous and, although she knows the photo is pretty conclusive evidence, she's still finding it hard to believe. He seems so into her. And why does he want to move in together if he's messing around with someone else behind her back already?

As she walks back across the field towards the stables and lorry park, Hattie feels utterly deflated. Mermaid's Gold did an amazing job on the cross-country, another confident clear round within the time. It's amazing to have won the class, and great to be able to add another round to their qualification runs and take another step closer to Badminton. But instead of enjoying the moment, Hattie just feels sad.

She tells herself to snap out of it. That she should be angry at Daniel, furious. And she knows she'll be okay on her own – she's done it before and she'll do it again. She can move Mermaid's Gold back to Robert's place in the short term; the goats, Gladys and Mabel, will be delighted to have their horse friend back.

She can get through this, Hattie knows that. But still, she feels sad. She really thought she had something special with Daniel. Now it seems that isn't true.

Reaching the stables, she heads along the rows to Mermaid's Gold's. The chestnut mare looks out when she hears Hattie approaching, and whinnies.

Hattie smiles. 'Hey, girl, let's get you back home.'

The smile fades from her lips as she says it.

Soon Templeton Manor won't be home.

'Great run,' says Fergus Bingley, riding towards his stable on a large grey gelding. 'Remember what I said, if you ever want to sell…'

'I remember. But like I said, it'll never happen.'

Fergus smiles. 'Very wise. But I'll keep checking, just in case.'

Turning away, Hattie lets herself into the stable with Mermaid's Gold to get the mare ready for travelling. She puts on the horse's protective leg boots and then the padded poll guard to protect the sensitive spot at the top of her head. Once the mare is ready, Hattie casts her gaze around the stable, double checking she's packed everything, then picks up the water bucket and leads Mermaid's Gold outside.

After emptying the water from the bucket, they head over to the lorry. Mermaid's Gold walks happily up the ramp and immediately starts tucking into her hay net as Hattie fastens the partition in place and puts up the ramp.

Climbing into the cab, Hattie takes her phone from her

pocket. The notifications on the screen tell her she has eight missed calls and four text messages – all from Daniel.

> Good luck on the cross-country. U will be amazing.

> How did it go?

> R u ok?

> Please H, I don't want things to be weird between us. I love you. I'm fine to wait until yr ready to move in. It's no big deal. Let me know u r ok. Please

Daniel's messages don't sound as if they're from someone who's messing her about. He sounds like a man who genuinely cares. Taking a breath, Hattie opens the message from Jem Baulman-Carter and for the first time takes a proper look at the photo.

She rereads Jem's message:

> YOU SHOULD KNOW THE TRUTH ABOUT DANIEL. Jem x

Tapping on the photo, Hattie switches it to full screen mode. The picture has been taken in what looks like a parking area at a yard but she doesn't recognise the place. In the background is the edge of a cab – it looks like Jenny the vet's lorry – and the back half of a large silver car. Hattie's stomach lurches and her heartbeat accelerates as she looks at Daniel and the unknown woman. But as she stares at the image, she starts to see more details. She enlarges the image so their faces are in closeup. Now the picture doesn't look quite as intimate. Daniel's expression makes it look as if he's feeling a bit awkward, and the woman is clearly crying. It looks more as if he's comforting her than being intimate.

She was wrong. This *isn't* a picture of two lovers.

Hattie's heart rate begins to slow.

Bunty was right. Jem Baulman-Carter is a bitch, and she seems to be set on causing maximum trouble. There's clearly a kind of clash between Jem and Daniel and, as Jem seems intent on dragging Hattie into it, she needs to know what's going on. Then whatever the issue is needs to be resolved. Her guess is that it has everything to do with whatever happened at Jem's hastily aborted jumping lesson. When she gets back, she'll ask Daniel for the full story.

As Hattie zooms out of the picture, something catches her eye. In the background of the picture, the silver car has a boot and backseat piled high with what look like rugs. Hattie squints at the image as she enlarges that section of the photo.

Her heartbeat accelerates again.

It's folded over, and only a small section of the logo and wording is visible, but lying in the pile of rugs is one that she recognises. She reads the partial word 'MINTON' and below it 'INNER', and sees the tatty hole just to the right of the wording, the work of a horse's teeth.

It's Daniel's Badminton Horse Trials winner's rug that was taken in the burglary.

The silver car must belong to someone connected with the tack thefts, or someone who has bought stolen property. Hattie needs to know which.

CHAPTER FIFTY-SIX

MEGAN

*I*t's months since she's been out-out, even if it's just to the pub. The minute they arrive at the Red Lion in Saundersford village, Megan remembers why, and regrets agreeing to come along tonight. Most people in the pub are men and it feels as if every one of them is staring at her.

'You okay?' asks Wayne as they approach the bar.

Megan nods, even though she isn't. She can't shake the thought that any of these people could be subscribers to her OnlyFans. They could have seen her virtually naked.

The bartender, a blond guy in a Red Lion polo shirt, is busy serving a group of rowdy lads to their left. A large telly is on in the corner showing what looks like a baseball game, and the men keep breaking off from ordering their drinks to yell at the action on the screen.

'That's Jimbo and the guys,' says Wayne. 'They bet on sports a lot so there's probably quite a bit of cash at stake.'

'Right,' says Megan. She guesses Wayne probably knows most people in here as it's his local. 'Are any of your friends here?'

'Kevin and Mucker are probably round the back playing pool,' says Wayne. 'When we've got our drinks, I'll take you over to meet them.'

'Great,' says Megan. She frowns. 'Mucker?'

Wayne laughs. 'Yeah, that's a bit of a long story, and a lot more fun to tell you it when Mucker's listening – his ears will go bright red.'

'Sounds intriguing,' says Megan, trying to relax. It'll be good to meet some of Wayne's friends, and the village pub is really very charming with its exposed original brickwork, timber-beamed ceilings, huge inglenook fireplace and traditional bar.

It takes a while for the bartender to get the sports fans their drinks. As Megan and Wayne wait to be served, a fifty-something guy with greying hair and a half-drunk pint sitting along the bar catches her eye and winks. Megan frowns. She doesn't know the man. Then she watches with growing horror as the guy nudges his friend, a bald man of a similar age sitting on the stool next to him, and nods in her direction. His friend looks straight at her, a leering smile spreading across his face.

Megan looks away quickly as she feels heat spreading across her cheeks.

Have they recognised her? Are they both subscribers to her OnlyFans?

'Well, well, well, it's Mr March himself,' says a jovial lady with wavy brown hair and a friendly, red-lipsticked smile. She stands in the doorway between the back-of-house and the bar. 'You've been quite the stranger these past couple of months.'

'Sorry about that,' says Wayne. 'Didn't the lads tell you? I've been laid up with a bad back and—'

'Yeah, yeah,' says the woman, laughing as she steps through the doorway and up to the bar. She glances at Megan, then looks back to Wayne and grins. 'I bet you've been laid alright.'

Wayne clears his throat, awkwardly. 'Rachel, this is my *friend*, Megan.'

Megan doesn't fail to notice the emphasis he puts on the

word. She tries not to show her disappointment that she's so clearly friend-zoned.

'Nice to meet you, Megan,' says the woman. 'I'm Rachel, the landlady of this place.'

'Hi,' says Megan, feeling increasingly self-conscious. It's then that she notices a copy of the 'Rural Pleasures' calendar is pinned up behind the bar. It's still open on March even though it's September now, and there's an orange sticker on it proudly stating: *Mr March drinks here.*

Rachel follows her gaze and grins again. She winks at Megan. 'Our Mr March has got quite the fan club.' She looks at Wayne. 'And quite an impressive reputation.'

Wayne shakes his head, laughing.

Megan doesn't know what to say. Other than Jem, Wayne's never spoken about women he's been with. And it's not like she expects him to; after all, they're only friends. It's very clear that there are no romantic feelings involved, at least not on his part.

'Anyway, your first drinks are on the house,' says Rachel. 'For you and your *friend*. Call it a welcome back gift from me.'

'That's kind, thanks,' says Wayne. He looks at Megan and doesn't seem to notice her discomfort. 'What would you like?'

She hadn't been intending to drink much, but right now she needs something to calm her nerves. 'A large glass of pinot, please.'

'Wine, huh?' says Wayne, smiling. He looks at Rachel. 'A pint of the local, and a large pinot, please.'

'Coming right up,' says Rachel, leaning over the bar and lowering her voice to a stage whisper. 'You know, I can pull a pint almost as fast as you pull women.'

Wayne laughs, but it sounds forced. Megan smiles to be polite, and tries to pretend that the idea of him with other women doesn't upset her.

Seemingly oblivious to any awkwardness she might have

created, Rachel gets their drinks and sets them down on the green bar towel in front of Wayne. 'Enjoy.'

He passes the wine to Megan before picking up his own pint.

'Thanks,' says Megan, but she knows her voice sounds strained and her expression probably looks similar. Pushing the images of Wayne and other women from her mind, she puts more jollity into her tone and adds, 'So are you going to introduce me to your friends?'

Wayne grins. 'Follow me.'

As they carry their drinks around to the pool area at the back, Wayne leans closer to her and says, 'Sorry about back there. Rachel loves to joke around.'

'It's fine,' says Megan, trying to sound unbothered. After all, Wayne's past conquests, or current ones, aren't any of her concern. At least that's what she tells herself. They're just friends; it's pointless getting jealous. But she does *feel* jealous. It sits like an ever-tightening knot in her stomach and she hates it.

'Here they are,' says Wayne, rushing up to the pool table and clapping his spare hand onto the back of a broad, ruddy-looking blond guy who's just about to take a shot. 'Alright, Mucker?'

The guy misses the pocket and the green ball rebounds off the cushion, stopping against a cluster of other balls. He shakes his head and looks back at Wayne. 'Well, I was until you screwed my shot.'

'Cheers for that, mate,' says a slim, black-haired guy with glasses and an almost identical outfit to Mucker – plaid shirt, old denims, battered leather work boots. He clinks his pint against Wayne's. 'I'm winning now.'

'Ha, you're welcome, Kevin.' Wayne gestures towards Megan. 'This is Megan.'

'Alright,' says Mucker.

'Are you any good at pool?' asks Kevin.

'Average,' she says, smiling. It's impossible not to like these guys.

'Good,' says Kevin, looking back at Wayne. 'Let's double up.'

'And there it is.' Wayne looks at Megan and gives a rueful grin. 'This bloke is always trying to find a way to beat me. Never does though.'

'Never say never,' says Kevin, giving a shrug. 'Tonight's the night, I reckon.'

'Doubt that,' says Wayne, laughing. 'But let's see what happens.'

It's easy to relax with Wayne and his friends, even though they're super competitive at pool. They're partway through the game, with her and Wayne a few up on Kevin and Mucker, much to Mucker's chagrin, when she gets the strong feeling she's being watched. She finishes her shot. Gets a high five from Wayne. And then turns towards the tables over near the bar.

A group of middle-aged men in cords and tweed are sitting at the nearest table to the pool area. From their flushed faces and overly loud voices, Megan reckons they're more than a few pints into their night. As she looks at them, one of the men, a bearded, greying guy in a tweed waistcoat, whoops. The man next to him, with a receding hairline and large gut, guffaws loudly. The waistcoated man, and the three other men with them, join in with the laughter.

Megan looks away quickly. Maybe they're laughing about something else.

She tries not to think about them or look in their direction as the end of the pool game nears. Kevin is trash-talking Wayne as he prepares to take the final shot, and larking about over by the pocket Wayne's aiming for to try and put him off. Wayne remains absolutely unflappable, and pots the ball with ease. He looks at Kevin and gives a rueful smile. 'Sorry, mate, it's just not your night again.'

Kevin shrugs good-naturedly. 'Story of my life.'

'We bloody did it,' says Wayne, pulling Megan into a hug. 'Shall we have another round to celebrate our victory?'

The hug takes Megan by surprise. It feels as if every nerve ending across her body is tingling with desire. But it's a friendly hug; it means nothing, right? Wayne friend-zoned her weeks ago. So, trying not to show how she's feeling, she gives a quick nod. 'Sounds good.'

A moment of confusion flashes across Wayne's expression, then he releases her from the hug. Turning to Kevin with a cheeky smile, he says, 'Loser buys the pints, mate.'

'Yeah, yeah, whatever,' says Kevin, but he's smiling. 'Same again?'

They give Kevin their orders and he heads off towards the bar. Wayne and Mucker are conducting a blow-by-blow analysis of the pool game but Megan feels a bit discombobulated. Telling them she's going to the ladies, she heads back around the bar, past the table of middle-aged men, who fall silent as she passes, and through the door and along the wood-panelled corridor to the toilets.

Sitting down on the loo, Megan massages her temples and wonders why she's so jumpy tonight. Ever since the two guys at the bar, and then the middle-aged men at the table, started staring at her, she's felt really freaked out. It's true they might have seen her OnlyFans, but what are the chances, really, of them ending up in the same pub as her? It's far more likely that they're just drunk. She's not going to let that spoil her evening with Wayne.

Feeling a little better, she finishes in the loos and heads back into the corridor. It's as she's coming out of the ladies that she almost runs straight into the man with a receding hairline.

'Well, hello,' he says, stopping in the middle of the narrow corridor. 'You're quite the filthy filly, aren't you?'

'I'm... what?' says Megan, taking a step back. 'I'm sorry but do I know you?'

'Not yet, but I must say we've all been rather taken with your pictures,' says the man, leering down at her. 'Sadly, tonight you seem to be wearing rather too much.'

Megan goes cold. Her original instincts were right: this man and his friends *have* seen her OnlyFans. 'I... I don't—'

'We were just discussing what you might charge for... a little extra?' says the man, raising his eyebrows.

'I'm not working tonight,' says Megan, feeling flustered. 'You can DM me on the platform if you want to ask me for exclusive content.'

'I was thinking something more intimate than content,' says the man, taking hold of her forearm and pulling her closer until she's pressed up against his large gut. 'Like a date.'

The coldness is replaced by heat as she realises what he means – he thinks he can hire her for the evening, or more. She pulls her arm from his grip. 'I don't do that.'

'Oh come on,' says the man, moving closer to her, and blocking the gap between her and the exit. He's so close, she can smell the stale sweat on his clothes and the beer on his breath. 'Everything has a price, and I'd be happy to pay a decent sum. All of us would. Maybe we can get a group discount?'

Megan feels nausea rising. She tastes bile on her tongue. She shakes her head. 'I said no, I don't do that.'

The man reaches out towards her again, grabbing for her wrist. His tone hardens. 'Come on, don't be such a bloody tease, tell me what it'd cost for a night with—'

'Get away from me,' says Megan, shoving him away and scuttling past before he can regain his balance.

'You little...'

Not waiting to hear the rest, Megan pushes through the door at the end of the corridor and hurries back to the pool area.

'Here she is,' says Wayne, smiling as she reaches him and his mates. 'I was just saying we need to tell you Mucker's origin story. After besting him and Kevin this evening, you've definitely earned the right to hear it.'

'Thanks,' says Megan, grabbing her jacket from the stool she laid it on earlier and pulling out her phone to book an Uber. 'But I need to go.'

'It's not even last orders yet,' says Wayne, confused. 'And we've got bragging rights over these boys until closing.'

Megan glances over her shoulder at the table of middle-aged men. The one with the gut and receding hairline is telling them something. Moments later, they all look over at her and stare. Shit. She *cannot* stay here. What if the guy comes over and propositions her again in front of Wayne and his mates? No. That can't happen. She shakes her head. 'I've ordered a cab and they're already on the way.'

Mucker and Kevin look awkward.

Wayne's frowning. 'But weren't we having a fun—'

'Thanks for a great evening,' says Megan, turning towards the exit so they can't see her lower lip quivering.

Before they can reply, she hurries across the pub and out into the dark night. It's still warm enough without her jacket on, and the sky is clear and full of stars. It should be the end to a brilliant evening, but instead everything feels ruined.

Megan hears the pub door open and footsteps hurry up behind her. She flinches and looks round, afraid the man with the receding hairline or his mates have followed her. But it isn't them.

'What's wrong?' asks Wayne. His tone is kind, and his expression is full of concern.

'I...' She wants to tell him, really she does, but she can't bring herself to repeat what happened with the middle-aged guy out loud. It's mortifying, far worse than what happened at Badminton. The way he and his friends leered at her makes her feel like a piece of meat, and the way he tried to restrain her makes her feel vulnerable.

'You can tell me,' Wayne says, as a silver Toyota – the Uber – pulls up at the curb.

She looks into his eyes, at the intensity of his gaze, and she so wants to tell him. But if she does, he might think less of her – think she's soiled in some way – and she can't have that. It's one thing to know that she sells pictures online, but quite another to come face-to-face with the men who've bought them. So she holds her emotions in and shakes her head. 'I'm sorry... but I can't.'

Running to the Uber, she climbs inside and buckles her seatbelt. It's only then that she looks back towards the pub, expecting Wayne to have gone back inside. But he hasn't. He's standing there, looking at her, his expression a mixture of confused and forlorn.

Megan bites her lip and fights back the tears of humiliation. She wishes she stood up for herself more. She should have told the man with receding hair just how disgusting his behaviour was, and how he didn't have the right to speak to her like that and that he should absolutely never touch her. But she didn't.

And, after running off like this, she wouldn't blame Wayne if he doesn't want to see her again.

Everything is ruined.

CHAPTER FIFTY-SEVEN

HATTIE

It's late in the evening by the time Hattie and Mermaid's Gold arrive at Templeton Manor and Hattie has settled the mare in her stable and given her some dinner. Daniel popped out to see them when they first got back but the atmosphere felt stilted and awkward. Hattie supposes she shouldn't have been surprised about that.

She messaged Daniel before she set off from Cotters Hall, telling him how great Mermaid's Gold had been, but also that they needed to talk. She's been feeling increasingly nervous as she's put Mermaid's Gold to bed. She's sure the relationship between Daniel and the woman in the photo is innocent enough, but there's something going on between him and Jem that doesn't make sense. He'd not wanted to talk about what happened with Jem in the lesson, but now Hattie needs him to. There can't be any secrets between them.

Having double checked the tack room is locked, Hattie gives Mermaid's Gold a Polo and tells her again how clever she is, before turning out the yard lights and heading back to the house. As she opens the back door, Poppet hurtles out to greet her, wiggling his body and tail back and forth at a hundred miles an hour and excitedly licking her hands.

Hattie leans down, stroking him. 'Hello, baby, have you been a good boy?'

'He's been very good,' says Daniel, from inside the kitchen. 'Although he did destroy one of Bunty's socks. I've said I'll get her another pair.'

Hattie takes off her boots and hangs up her competition jacket in the boot room cupboard, shoving the rest of her competition clothes – breeches, shirt and everything – straight into the washing machine.

She turns towards the kitchen. Her throat feels a bit dry, and she can feel butterflies fluttering in her stomach. But she can't back out now, they need to have this conversation. She steps through the doorway into the kitchen. Daniel's over by the Aga, dishing out something that smells amazing. The table is set for two. Michael Bublé is playing on the tiny speaker over the mantle, and there's even a couple of lit candles in the centre of the table.

'Wine?' asks Daniel, turning towards her.

'Sure,' says Hattie. It might calm her nerves.

Daniel hands her a glass of white wine. 'I thought you might be hungry after the long day you've had.'

'Thanks,' says Hattie, feeling a bit uncomfortable at all the effort Daniel's gone to. 'You didn't have to cook.'

'I wanted to.' Daniel smiles. 'So what did you want to talk about? It sounded important.'

'It is,' says Hattie. She takes a deep breath and holds his gaze. 'I need to know what happened between you and Jem Baulman-Carter.'

Daniel's mouth hangs open. He shakes his head. 'Nothing's happened. I don't know what you mean.'

'Don't fob me off,' says Hattie, her tone firm, serious. 'I know something must have gone on between you.'

Daniel stares at her. He frowns. Exhales hard. 'Look, I didn't tell you because it really was nothing, but when she came for that jumping lesson, Jem came onto me. I told her I wasn't interested, obviously, but she got pretty pissed off about me rejecting her advances.'

'And that's it?' says Hattie, putting her wine glass down on the table.

'Of course,' says Daniel, stepping towards her and taking her hands in his. 'You're the only person I want to be with.'

Hattie looks into his kind, eager face and believes him. 'Okay. So is that why the lesson finished early?'

'She didn't want to stick around once I'd turned her down. I didn't lie when I said the lesson had gone badly and that she'd been weird with me after I'd ridden her horse, and that she'd decided she didn't want to jump after all – that's all true. I was just too embarrassed to tell you about her coming onto me and, to be honest, it gave me flashbacks to what happened with Lexi. I thought I was going to have a panic attack.'

Hattie squeezes his hands. 'I get that. But Jem's had it in for me, for us, ever since it happened.'

Daniel frowns. 'How do you mean?'

'Well, firstly, when we were at the Lounge celebrating your win at Badminton I found her crying in the ladies' loos. I tried to help her, but instead she verbally attacked me and said that you aren't loyal and that you had devilish ways.'

'Really?' says Daniel, looking surprised. 'Why would she do that?'

'I didn't know at the time, and the description of "devilish ways" didn't ring true with anything that I know about you, so I tried to forget about it. But then earlier today she sent me this.' Hattie takes out her phone and brings Jem's message up before holding the screen out for Daniel to see.

'That's Megan,' says Daniel, looking back at Hattie. 'I went and picked her horse up from Jem's yard this morning. Jenny was there yesterday and said Jem was bullying Megan horribly. The poor girl was very distressed. Jenny said I could use her lorry to pick up the horse, and when I arrived there this morning the atmosphere was deeply unpleasant. Jem was furious that Megan was leaving and said a lot of nasty things until Megan ended up in tears.' He pauses, reading the message from Jem. He shakes his head. 'It's ridiculous. I only met Megan a few minutes before this picture was taken.'

'She's trying to break us up,' says Hattie, feeling the anger building inside her. 'That's why she sent me this picture.'

'Why would she be so vindictive? Just because I didn't want to sleep with her?' Daniel shakes his head. 'She's just as bad as Lexi.'

Hattie nods. It does seem Daniel is a bit of a magnet for possessive, rich women. 'There's something else. I've already told the police – I called them when I was driving back here.' She taps her figure against the photo. 'In the boot of this silver car, folded in with some other rugs, is The Rogue's Badminton winner's rug.'

'Really?' says Daniel, squinting at the phone.

'Here,' says Hattie, enlarging the section of the image with the silver car. 'Can you see it now?'

'Bloody hell,' says Daniel. 'You're right. It's got the hole he munched out of it and everything.'

'Yeah,' says Hattie. 'So someone at Jem's yard must have a connection to the burglaries. Either they've bought the rug from somewhere the stolen items were taken, or they were involved in stealing them.'

'Seems risky for them to just leave them on display in the car,' says Daniel. 'What did the police say?'

'Just that they'd check it out,' say Hattie. 'So I guess we just have to leave it to them.'

'Let's hope it helps them find the thieves and the rest of our stuff,' says Daniel. He gestures towards the table. 'Anyway, you must be starving. Take a seat and I'll bring dinner over.'

'Thanks,' says Hattie, sitting down at the table. Suddenly she's feeling super hungry.

Daniel's done an amazing job. The table looks beautiful, so romantic, and as he spoons the spaghetti onto their plates, it looks and smells delicious.

Sitting down opposite her, Daniel takes her hands in his again. 'You know I'm only interested in you, right? I love you, Hattie, I really do.'

Hattie smiles. 'I love you too.'

It's a perfect romantic moment, but as they clink glasses and Hattie takes a sip of wine it tastes like ashes on her tongue. She feels bad, a hypocrite. After all, she doesn't want Daniel to have any secrets from her, but she's the one who isn't telling the whole truth.

CHAPTER FIFTY-EIGHT

MEGAN

As Rosalie plonks a carrier bag onto the kitchenette countertop and starts rummaging around inside it, Megan takes a bottle of wine from the fridge. It's been two days since the incident at the pub and Megan is still feeling down, although she's trying to be more upbeat for Rosalie's sake. The truth is, Megan's worried. She's logged into OnlyFans a couple of times, and the DMs are mounting up, but she hasn't felt motivated to reply. She's got a decent amount saved up from the past few months, but she won't be able to live off those savings forever. 'Wine?'

'Great,' says Rosalie, leaving a couple of oven pizzas on the counter and carrying the bag and the rest of its contents across to the sofa.

'Coming right up,' says Megan. Taking a couple of glasses from the shelf over the sink, she glances across the tiny studio flat towards the shower room; the sour smell in there has abated a little over the summer but it'll be back as soon as the weather turns cold. And the ridiculously expensive-to-run electric heater barely coughs out any heat so the damp will return along with it.

Megan shivers. If she can't face OnlyFans, she's going to need to find another job. She's not sure she can do another winter in this place.

As Megan opens a bottle of wine and fills the glasses, Rosalie opens a family bag of sea salt crisps and a tub of salsa and puts them down on the sofa.

Megan sits down on the bed and hands her friend a glass of wine. Raising her own, she clinks it against Rosalie's. 'Cheers. I need this.'

Rosalie waits until Megan's had a big gulp of wine before starting with the questions. 'So, what happened? Tell me everything.'

Megan exhales loudly. 'It was a total disaster.'

'Because?' Rosalie makes a winding signal with her hand. 'I need more details.'

'There were some men in the pub who subscribe to my OnlyFans.'

'Ah. Tricky,' says Rosalie, her tone sympathetic.

'It was more than that. They wanted to hire me to have sex with them – all of them, together.'

'Shit,' says Megan. 'How did Wayne handle that?'

Megan takes a gulp of wine. 'I didn't tell him.'

Rosalie frowns. 'Why ever not?'

Megan looks down. 'I didn't want him knowing those men thought they could just buy me.'

'But he knows all about your OnlyFans, doesn't he?' says Rosalie. 'And you're not together, right?'

'Yes, and we're not.'

Rosalie looks puzzled. 'Then why not tell him? I reckon he'd be as pissed off as you and certainly not judge *you* for it.'

'Maybe, but I didn't want to take the risk.'

Rosalie frowns. 'But if you're just mates, why would he mind even if you did want to sell a night of passion to the highest bidder?'

'Because... I just didn't want him to know, okay?'

'Hmmm... interesting,' says Rosalie, cocking her head to the side. 'I see it now. You're not together but you *want* to be.'

It's a statement, not a question. Megan doesn't reply.

'I'm right, aren't I?' says Rosalie. 'And from the look on your face I'd say you've got it bad for him.'

'What?' says Megan. 'Why would you think that?'

'It's obvious,' says Rosalie, shaking her head. 'Your expression says it all. Does he know?'

Megan blushes. 'I hope not.'

'You know he's the most awful shagger, don't you?' asks Rosalie, taking a sip of wine. 'I mean, from what I've heard he's very good at the actual shagging, but then he's had a lot of practice. He's a real fuckboy.'

'Thanks, I'd got that impression,' says Megan, grabbing a handful of crisps from the bag between them. 'Anyway, nothing's going to happen. I've been very clearly friend-zoned.'

'You mean he's never tried anything?' says Rosalie.

'Never,' says Megan, sadly.

'Wow.' Rosalie raised her eyebrows. 'You must be the only girl in the county then.'

'Thanks.' Megan shakes her head. 'Way to make me feel good about myself.'

'No, I think it's a good sign,' says Rosalie, thoughtfully. 'You've got an actual relationship with him, not just a one-time thing.'

'An utterly *platonic* relationship,' says Megan. She can't see why Wayne's lack of interest is a good thing. If he usually shags anyone, the fact he hasn't tried to get it on with her seems a pretty clear statement he's not interested. 'Anyway, enough about me and Wayne. I've got other stuff to worry about, like what am I going to do about OnlyFans? And planning my campaign to upgrade to Medium with Velvet next season.'

'How's he doing at Daniel's yard?'

'He loves it,' says Megan, smiling as she thinks about how

happy Velvet is now. 'He gets turned out all day with the other horses and ad lib hay – he thinks he's in heaven. And Willa Alton, the American dressage trainer who helps Hattie and Daniel with their flatwork, has said she'll give me some lessons once she's back to full strength.'

'I've heard she's great,' says Rosalie, finishing her wine and grabbing the bottle to refill her own glass and top up Megan's. 'And I'm glad she's recovering well from the attack. That was so awful.'

'Totally.' Megan nods.

'So what are you thinking about OnlyFans?' asks Rosalie. 'Are you going to let a few random arseholes dictate your life?'

'I don't want to,' says Megan, cautiously.

'Then don't,' says Rosalie, taking a couple of crisps, dipping them into the salsa and popping them in her mouth.

'I just feel so frustrated that I didn't tell that guy how wrong his assumptions and his behaviour was,' says Megan, shaking her head. 'I mean, I told him I didn't do that sort of thing, but I can't help feeling I should have been more forceful.'

'Then do it – tell him,' says Rosalie. 'What's stopping you?'

'It happened days ago. The moment's gone.'

'Has it, though? Isn't he one of your subscribers?' asks Rosalie. 'Because if he is, you can reach him through your posts or whatever you call them on there.'

It's a good point, thinks Megan. Anything she puts on her OnlyFans can be seen by all subscribers. Maybe there is a way to get her thoughts across. She nods, smiling. 'You're right. Maybe it isn't too late.'

'That's more like it,' says Rosalie. 'You show him what's what, the creepy arsehole.'

Show him, thinks Megan, smiling as the spark of an idea comes to her. She nods again, more decisively this time. 'I bloody well will.'

'Good,' says Rosalie.

'Anyway, sorry to go on about all my stuff,' says Megan. 'How are you? I hope Jem isn't being too much of a bitch.'

Rosalie rolls her eyes. 'She's worse than ever. Honestly, how I don't kill her on a daily basis is a miracle.'

'Then leave.'

'Yeah.' Rosalie looks conflicted. 'I could.'

'It's almost the end of the season.' Megan raises an eyebrow. 'You said that's when you'd start looking.'

'True,' says Rosalie, although her tone is rather non-committal. 'I'll talk to Peter first though, and see what he's planning. He's said several times he can't continue working for her. I know he's pissed off with her constant bitching. It's like she believes the world begins and ends with her, and now her Instagram followers are deserting her, she's even more unbearable.'

'What's happened to her Insta?' asks Megan. She's not looked at Jem's grid since she left the yard.

'She did a couple of videos where she was complaining about how hard she works and everything, you know, her usual-type monologue, and people turned on her in the comments. Instead of ignoring them, she doubled down and got called things like "poor little rich girl" and a lot worse. Then they started unfollowing.'

'Ouch,' says Megan. She knows how much Jem's Instagram followers meant to her.

'Exactly,' says Rosalie. 'It almost makes me feel sorry for her, but after that stunt she pulled back in the spring when she deliberately rode into me, and how she treated you, and all the shit things she's said to me and Peter, my sympathy doesn't last long.'

'I can understand that.'

'But I'll miss the horses. They're a good bunch. I hate the thought of leaving them.'

Megan nods. She can only imagine how horrible it must feel

to leave the horses you've cared for and not be able to see them again. 'Well, it's your choice, obviously. I just hate that she takes advantage of you, both of you, and treats you like crap.'

'Me too,' says Rosalie, exhaling hard. 'Me too.'

CHAPTER FIFTY-NINE

JEM

The two police officers are nice enough, but she really doesn't have the time to deal with them this morning. She has horses to ride and then a cut and blow dry at the salon in London. She absolutely can't miss her appointment with Frederick; they are virtually impossible to get. The police officers, or detectives or whatever they are, don't seem to appreciate this at all. They keep banging on about needing to find the burglars, but they don't seem to understand it's too late. The worst happened several months ago – she's already been burgled.

They are insistent, though, and so here she is watching as they search Tyler's silver Audi, and then the horsebox and the yard. It's dull, but they've said that they want her with them as they search. They'd have liked Tyler to be here too, but he's off with some friends and isn't answering his phone, so she's said that she'll get him to call them later. They didn't look too happy about that, but what else could she do? It's not like they're the criminals, is it? She's a victim of the burglars.

Sitting down on the wall of the flowerbed in the centre of the yard, Jem takes out her phone again. She's about to check her

Insta when she notices Rosalie standing in the doorway of the tack room, watching the police rather than doing her job.

Jem glares at Rosalie until the groom notices she's looking at her, then says, 'You should be getting on with your work. I'll need to ride Starchild first, and I don't want any delays.' She pointedly glances across at the chestnut gelding looking over his stable door. 'It looks like you haven't even bothered to start getting him ready.'

Rosalie's cheeks flush. She turns her head back into the tack room, no doubt muttering something to Peter, who is in there cleaning tack, then looks back at Jem. 'I'll get onto that in a minute. I've been busy this morning.'

'Welcome to my world,' says Jem. 'See that you do it quickly.'

As Rosalie makes no sign of moving, Jem rolls her eyes and feels increasingly irritated. She pays these people to do a job. She just wishes that they'd pull their weight.

The police officers are still having a look around the yard. They're currently poking about in the feed room, which has made all the horses look out of their stables in the hope they might get a second breakfast.

Sighing, Jem taps her phone and brings up Insta. She put up a new post yesterday evening – a picture of her glass of champagne and a tin of out-of-date Golden Oscietra caviar with some of the caviar on a cracker with a bite taken out. She'd used the hashtags #hardtimes #makedo #creditcrunch – which are some of the top trending hashtags at the moment – but the post has had a fraction of the likes that she was getting a few weeks ago. It's been the same with all her posts lately, although this one seems to be doing especially badly. Then she feels her chest constrict as she realises that she's lost several thousand more followers too.

Why is this happening?

Jem scrolls down to the comments. She inhales sharply as she reads them.

PONYGRL3975

so out of touch

DRESSAGEYY3

not for me. I'm out. Unfollowed

YIPPIP:

Caviar? Seriously?!!!!!

HAPPYTIMES19276

Obvs not living in real world

RISINGTROTTER

You make me sick. You think you're having a hard time but you have no idea. Pathetic #pityparty for one

ANDAGAINFORTHEWIN

Ridiculous. @Ponygrl3975 called it – so out of touch

CENTRELINEWOBBLER

Just another poor little rich girl

Jem keeps scrolling. Her hands are shaking as she slides her finger across the screen. There are hundreds of comments, all along the same theme – she's out of touch, doesn't know what living frugally is, she's just some overprivileged rich girl.

She doesn't understand. They love her, loved her, just a few weeks ago. Why have they turned on her now? She's still the same person.

Don't these people understand how busy she is? How hard she works?

Why don't they understand that eating out-of-date caviar is slumming it – everyone knows it's never as good as it should be?

Why don't they care?

Why don't they love her?

CHAPTER SIXTY

HATTIE

Having come over to Templeton Manor for the afternoon to cast a watchful eye over Daniel and Hattie's dressage in lieu of Willa, who is still convalescing, Lady Pat joins them for a tipple afterwards to plan the last part of the season. Daniel isn't doing another five-star competition this autumn, not wanting to put too much strain on The Rogue in his first season back after injury. Hattie's campaign is focused on getting qualifications in place so that next year she can have a crack at Blenheim Horse Trials.

It's a gorgeous late summer evening. The scent of the roses carries on the warm air and the birds happily twitter in the trees around the garden. Sitting outside on the patio, an almost empty bottle of white wine on the table and the crackers and cheese Daniel put on a platter almost finished, the conversation turns from the last few events of the season to the tack thefts.

'So what news have you had after you sent over that photograph?' asks Lady Pat, taking one of the last crackers and popping it into her mouth.

'The police said the silver car was empty when they went to Jem's yard, and that there's not enough of Daniel's Badminton winner's rug on show in the photo to conclusively prove it was that,' says Hattie, angrily. 'They spoke to the car's owner, but they said they'd just had old rugs in the boot that they were taking to the dump for recycling.'

'And they believed them?' asks Lady Pat.

'It seems so,' says Hattie, rolling her eyes. 'They wouldn't even tell me who the car belonged to.'

'How frustrating,' says Lady Pat, taking a sip of wine. 'Have they got any other leads?'

'No,' says Hattie, shaking her head. 'Even though there've been two more burglaries in the past month. It's bizarre that they haven't any idea who is behind it.'

Daniel puts his empty wine glass down on the table. 'At least our insurance paid out. For the people burgled who weren't insured, it's a nightmare. That's what happened to Megan when she was at Jem Baulman-Carter's yard. The yard was insured but not Megan's tack.'

Lady Pat frowns. 'Well, that doesn't sound right at all. Surely Megan's things would have been covered by the yard policy?'

'I bet it was, but Jem Baulman-Carter isn't a very nice person so...' Hattie shrugs.

Daniel says nothing. Over in one of the paddocks, a horse whinnies.

'Anyway, it seems like the photo was a dead end as far as the police are concerned,' says Hattie, taking the last piece of cheese from the platter. Poppet, who has been chasing butterflies across the lawn, hurtles back to Hattie, his gaze fixated on the cheese.

'I once dated the chief of police, you know,' says Lady Pat. 'He was rather smitten with me, as I remember it. We've kept in touch over the years.'

'Any romance going on?' asks Hattie, raising an eyebrow.

Lady Pat waves away the question. 'Nothing like that. He's a happily married man. But we get coffee together every month or so. Only the other week, we were talking about the tack thefts and he said his officers were stumped.'

'Well, maybe they're just not very good at their job,' says Hattie, breaking the piece of cheese in two and giving one to Poppet, sitting to attention at her feet, and eating the rest herself.

'Or overwhelmed with too much work and too many cases,' says Daniel.

'Indeed. But either way, that's not good enough,' says Lady Pat, thoughtfully. She drinks the last of her wine, then nods decisively. 'Okay, leave it with me. I'll have a word.'

CHAPTER SIXTY-ONE

MEGAN

It seemed like a good idea before, but now she's about to upload the picture to OnlyFans, Megan's feeling nervous. She studies the image of herself that she's spent the morning creating. It's different to anything she's posted before, very different, and she knows that it's bound to irritate and even alienate some of her subscribers.

In the photo, she's wearing a pink cropped vest, a tiny pair of pink Lycra shorts and a pair of high-heeled brown suede knee-high boots. Across her shoulders, arms, chest, tummy and legs, she has positive affirmations painted onto her skin – model, intelligent, kind, worthy, human, strong, enough, learning, hopeful, entrepreneur, loved, businesswoman, and many more. She's grateful that Rosalie stayed over last night and was able to help her with the painting before she returned to the yard – there's no way it would have been so neat, or readable, if she'd had to do it all herself.

At the bottom of the photo, she adds the caption. She types a couple of sentences, then deletes them. Starts again, then deletes them again. She sits for a moment. When she first thought of doing this, she'd wanted to make it more personal to the men she'd encountered at the pub, but now she's thinking she should make it broader. It's about her knowing and being confident in her own worth, and letting them know that. They say a picture tells a thousand words, and she's going to let the image convey her message. A short caption will do. Slowly she taps the words across the bottom of the photo: *Don't let anyone else determine your worth.*

Satisfied she's got it right now, she clicks the button to upload the image and watches as it goes live onto her OnlyFans. Then she switches from OnlyFans to Instagram and does the same.

Finally finished, she turns her phone off and heads to the shower. She'll scrub off the paint now, and then head over to see Velvet. As she switches on the water and steps into the tiny shower cubicle, Megan smiles to herself. Whatever the reaction on social media, she feels lighter – happier – than she has done since the incident at the pub. She's not going to let a few arseholes chase her from OnlyFans. She's going to keep making content until she has enough money to buy her own flat, and then she's going to find herself a new job – something she's passionate about.

But before that, there's something important she needs to do.

CHAPTER SIXTY-TWO

HATTIE

In the last few days, the weather has turned from summer into autumn. The air is cooler and the leaves on the trees are beginning to turn yellow and orange. Soon they'll fall to the ground, a sure sign that autumn is here.

As they reach the bottom of the gallops, Hattie feels Mermaid's Gold start to jig, impatient to be off on their third and final run up the track. Turning towards Daniel, Hattie says, 'Are you ready?'

The Rogue blows out hard as if saying yes. Daniel smiles. 'Yep, let's do this.'

Turning, they move from walk to trot and then into a canter, letting the horses lengthen their strides into a gallop as they start the climb up the hill.

Mermaid's Gold and The Rogue gallop side-by-side, although the little mare is always sure to have her nose a couple of inches ahead of the gelding.

The speed is exhilarating. This is the last time they'll visit the gallops until next year. The last events of the season are coming up and then the horses will be turned out to pasture for a couple of months' holiday while Hattie helps Jonathan Scott with some of his trickier horses and Daniel focuses on his own youngsters.

Reaching the turn, the horses power on around the corner and along the final straight. Mermaid's Gold loves the gallops and never seems to tire. Every moment riding the mare is a joy. It makes Hattie feel so lucky.

Her relationship with Daniel makes her feel lucky too.

As they bring the horses back to a walk, Hattie looks across at Daniel. She needs to tell him. It just doesn't feel right to keep it from him anymore.

Glancing across at her, Daniel frowns. 'You okay?'

'There's something I need to tell you,' says Hattie, letting Mermaid's Gold have a long rein so she can stretch out her neck as they walk back down the gallops to the gate.

'Okay,' says Daniel, looking a bit worried. He gives The Rogue's neck a rub. 'So tell me.'

Butterflies flutter in her stomach. 'Just before Christmas last year I found out who my father was. He was Lady Pat's husband, but he had a relationship with my mum for many years. I never knew, and neither did Lady Pat. She found out after Sir Harry died.' Hattie takes a breath. Daniel's expression is hard to read. 'Lady Pat told me when she signed Mermaid's Gold over to me. When I finally opened the trunk that my mum left me, I found a letter from her in there that explained everything. I also found a savings account in my name that my father had set up when I was born. He'd put money into it every birthday I had. The balance is currently around three-quarters of a million pounds.'

Daniel raises his eyebrows. 'Wow, Hattie. That's huge.'

She nods. 'I know. Look, I didn't tell you partly because it didn't feel real and partly because I don't know what I should do with the money, whether I should buy my own place or invest it in something or…' Hattie shrugs. 'Or whatever people do when they have that much money. I wasn't ready to talk about it – the whole thing made me feel too emotional. I didn't even know how to have that conversation. But, as the months have gone on it feels wrong not to tell you.'

Daniel looks thoughtful. 'It must have been a massive shock.'

'It was,' says Hattie. 'I wish my parents had been alive so I could talk to them about it. I feel so sad that they felt they needed to keep it a secret from me my whole life, but then happy that rather than being alone, I had family I hadn't known about – Lady Pat is like an aunt to me, and Robert is actually my half-cousin.'

'It must have been a lot to process,' says Daniel, gently, riding The Rogue closer to Mermaid's Gold and reaching out to give Hattie's hand a squeeze.

'It was,' says Hattie, nodding. 'But don't you hate me for keeping it from you?'

'Why would I hate you?' says Daniel. 'You were still working through it yourself.'

'But the money. That amount would be enough for a new roof on Templeton Manor and a bunch of other repairs, I felt so—'

'Hattie, that's *your* money,' says Daniel. 'Why would I expect you to use it on my house? It's for you, and only you, to decide what you use it on.'

CHAPTER SIXTY-THREE

WAYNE

He's feeling rubbish. Not ill, but pretty down. So Wayne's doing the thing that always cheers him up and that's cooking. Except this time it isn't really working, or at least not yet anyway, and he's already been at it for a few hours.

As he cooks, he thinks about the strange request from Lady Pat. Yesterday was his last day shoeing at Jem Baulman-Carter's yard. After how she behaved towards Megan, he couldn't stomach seeing her, so he gave her notice and terminated her as a client. Not that Megan even knows. She still isn't answering his calls and messages.

Anyway, earlier in the day he'd been shoeing at the home of Sandy Lancaster, and Lady Pat had been there. She and Sandy had asked him to tell anyone and everyone at Jem Baulman-Carter's yard that the Lancasters are away this weekend for their anniversary. They'd said it was something to do with finding the tack thieves – that they were laying a trap – and Wayne had been happy to help. After all, Jem had told the police *he* was behind the thefts, so if the jumped-up little madam was the criminal mastermind all along he wants her to get her comeuppance.

A loud yelp pulls him back into the moment. Albert and Dora

have both been keeping a keen eye on what's going on in the kitchen, and have become even more interested since Wayne started making the filling for the beef-and-ale pies. Every few minutes, Dora gives a loud mew, and Albert dances around Wayne's feet – the pair of them begging for scraps in their own way.

'Not yet, you guys,' Wayne says, putting on an upbeat voice for the sake of the animals. 'I've already told you that you can't have any until it's cooked.'

Dora mews more pitifully. Albert puts his front paws up on Wayne's thigh and scrabbles at his jeans, gazing at him with big, mournful eyes.

Wayne can't help but smile as he shakes his head. 'You guys, I said—'

He's interrupted by a knock at the front door. Setting his knife down, he pushes the chopping board with the beef fillet and the bowl of pie filling to the back of the worktop so it's harder for the animals to get at it, and then walks across to the door.

'I'm watching you,' says Wayne, keeping eye contact with Dora and Albert as he walks. 'Don't you try and steal.'

He's still keeping watch on the animals as he opens the door.

'Hi.'

Wayne flinches at the sound of her voice. As he turns to look at her, he can't believe she's really here standing on his doorstep. 'Megan? Hi.'

Damn, she looks good.

They stand for a moment, neither speaking.

A crash from the kitchen breaks the silence. Wayne glances towards the noise and sees Albert is bouncing up and down trying to reach the meat on the chopping board, and Dora, having jumped onto the worktop and knocked off a rolling pin, is just about to stick her head into the bowl.

'No!' Wayne rushes towards them. 'Stop, Albert, no. Get down, Dora, you naughty cat.'

Dora yowls angrily when he picks her up from the worktop and puts her back on the floor. Her tail thrashes back and forth as she struts angrily towards the sofa. Albert looks up at him dolefully and whines. He shakes his head. 'What are you guys like?'

'Can I come in?' asks Megan, sticking her head around the front door. 'Oh wow, something smells good.'

Wayne gives her a rueful smile. 'I thought I'd do some batch cooking.'

'Nice.' Megan's expression turns serious. 'I'm sorry I didn't reply to your messages.'

'It's okay,' says Wayne, avoiding her gaze.

'No it isn't.' Megan closes the front door behind her and walks across to join him in the kitchen. 'So I want to explain.'

Wayne feels a bit sick. If she's here to bin him off, he wishes she'd have just messaged him. 'Look, I really am sorry about what Rachel said in the pub. I could tell you felt a bit uncomfortable about her implying we were together. I never meant for you to—'

'It wasn't that.' Megan holds his eye contact. 'I was embarrassed about something else that was said.'

Wayne shakes his head. 'Was it the stuff about me being a serial shagger? I know that might be a bit off-putting but I'm—'

'It wasn't about you,' says Megan. 'There were some men in the pub who recognised me from my OnlyFans. When I came out of the loos, I found one of them in the corridor. He blocked my exit and propositioned me, asking how much I'd charge for sex with him and his friends.'

Wayne clenches his fists. Feels disgust and anger building like a pressure in his chest. 'What the hell? What right did he think he had to—?'

'He didn't want to take no for an answer,' continues Megan. Her cheeks flush and she looks away as she speaks. 'That's why I left in a hurry and haven't been in contact. I was embarrassed to tell you and I felt really rubbish about it for a while.' She takes a breath. Looks back at Wayne. 'But then I realised that just because that man made that misinformed assumption, it's not my problem. I refuse to let him dictate how I feel about myself.'

'Too right,' says Wayne. The anger inside him shows no sign of dissipating. 'I'm so sorry you had that happen. I wish you'd pointed this joker out to me. I'd have—'

'Thanks, but I'd rather fight my own battles.' Megan smiles. 'I've dealt with it in my own way.'

'Okay, okay. I understand that,' says Wayne. He hates that Megan experienced harassment from some arseholes in the pub and he hadn't even known. What sort of a friend is he? He should have been looking out for her.

'You're awfully quiet,' says Megan, nudging him with her elbow.

He meets her gaze. 'Are we okay?'

Megan's smile broadens. 'Of course.'

It's as if a weight has been lifted from his shoulders. 'And you're not upset about the stuff Rachel said?'

Megan shakes her head. 'Why would I be? We're just friends.'

It's true, thinks Wayne, but he wants them to be more than that. Far more. This feels like his cue to tell Megan how he feels and ask her out on a proper date. He's never really taken someone on a proper date before – usually he's either propositioned or just falls into one-night hook-ups. But it's time to change that. Yes. He's going to do it now. He feels his heart rate accelerate. Clears his throat. 'What if we—'

'Sorry, hang on,' says Megan, reaching into her bag and pulling out her phone. It's vibrating: a call rather than a message. 'Let me just get this.'

'Okay.' Wayne tries not to show her how deflated he feels. As Megan answers, he busies himself with tidying up the kitchen, putting used pans and utensils into the dishwasher, and then continuing to make the pie filling. The call is going on a bit but, although she sounds animated, excited even, Megan's side of the conversation is mainly 'yes', 'no' or 'I see'.

Six minutes after she answered the call, Megan ends it.

When Wayne turns round, she's standing there with a shocked expression. 'Everything okay?'

'Yeah… I.' She frowns, and taps the phone screen. Her eyebrows rise. 'Oh, wow.'

'What is it?' says Wayne.

'A post I did earlier has gone viral. I hadn't realised as I turned my phone off right afterwards and only switched it back on when I arrived here.' Her voice is halting, and there's a quiver to it, the shock clear in her voice. Megan widens her eyes. 'That call was from Agency 12, one of the top modelling agencies in London. They want to sign me.'

CHAPTER SIXTY-FOUR

JEM

It's like something out of a TV show. One moment she's asleep beside Tyler, the next a swarm of combat-gear-wearing police storm into the bedroom and grab her boyfriend.

'What the...?' Jem pulls the duvet up to her chin, covering herself and wishing that she wasn't sleeping naked.

'Police. Stay where you are,' shouts one of the officers.

Jem does as she's told.

She watches as Tyler is pushed to the ground and his hands are handcuffed behind his back. It's only when they pull him back up to standing that she sees the black eye. 'What happened to your...?'

'No talking,' says another officer, her tone no-nonsense. They pick some clothes up from the chair on Jem's side of the bed and throw them to her. 'Get dressed.'

Jem does as the officer says but her mind is whirring. Tyler didn't have a black eye last night when he left to go out with his mates. Did he get into a fight at the pub? Did he hurt someone – is that why the police are here?

A burly officer, who Jem assumes is in charge, stands in front of Tyler. He speaks loudly and clearly, making sure there's no doubt in what he's saying. 'Tyler Jordan, you're under arrest for the attempted burglary of Picketpeace Grange, the home of Mr and Mrs Lancaster, and for nine additional counts of tack theft across the county.'

'Tack theft?' says Jem, looking towards the female officer and forgetting that she was told not to speak. 'But my yard was burgled. Why would he steal from his own girlfriend?'

'You'll have to ask him that yourself,' says the female police officer. 'But later, because right now he's coming to the station and we need to take a statement from you about his whereabouts last night and on a number of other nights over the past few months.'

'Okay,' says Jem. It's a lot to process. This sort of thing never happens to people like her. She's not a criminal. She's important.

Oh God, what will Mummy and Daddy say?

She watches as two officers frogmarch Tyler towards the door. As they reach the doorway, Jem calls out. Not speaking be damned. 'What did you do, Tyler? What the hell did you do?'

Tyler turns and glances at her. He says nothing, but his expression tells her everything she needs to know. He's guilty. One hundred percent. Then the officers march him through the door and along the landing to the stairs.

Jem shakes her head as the fury rips through her. Clenching her fists, she yells at his retreating form. 'You total loser. You're dumped. I never, ever want to see you again.'

CHAPTER SIXTY-FIVE

MEGAN

Megan takes extra care getting ready. She knows Wayne's seen her without make-up and, of course, she was crying the first time that they ever really spoke, just after the thieves stole her tack, but she wants to look properly nice tonight. They're going to Daniel and Hattie's end-of-season yard meal together, and she has something important that she wants to ask him.

It's only been a few days since she signed with the modelling agency, but so much has changed already. Firstly, she already has a booking for a modelling job next week, and she's super excited. She's also hired an accountant and they've gone through her finances in detail and worked out her taxes. As a result, she now knows she's got enough money to buy a small apartment, and for her and Velvet to live comfortably for quite a while. She's grateful that OnlyFans enabled her to do that, but she needs to move on, so this afternoon she deleted her account on the platform, and her other social media. She's had enough of the digital side of life; she's going back to being analogue.

She hears the toot of a car horn and looks outside. Sure

enough, Wayne's van is parked by the curb, waiting. Pulling on her blue tweed jacket, she smooths down her black mini dress and slips her feet into her heeled knee-high suede boots. Grabbing her bag, she moves across to the door. Before she opens it, she takes a breath to steady herself.

This is it.

Then she exits the flat and strides down the pathway to meet Wayne.

Opening the passenger door of the van, she climbs inside. Usually the cab is filled with junk – the debris of old sandwich packaging, empty crisp packets, and half-drunk cans of Coke and take-away coffee cups. But this evening the cab is pristine, tidy and clean, with the footwells freshly hoovered. She sits down and turns towards Wayne.

'Hey,' he says, raising his hand in greeting. 'You alright?'

Be bold, Megan tells herself. 'I thought you might come and knock on my door, isn't that what dates do?' she says, her tone playful and teasing.

Wayne looks confused. 'So is this a date?'

Megan feels her stomach flip. She's suddenly even more nervous. 'Would you like it to be?'

'Hell yes,' says Wayne, without hesitation. 'I've been trying to get the courage up to ask you on a proper date for ages, but I thought I'd been friend-zoned.'

'OMG, what are we like?' says Megan, laughing. 'I've wanted to tell you how I feel for ages, but I thought you just wanted to be friends.'

Wayne smiles. Shakes his head. 'What a pair.'

'Totally,' says Megan.

She looks at him: the sexy twinkle in his eyes, the day-old stubble across his handsome face, and his cute, dishevelled bed hair, and can't believe that she's been so worried about telling him how she feels. He's a good friend, and hopefully he's about to become a whole lot more.

Be bold, she reminds herself.

Throwing caution to the wind, she leans across and kisses him.

CHAPTER SIXTY-SIX

HATTIE

The pub restaurant is busy tonight. Hattie's glad they booked a table as it would have been impossible to get one big enough otherwise. This season might have had its share of ups and downs, but tonight they've got a lot to celebrate.

'Shall we start with champagne all round?' says Lady Pat from her seat at the head of the table. 'My treat.'

There are nods from the group. The whole yard is here. Eddie and Jenny are sitting opposite her and Daniel, Bunty is on Eddie's other side, with her boyfriend Tom next to Daniel, and Megan is sitting beside Hattie, with her boyfriend Wayne sitting opposite.

'Lovely idea,' says Hattie.

Daniel smiles. 'Thanks, Lady Pat, much appreciated.'

Lady Pat waves his thanks away. 'It's the least I can do. It's so jolly being involved with a yard like yours. You should all be very proud of what you've achieved this year.'

'Hear, hear,' says Eddie. 'This season has been a great one.'

'Well, the second half was better for some of us,' says Hattie, giving a rueful smile as she holds up the wrist she damaged earlier in the year.

'But not all,' says Lady Pat, putting her hand over her heart. 'Sometimes the body isn't as willing as the mind would like.'

'True,' says Hattie, remembering Lady Pat's mini stroke a few months ago. She's recovered amazingly well, thankfully.

'Although if I hadn't been laid up in bed, I might not have had as much time to devote to puzzling out the tack thefts,' says Lady Pat. 'And I do think Teddy appreciated my help.'

'Teddy?' says Bunty. 'Who's that?'

'An old friend,' says Lady Pat, smiling secretively. 'Who happens to be the current chief of police.'

'Well I'm glad they caught them,' says Wayne.

'I'm sure that came as a big relief,' says Lady Pat, with a definite sparkle in her eye as she turns to Wayne. 'Especially seeing as the police seemed to have you in their sights for a long while.'

'Yeah. It felt pretty liberating, for sure,' says Wayne. 'And it felt good to help out.'

Hattie frowns. 'Help the police?'

'Not exactly,' says Wayne, his gaze flicking towards Lady Pat.

Hattie raises her eyebrow. 'Lady Pat?'

Lady Pat laughs. 'I didn't do much, dear, but seeing as you'd already uncovered the identity of one of the perpetrators with that photo, it was just a question of helping the police catch the blighter. Seeing as the officers sent to Jem Baulman-Carter's yard came up empty, I thought I'd give them a little more to work with.'

'Like what?' says Daniel.

Everyone is silent, waiting for Lady Pat to elaborate.

Lady Pat shakes her head, but she's smiling. 'Well, Wayne here spread the word that the Lancasters, some dear friends of mine, would be away for the weekend, but that, of course, wasn't the case. Instead, Arthur Lancaster, who is a rather handy fellow, installed six fancy new security cameras around the yard area, and two more inside the tack room. They were very small and hidden, so they'd go undetected by any burglars. He also decided he fancied a little sit-down in the tack room after dark, with the door locked and the lights off, naturally.' Lady Pat smirks. 'When the burglars turned up and broke in, they found Arthur and his trusty broom in situ. There was a bit of a scuffle, and the balaclava of the ringleader was pulled off. Arthur tried to restrain the fellow, but he fought back and although Arthur landed one decent punch the chap managed to get away. It didn't matter though, because by that time both the man's face, and the number plates of the two vehicles used by the criminals, had been recorded on the hidden security camera feeds. The Lancasters simply put a call in to the police, gave their statements and handed over the footage. Job done.'

'You orchestrated a sting operation?' says Daniel, the admiration clear in his voice.

'Genius,' says Hattie, impressed. 'But weren't the police annoyed?'

'Oh, I don't think so,' says Lady Pat, waving away her concerns. 'Dear Teddy knows how I can be, and he was happy to roll along with it. After all, his officers managed to arrest and charge all four of the burglars behind the tack thefts. So it's a big coup for him and the local force.'

'I can't believe Jem Baulman-Carter didn't know what her boyfriend was up to,' says Jenny. 'I mean, they lived together. Surely she would have seen or heard something to make her suspicious?'

'I seriously doubt it,' says Megan, a slight bitterness to her tone. 'Jem is the most self-absorbed person I've ever met.'

'She's definitely that, and then some,' says Wayne, nodding.

'At least we're free of her now.'

'Yeah, for sure,' says Wayne. 'After the way she treated you, there's no way I'll step foot in her yard again.'

The waiter comes over to serve them the champagne, popping the cork with a flourish and then pouring it into flutes.

Tom leans closer to Daniel and Hattie. He looks nervous. 'Bunty and me have got something to ask you, mate.'

'Sure,' says Daniel.

'I'd like to move in with Tom,' says Bunty, the nerves clear in her voice. 'I know the terms of my contract say I need to live in so I'm on-site to deal with any out-of-hours issues with the horses, but Tom's farm is only over the hill, it's a five-minute drive at the most, so I'd still be super close. I don't want to cause trouble, really I don't, but me and Tom are happy together. We want to take our relationship to the next level.'

Hattie's not surprised by the question, but Daniel looks blindsided. It takes him a moment to get his thoughts together. During that time, Bunty's face flushes red and Tom reaches across the table to hold her hand.

'Okay,' says Daniel.

'Are you saying yes?' asks Bunty.

Daniel smiles. 'Of course I am. Tom's farm borders Templeton Manor; you'd be practically on-site even living there. I'm fine with it.'

'Thank you,' says Bunty, grinning.

'Thanks, mate, you're a star,' says Tom, clapping his hand against Daniel's back.

As Bunty and Tom start planning the date of the move, Hattie moves closer to Daniel. 'You okay?'

'Sure,' says Daniel. 'It's not far, and who am I to stand in the way of young love.'

Across the table, Eddie clears his throat loudly. When everyone's stopped talking and is looking at him, he starts to speak. 'We've got some news,' he says, looking at Jenny.

Lifting up her left hand, Jenny shows off a gorgeous, square-cut diamond ring. 'I said yes!'

'Oh wow! Congratulations,' says Hattie. Standing, she pushes back her chair and stretches across the table to hug first Jenny and then Eddie. Daniel does the same. There are tears in his eyes as he congratulates the pair.

'Looks like we're going to need some more champagne,' says Lady Pat, raising her glass to salute Jenny and Eddie. 'Congratulations.'

After the congratulations have all been said, and they've ordered their food, Daniel slowly gets to his feet, champagne flute in hand. 'I don't like giving speeches, so this will be short, but I think I need to say something to mark this occasion. Firstly congratulations to Jenny and Eddie, you are amazing together.'

There are murmurs of agreement around the table and more congratulations.

'It's been a great year for the yard,' says Daniel, continuing. 'The youngsters are coming on well, The Rogue and I are on the World Class Programme, Hattie and Mermaid's Gold are well on their way to qualifying for next year's Blenheim, Jenny and Dinky are putting in solid performances at Intermediate, and Megan and Velvet Mimosa have qualified for the summer dressage championships.'

'And Megan's just been signed by a top model agency in London,' says Wayne, proudly.

'It's true.' Megan smiles. 'I've already got my first job booked in. I can't say the name of the client, but it's a high-end designer brand.'

'That's marvellous, dear. Well done,' says Lady Pat. She looks at Wayne. 'And speaking of modelling, will there be another charity calendar for next year?'

Wayne blushes. 'Yes, ma'am. We're due to shoot it next month.'

'Well that's quite wonderful,' says Lady Pat. 'I shall look forward to seeing it.'

Hattie raises her glass of champagne and looks around the group. 'Congratulations, everyone. This season has been challenging at times but I think we've all come out on top.'

'To everyone,' says Daniel, raising his glass. 'I feel very lucky to have such a great bunch of people, and horses, in my life.'

Their friends all raise their glasses and repeat, 'To everyone.'

As they sit back down, Lady Pat talks to Jenny and Eddie, having another look at the ring, Tom and Bunty are busy chatting about when to move Bunty's stuff, and Wayne and Megan are staring into each other's eyes.

Daniel leans closer to Hattie. His expression is a little sad. 'It feels like the end of an era. I mean, I'm super happy for Eddie and Jenny, and Bunty, of course I am, but it feels as if so much is about to change.'

Hattie knows this is the right moment. After all, she told Daniel the secret she was keeping from him and he was cool with it. She loves being with him. Loves him. She's ready. 'Do you think you could handle one more change?'

Daniel looks slightly alarmed. 'Like what?'

Taking his hand, Hattie looks up into his kind, handsome face, and smiles. 'How about we move in together?'

A grin spreads across Daniel's lips as he pulls her closer and kisses her. 'That, I would love.'

AFTERWORD

Firstly, I'd like to thank you, the reader, for reading this book. I really hope you enjoyed it as much as I enjoyed writing it. Please let me know your thoughts by posting a review on Amazon; it would really mean a lot.

Getting a book prepared for publication takes a brilliant team. I'd like to say a huge thank you to the brilliant author Ed James for mentoring me through the process, to John Rickards, top copyediting guru, to Victoria Goldman, excellent eagle-eyed proofreader, and the brilliantly creative Louise Brown for the cover design – you are all awesome. A big shout out to my family and friends for all your support and encouragement – and massive thanks to those of you who read the early drafts.

If you'd like to find out more about me, you can hop over to my website at joniharperwriter.com and check out my socials via Instagram @joniharperwriter or Facebook @joniharperwriter – it's always great to connect.

You can also stay up to date on my book news by signing up to my Readers' Club – turn the page to find out more!

Until next time…

Joni x

THE CHASE

A FREE LEIGHTONSHIRE LOVERS SHORT STORY

Join the Joni Harper Readers Club and get access to THE CHASE – a free short story set in and around Leightonshire and the equestrian world.

I've also included a bonus short story along with it – THE TROT UP.

As a member of the Readers Club you'll receive book and writing news updates and have the opportunity to enter exclusive giveaways. It's all completely free and you can opt out at any time.

To join, follow this link **joniharperwriter.com** and click on **Join My Readers' Club**.

GRIT & GLAMOUR

LEIGHTONSHIRE LOVERS SERIES BOOK ONE

Horse whisperer Hattie Kimble dreams of winning the prestigious Badminton Horse Trials and representing Great Britain at the Olympics, but without a job or a horse she's further from her goal than ever. When she takes a housesitting assignment in Leightonshire county – right in the heart of horse country – her luck begins to change and she's asked to work with a talented event horse who has lost her trust in humans. Hattie wasn't looking for love but when she meets Daniel Templeton-Smith at her first horse trials she can't deny the instant attraction. Should she follow her dream or her heart, or can she do both?

Event rider Daniel Templeton-Smith is broke. When he can't see any other way to pay the bills for crumbling Templeton Manor, he accepts an offer from alpha female Lexi Marchfield-Wright that involves more than just riding horses. As his career takes off, and he meets and starts falling for Hattie Kimble, he realises the price of success might be too high. But Lexi won't let him break their arrangement, and sets out to sabotage the developing relationship between Daniel and Hattie, whatever it takes.

GRIT & GLAMOUR is a spicy, adrenaline-fuelled equestrian sports romance set in the rural idyll of Leightonshire county and the high-octane world of eventing. Feelings grow and hearts are shattered, promises are made and friends are double-crossed, and as emotions reach breaking point, feuds erupt at the end-of-season winter ball, with devastating consequences.

https://mybook.to/PUVaD

TINSEL & TEMPTATION

LEIGHTONSHIRE LOVERS SERIES BOOK THREE

It's December and event rider Daniel Templeton-Smith has been invited to jump in the Eventers vs Showjumpers competition at the London International Horse Show. With his top horses and girlfriend, fellow eventer Hattie Kimble, he sets off in the horsebox for a fun week in London. Little does he know that his nemesis from the past is also heading for London, and they're out for revenge.

Up and coming show jumper Maisy Cooper has qualified for her first London International but the pressure is getting to her. When she shows up drunk to walk the course on the first day, it looks as if her dream of competing might be over before she's even set foot in the arena. Then she meets show jumping heart-throb Joe Broughton and everything gets a *lot* more complicated.

Wayne Jefferies is thrilled to be one of the on-site farriers at the London International this year. Loved-up with his girlfriend, the model Megan Taylor, he's hoping the week in London can be a romantic getaway too. He's got a special secret planned, if only the crowds would stop besieging Megan everywhere they go.

TINSEL & TEMPTATION is a spicy, adrenaline-fuelled equestrian sports romance set in the heart of London at the glamorous week-long

London International Horse Show. Trophies are won and dreams are shattered, lovers are made and enemies are out for vengeance, and on the final night of the horse show tensions reach fever pitch, climaxing as the fairy tale Christmas finale takes place and the commentator wishes the audience a Merry Christmas.

Coming 28th November 2024...
Pre-order now:
https://mybook.to/lxCxH

ABOUT THE AUTHOR

Joni Harper began riding horses almost as soon as she could walk and started her competitive horse riding career aged six years old. She was a keen member of the Pony Club and as an adult rode successfully for many years in British Eventing competitions. She's been a Pony Club instructor in the UK, a Riding Counsellor in the USA, and has mucked out more stables than she can possibly count. She also trained as a horse whisperer. Joni has an MA in Creative Writing and loves to write about horses, the countryside and goings on in rural communities.

Printed in Great Britain
by Amazon